THE TATTOOED

MAN

ADVENTURE AND MYSTERY STORIES
BY HOWARD PEASE

Stories about Tod Moran

NIGHT BOAT
THE BLACK TANKER
HIGHROAD TO ADVENTURE
THE SHIP WITHOUT A CREW
WIND IN THE RIGGING
HURRICANE WEATHER
FOGHORNS
THE JINX SHIP
SHANGHAI PASSAGE
HEART OF DANGER

Other Mystery and Adventure Stories

JUNGLE RIVER
SECRET CARGO
THE GYPSY CARAVAN
THUNDERBOLT HOUSE
THE LONG WHARF

THROUGH YOUR LOCAL BOOKSTORE OR LIBRARY YOU CAN
OBTAIN THE ABOVE TITLES—ALL PUBLISHED BY DOUBLE-
DAY AND COMPANY OF NEW YORK.

THE
TATTOOED
MAN

A MYSTERY BY
HOWARD PEASE

ILLUSTRATED BY
RALPH RAY, JR.

ROCKEFELLER CENTER, NEW YORK

THE PRINTING HISTORY OF
THE TATTOOED MAN

Doubleday edition published September, 1926

1st printing ....February, 1927
2nd printing ....August, 1927
3rd printing ....January, 1929

Young Moderns edition published January, 1930

1st printing ....January, 1930
2nd printing ....July, 1931
3rd printing ....January, 1934
4th printing ....January, 1935
5th printing ....January, 1936
6th printing ....January, 1937
7th printing ....September, 1947

Comet Books edition published June, 1948

1st printing ....February, 1947

2nd printing ....July, 1948

DESIGNED AND PRODUCED BY THE SANDPIPER PRESS

This *Comet* Book includes every word contained in the original, higher-priced edition. It has been printed from new plates made from completely reset, large, easy-to-read type. It is published by arrangement with Doubleday and Company, Inc.

Printed in the U. S. A.

CONTENTS

PART ONE

THE OCEAN TRAMP

I.	MISSING—AND GUILTY	1
II.	GRINNING DRAGONS	10
III.	S. S. "ARABY"	19
IV.	THE CABIN AFT	30
V.	OUTWARD BOUND	39
VI.	MAN OVERBOARD!	48
VII.	THE LIFEBOAT	58

PART TWO

THE FIGHT IN THE FORECASTLE

I.	SOUTHERN WATERS	71
II.	THE ENMITY OF RED MITCHELL	82
III.	SHARKS	89
IV.	MOCK WOO OF PANAMA	102
V.	TO COLON! TO COLON!	111
VI.	TOD SHOWS HIS FISTS	118
VII.	BLACK GANG VS. DECK CREW	128
VIII.	CAPTAIN TOM JARVIS	136

PART THREE

ON THE TRAIL OF NEIL MORAN

I.	A SECRET MEETING IN MARSEILLES	147
II.	THE THIRD-CLASS COMPARTMENT	156
III.	AT THE VILLA PARADIS	166
IV.	THE PRISONER	173
V.	ESCAPE	178
VI.	THE STORY OF THE "ANNIE JAMISON"	192
VII.	SHANGHAI PASSAGE	200

PART FOUR

THE DOOMED SHIP

I.	HIGH ADVENTURE	211
II.	MR. HAWKES SHOWS HIS HAND	220
III.	IN THE STOKEHOLE	229
IV.	MIDNIGHT	239
V.	ABANDON SHIP!	248
VI.	"I TAKE COMMAND, MR. HAWKES."	259
VII.	MAKING PORT	268

ILLUSTRATIONS

She rose on a swell, then plunged.   *frontispiece*

His mouth contorted in a snarl . . .   *page 70*

The stones sang with their eager steps.   *146*

"Get busy! Pressure's down ten pounds!"   *210*

SHE ROSE ON A SWELL, THEN PLUNGED.

PART ONE

THE OCEAN TRAMP

SAN FRANCISCO
Tues., February 24
FOR MARSEILLES and GENOA.—
European-Pacific Co's Stmr *Ar-
aby*, Capt Ramsey—(Freight
Only) Leaves Powell St (Pier
43) at —— pm.

San Francisco *Shipping Guide*

I : MISSING—AND GUILTY

SEA FOG hazed like spindrift along the San Francisco
water front. Tod Moran, coming from the echoing
halls of the Ferry Building to the Embarcadero, paused
uncertainly upon the damp pavement. On train and
ferry, he had been leaping gloriously through pages of
high romance with a gentleman adventurer and his "noble, brave men of the sea," and now, upon stepping out
of the rose-tinted covers of his book, he was momentarily
startled, as though he had strayed into another world.

About him were the strange, muffled sounds of a February morning when the city is smothered in mist: the

1

distant clang of cable cars, the hoarse cries of newsboys, the dull rumble of trucks and drays passing in the gloom like ghosts. Tod noticed a policeman standing near by, and at once approached him.

"Can you please tell me," he asked, clutching the rose-coloured book in a nervous hand, "how to get to Pier 43? I want the European-Pacific Steamship Company."

"Never heard of that line," the officer replied; "but you'll find Pier 43 straight down the docks to your right. A bad neighbourhood—that. Know any one there?"

Tod shook his head. "No—nobody."

The officer surveyed him from head to foot, noting the boy's worn clothes which tightly fitted his lithe young frame, his sandy hair beneath its cap, and the eyes, clear and gray, that shone keenly from his tanned face. "Oh, a stranger to San Francisco, eh?"

"Yes, sir; I just got in from up-river this morning. I'm looking for my brother. He works for the European-Pacific Company—or used to."

The policeman gave him a quizzical glance. "Don't you know?"

"I haven't heard from my brother for six months. He was purser on a passenger freighter." The boy's mouth trembled; his voice grew husky. "I'm afraid— something has happened."

The policeman waved him on. "Straight down the Embarcadero—almost to Fishermen's Wharf."

With the words of thanks lost on his lips, Tod Moran turned away. In soft, impenetrable folds, the mist lay about him. He walked slowly, his eyes strained ahead into the dripping grayness. Soon, the noise of the Ferry

was left behind; he passed great open doorways leading
to covered piers where lay ships from the seven seas.
He read the names as he passed: The China Line. The
Java-Pacific S. S. Co. Great steamers that plied to and
from the Orient. He glimpsed huge cargoes in the dim
warehouses. Now and then, an open space gave him
sight of the bows of mammoth liners that loomed sombrely above him. Occasional figures passed: sailors on
shore leave from battleships at anchor in the Bay, swaying seamen from Australian windjammers, groups of
chattering Orientals from the Toyo Kisen Kaisha Line.

At No. 39 the covered piers ended. Beyond lay open
docks. Here a breeze swept in from the Golden Gate
with a keen zest that made Tod hurry forward and
brought drops of moisture to his face. He went by a barkentine with masts and spars that imperceptibly vanished above—some copra trader, he knew, in port from
the South Seas. The next pier was No. 43.

A wharf office, small and ancient, first detached itself
from the pearled obscurity. Tod drew near and read
over the door:

THE EUROPEAN-PACIFIC S. S. Co.

Now that he had arrived at his destination, he was
reluctant to enter. He walked back and forth for a moment, debating what he should say to the manager. After
all, perhaps his fears were groundless; his brother might
have had a bad passage out, and in port, of course, a
purser was always busy. Yet Neil had never failed to
write before. He knew how his younger brother looked
forward to receiving a letter stamped Marseilles or
Genoa or Port Said. Perhaps Neil was ill with fever

again—that jungle fever which he had contracted upon a voyage up the Amazon for cacao. With renewed anxiety, Tod returned to the office and opened its begrimed glass door.

Behind a counter facing the entrance, a girl sat typing, her slender hands flying deftly over the keys. She glanced up from her machine with a questioning smile. Her eyes were kind, Tod saw, and her hair the colour of bronze.

"Could I—could I see the manager?" Tod stammered.

"He's outside just now," the girl answered quickly. "Will you wait?"

Tod seated himself on a bench near the door. His gaze strayed past the girl and settled upon a glass door leading to a rear office. In black letters on the glass were the words:

JASPER SWICKARD
MANAGER

At the sight of the name, Tod's restlessness increased. With a nervous movement of his hand, he rose and crossed to the counter. "Do you think," he asked, "that the manager will be back soon?"

"Oh, yes; he's just outside on the *Araby*."

"Is that the ship?"

"Yes; you'll find Mr. Swickard there—if it's very important." A smile played at the corners of her mouth.

"It is important," Tod rejoined. "I'm looking for my brother. It's been several months since I've heard from him."

At his words, the girl turned and directed upon him

a startled gaze. The smile left her lips. "Your brother?" she uttered softly. "And his name?"

"Neil Moran."

Tod, leaning over the counter, saw the blood drain suddenly from her face. Her glance fluttered past him out the door to the wharf; then she rose and quickly crossed to the counter. "Of course; you're Tod," she said with a little catch in her voice. "He told me of you—often."

"Neil? You know my brother?" Tod questioned eagerly.

The girl glanced over her shoulder and raised a warning hand. "We've only a moment. . . . Don't let Mr. Swickard know I've been talking to you."

"Yes, but Neil! Where is he?" Involuntarily, he lowered his voice to match her tone. "What's happened?"

"I wish I knew. . . . Hush—Mr. Swickard!"

She slipped back to her desk, and a light run of chatter came from her lips. "In just a moment. You don't mind waiting, do you? He's busy this morning."

Tod looked up. The outer door had opened and the manager of the European-Pacific Company entered. Crossing to a desk, he hurriedly glanced through some papers in a file. Tod watched him closely. He saw a slender, well-dressed man of thirty-five or forty, with sleek dark hair over eyes narrow and crafty.

"Mr. Swickard," said the girl, "a young man to see you."

"I'm busy, Miss Murray, as you see," snapped the manager. "What's he want?"

Tod spoke up. "I wanted to ask you about—my brother."

"Your brother?" The man turned slowly to face the boy; his beady black eyes narrowed to mere slits. "Who are you?" he said in even tones. "What's your name?"

"Moran—Tod Moran, sir."

Mr. Swickard stared impassively. Only his long white fingers, which gripped the desk behind him, gave evidence that he was disconcerted.

It was Tod who first broke the silence. "I came to ask you about my brother—about Neil."

Mr. Swickard's smooth-shaven face, dark where the beard showed through, broke into a smile. "So Neil Moran has a brother! I didn't know he had any relatives."

"Oh, yes," said Tod. "There's just the two of us."

"Oh, I see."

Tod followed his glance to the girl at the typewriter. She was bending over her shorthand notes, but Tod knew that she was listening, watching.

Mr. Swickard frowned. "Come into my office, Moran. I'm very sorry—but I have unpleasant news for you." He turned to his private office.

Tod cast a frightened glance at the girl; in her eyes, he saw reflected the fear that clutched his heart. As he stumbled through a swinging gate past the counter, the girl met him with bravely lifted head. She said not a word, but Tod read in her white, strained expression her warning: "Careful! Something's wrong. Find out!"

The private office of the manager of the European-Pacific Steamship Company was a tiny place containing only an old roll-top desk and two chairs. The manager seated himself and, swinging round, motioned Tod to the other chair. The boy faced the gray light of a window through which the bow of the S. S. *Araby* was just visible. Mr. Swickard's face, he noted, was in the shadow.

"So you are Neil Moran's brother," began the manager, as if he meant to be friendly, even though he had a sad and unpleasant duty to perform. "Where do you live?"

Tod gulped. "At Stockton, on the San Joaquin. I've been going to high school there—and working."

"Your brother, I suppose, helped you—financially?"

"Yes, sir. I never earned quite enough to keep me going, so every month Neil sent me something. He wanted me to get an education. He was going to help me through the university, too."

Mr. Swickard regarded him with apparent unconcern. "Well, that's too bad. You probably won't be able to go on with your schooling—now."

"You mean—Neil? Something's happened to Neil?" Tod's hands trembled; as he leaned forward his face grew pallid. "What is it, Mr. Swickard? Tell me—where is Neil?"

A smile, cold, indifferent, settled upon the man's thin

lips. "I'm sure I don't know, my boy, or I'd tell you. In fact, I'd like to get these hands on him—the cur!"

In his quick sense of relief, Tod scarcely noted the man's last word. "He's safe, then?" he cried.

Mr. Swickard did not answer. He met the boy's anxious, questioning glance with a gaze as sharp as steel. In those relentless eyes, Tod saw bitter animosity reflected. Bewildered, he arose and stepped back against the thin boards of the wall.

"What—what do you mean, Mr. Swickard?" he stammered, with dry lips.

"Neil Moran has absconded," the manager announced coolly. "That's what I mean—run off with the ship's money! Now I understand why he wanted more—to send his young brother to college."

Tod choked with astonishment and anger. "It's a lie!" he cried hotly. "It's a lie, I tell you! Neil would never do that. I know it!"

"Now, don't get excited, Moran," Mr. Swickard smoothly went on as he raised his hand to stroke his sleek black hair. "Sit down and let's talk it over. Of course, I realize that this must be a blow to you—so sudden, you know, and—unexpected."

Tod did not sit down. He stood outlined against a shipping guide upon the wall, his head held high, his eyes blazing scorn at his tormentor. "All right, Mr. Swickard. Go on!" he challenged. "Tell me about it. I'm listening."

The manager coughed slightly. "It hurts me deeply," he began in a suave voice, "to inform so youthful a person as yourself, Moran, of the guilt of a brother. Truth to tell, it was also a surprise to me. Neil Moran, as you know, was purser on our cargo carrier, the *Panama*, a much larger steamer than the one moored outside. The *Panama* sailed by way of the Canal for New York and Liverpool. I began to suspect your brother of crooked entries soon after. I cabled to England, but the ship had already departed. My agent there sent a wireless to the captain, explaining matters. Unfortunately, he failed to act and unwittingly allowed your brother to escape at the next port of call." Mr. Swickard paused and, taking a long cigar from his pocket, lighted it.

Tod, with fast-beating heart, watched the man puff slowly. "At what port, Mr. Swickard?" he asked in as calm a tone as he could muster.

"Bordeaux. His ship was bound for Mediterranean ports."

"Neil is in France, then?"

"I suppose so. We did not put the police upon his trail, though I believe now that we should have done so. He's only twenty-three or -four, isn't he? Well, we thought perhaps he'd learned a lesson. You realize, of course, that he is finished as far as his future is concerned with ships out of San Francisco. Too bad—he was a bright young fellow, too."

Tod let the words sink in. Neil guilty of embezzlement? Never! Not if he knew him—and who knows a fellow better than a brother does! No, in spite of the unruffled voice and the glib story, Tod was not convinced. He decided, however, to say nothing of this just then.

"It's queer that Neil hasn't dropped me a line from France," Tod rejoined. "He always did at every port— a post card, at least."

A smile twisted the man's lips and eyebrows. "Don't

you see?—he is ashamed. You may never hear from him—for a long time."

Something in the tone, something keen and cruel as a sword thrust, made Tod inwardly tremble. Was this a threat? A conviction? Whatever it was, it made the boy certain of one thing—Jasper Swickard knew more about Neil than he told.

"Well, my boy," continued the manager, "what are you going to do now?" He leaned forward, a questioning expression upon his dark, thin face.

"Oh, I don't know—really. Go back to Stockton, I guess."

"Yes, that's the best thing for you. Go back to your job and stick there. That's the only way to be successful. Only don't follow in your brother's footsteps—or you'll get into trouble."

Tod's face flamed. "I'll never believe that of him—never! . . . Good-day, Mr. Swickard. But I'm not going home. I'm going to find my brother—I'm going to find Neil."

II : GRINNING DRAGONS

IN THE outer office, the girl looked up from her typewriter. "I want to talk with you," she whispered quickly. "Go straight across the wharf to the bunkers. Wait there!" Almost at once, she turned to her shorthand notes; the keys of her typewriter clicked in cadence.

Without a word, Tod passed out to the gray wharf where the fog pressed about him like the gloom about his heart. Mr. Swickard's story, Neil's guilt—what did it mean? What was the mystery behind his brother's disappearance?

Safely screened behind the coal bunkers, he watched the little office, and presently he saw Jasper Swickard come out and drive off in an automobile. A few minutes later, the girl came hurrying toward him. Her eyes were starry with eagerness; her voice was breathless.

"I listened—I heard it all," she said defiantly. "Well, do you believe it?"

"No—no!"

"You're right, Tod. It's a lie—a lie!"

Tod looked keenly at her. With a sudden flood of thankfulness, he realized that here was a friend and an ally.

"Neil's alive, thank God," she went on; "of that I'm certain. But where he is, or how——"

"What's it all about?" the youth queried, bewildered.

"Listen, Tod, it's this company that's crooked—not Neil. I have no proof, but I know it! Ever since I came here to work, a year ago, I felt something was wrong."

Tod stared. "You mean the European-Pacific Steamship Company?"

"Yes. The name sounds big, doesn't it? It really is a flimsy little firm, though—and only a few years old. It had its birth during wartime. It has only two freighters: the *Panama* and the *Araby*. These men are crooks, I tell you; and what they've done to Neil——" She paused and pressed her hands together till the knuckles showed white.

"If I could only find him!" Tod began. "I'll do anything, Miss—Miss——"

"Murray," she helped. "Sheila Murray."

"Anything, Miss Murray. What can I do?" He gazed
about him helplessly. His last words to Mr. Swickard
now seemed boyish indeed.

"There's Captain Ramsey," broke in the girl. "He's
going into the office. I must run. Wait for me here."

Tod watched her till she entered the office, then he
seated himself on an iron bollard near by to think things
over. Strange! What did it all mean? Neil had sailed as
purser on the *Panama* six months before. It was his second trip on that boat. He had visited Tod in Stockton
and had seemed as gay, as carefree as always. Then this
silence.

Tod raised his eyes. The *Panama* had berthed at this
very dock. He rose and strolled forward, his hands thrust
deep into his pockets, his book beneath one arm. Another
freighter lay at her moorings there now, with a dozen
longshoremen at work loading her. A donkey engine
screeched; a winch whirred; a great wooden arm came
from the steamer and, picking up several boxes in a rope
net, swung the cargo across the water and deposited it
down the forward hatch.

Entranced for a moment, Tod watched the scene. Here
was a steamer making ready for sea, her single funnel
sending forth a thin spiral of black smoke to mingle
with the leaden mist about her. She was filling her holds
with mysterious cargo to be taken to some far port of the
world—Hong Kong, perhaps, or Sydney—London or
Constantinople. It was such a picture as Neil had told
him of, but never before had he been fortunate enough

to see. He breathed with delight; a sense of rapture, surging through him, mounted to his brain.

On the ship's bow he made out the word: *Araby*. The freighter *Araby* of San Francisco! The name brought to his nostrils a breath of the East, a perfume of spices and sandalwood, a vision of enchanted azure waters and swarming ports, of flashing golden sunlight and heavy tropical heat. What a marvellous vessel she was!

His eyes ran eagerly over her. Her steel hull was brick-red with rust; her wooden superstructure, once white, was now a dirty gray. She was blunt nosed, obviously built for her carrying capacity; she was old, too, and battered by seas until now she appeared like an ancient, fabulous sea horse come home from the wars in honour, her last days of repose well earned. No days of rest and decay, however, awaited her here; she was being loaded again for a distant port. Perhaps this was the end she desired: to die, not peacefully in the shallows of Sausalito, but bravely upon the high seas, her bows breasting the swell of a coming storm. Possibly, Tod instinctively caught the feeling of this ocean tramp bound by stout

ropes and cables to the wharf. To him she was romance
and adventure, all the glamour of an immortal galleon
about to break bondage and nose her way past headlands to the open sea.

A boatswain's whistle suddenly shrilled near by. At
once the derrick hoisted its net of cargo. Tod, at the opportunity, darted past the group of toiling stevedores to
the edge of the wharf, back of the cabins amidships. He
wanted to see the *Araby* more closely. Yes, she was just
such a vessel as Neil had told him of, only not so large,
of course. There, above him, was the bridge where the
captain walked; there were the wheel and chart room
behind; there was the boat deck with lifeboats swinging
upon davits. Below this, back of those portholes, were
the officers' quarters, and forward would be the forecastle where the crew bunked.

A sudden clatter of tinware focussed his attention
upon the cabins amidships. In a narrow sheltered alleyway, an open door showed a line of pots and pans.

"It must be the kitchen," Tod thought. "No—the galley, Neil called it. Gosh, what a racket! Somebody's getting killed!"

Indeed, from the noise, it was apparent that a battle
of some sort was ensuing in the ship's galley. A figure
abruptly issued from the door and rolled down the
alleyway. Next came a volley of curses such as Tod had
never before heard. They continued to roll forth like an
enemy's bombardment at dawn. The voice was deep,
bellowing, thunderous.

"Golly, this is the real stuff!" Tod acknowledged to
himself. "That's a sure-enough sailor!"

For a second, the voice died down, and Tod saw the

figure on the deck pull itself together and rise. It proved
to be a Chinese youth with a yellow, terror-stricken face.
At his first movement toward the open door, the abuse
at once recommenced.

"Drop the butter, will you—you blasted heathen!"
roared the voice. "Git out! D'yuh hear? Git, before I
twist off yer dirty yellow face!"

The unlucky culprit who had dropped the precious
butter gave a jump for the ship's rail. Tod thought for a
horrified moment that the fellow meant to leap into the
black, greasy waters below. But he didn't. He cowered
there, turning terrified eyes down the alleyway.

"Me no mean to!" he gasped in a sibilant whisper.
"Ming work allee time. Me can do."

"Can do!" bellowed the voice like thunder. "Yeh, you
blasted Chink, you can do one thing—you git!"

Tod's spellbound gaze left the Chinese boy and went
to the galley door beyond. His eyes widened in amazement. The owner of the voice stood in the doorway.

It was evidently low tide, and the freighter heavily
loaded, for the main deck was almost level with the
wharf. Tod stared. Just a few feet away stood the half-
naked figure of a man. He was of huge stature, clothed
only in a pair of short rolled seamen's pants. His great
hairy legs were firmly planted upon the deck; his herculean shoulders gleamed from the heat of the galley;
his teeth flashed angrily in a flushed face as he emitted
another volley of oaths.

It was no longer the curses that amazed Tod; neither
was it the massive tower of strength standing so near
him. As in a trance, he gazed at the strange pictures
which appeared painted upon the man's body.

"Why—he's tattooed!" Tod muttered. "Tattooed—all over!"

It was true. The cook's torso, from the waist up, was a mass of minute tattoo work. A Chinese dragon of red and green lay coiled upon his body with two long necks writhing up to the man's immense chest, where the evil heads grinned broadly. The thing was uncanny. As the man in his anger breathed heavily, the two-headed dragon seemed to twist and sway, the red eyes to dart fire and hatred.

"I won't have a Chink in this galley," bawled the cook. "Gut me, if I will. Git out—and git quick! Savee?" He threw out a hairy arm, muscular as a blacksmith's, and Tod saw that a blue snake lay wound about it. The other arm was a network of stars, like the quivering spiral of the Milky Way.

"Holy hemlock!" gasped Tod. "He ought to be in a circus. I'd pay a quarter to see him, any day!"

The Chinese boy gave the cook a supplicating glance. "Me good boy," he said in his queer pidgin English. "Me can do. Me work long time in house in Flisco."

"In a house!" roared the tattooed man. "I'm a swab-headed deck hand if he ain't said a house! Blast yer yellow hide! You git—before I throw a cleaver at yuh."

The Chinese boy edged along the rail. "Yes—me go. Me no likee this ship. Goo-bye!"

Tod watched him dive into a doorway and appear a moment later with a bundle. He pattered along the deck to the gangway and came ashore. Tod smiled; but as his gaze came back to the huge figure of the tattooed man, the smile vanished. The cook's eyes were turned upon him in a way that froze the boy to the spot. He felt as a tiny beastie of the wood might feel when suddenly confronted by a barbaric jungle monster. Unconsciously, he shuddered, repelled yet fascinated.

The cook gave a short, deep laugh and disappeared into the galley. Tod breathed more freely. "Golly, what a man!" he muttered, as he made his way back to the bunkers.

Sheila Murray was already coming toward him. "Why —what's wrong?" she asked. "You look as if you'd seen a ghost."

"A ghost? Oh, no—just a tattooed man," Tod answered. "What's the news?"

The girl regarded him intently. "Tod Moran, have you ever wanted to go to sea?"

"Go to sea!" he echoed. "I've always wanted to! I've dreamed about it—read travel books and sea books galore. Neil always wanted me to stay in school, though."

"Well, you're going to sea now—if you will."

"Now?"

"Yes, you can sail to-morrow morning as mess boy on the freighter *Araby*."

"Mess boy on the *Araby!*"

"Yes—don't repeat my words like a ninny." She smiled wistfully. "Oh, how I envy you! I wish I weren't a girl. But I am; so here I must stay. But you, Tod Moran, can sail for the Mediterranean by way of the Panama Canal—if you will."

Tod's eyes glowed. "Just watch me. And you think I might find Neil?"

"I don't know—but it's a chance. Listen: Mr. Hawkes, the mate, was second officer on the *Panama*. He knew Neil. He must know what happened. He left the steamer in Marseilles and came home on a Dollar boat when the *Panama* went on to South Africa. Make a friend of Mr. Hawkes. Get the truth from him. Find when Neil left ship, and trace him through the shipping offices or the American Consul."

"I'll do my best," Tod returned, athrob with hope. "How will I get the job?"

"You already have it. Captain Ramsey just came into the office and said the cook demanded a new mess boy. He's going to get rid of the Chinaman to-day."

"He already has. The Chink just left."

"Good. I told Captain Ramsey that I had a young friend who was just the person for a ship's boy. You'll make the beds in the officers' quarters, wait on the table, and help the cook."

Tod gulped. "Help the cook!"

"Didn't I tell you not to repeat my words?" Sheila Murray laughed. "You won't mind peeling potatoes, will you?"

"No," Tod murmured weakly. "I'll do anything for Neil. But the cook—that tattooed man?"

"Yes, isn't he a scream? Oh, if only Barnum were alive!"

Tod glanced across to the *Araby*, where the derrick was hoisting cargo. He could vaguely make out the galley portholes. "I was just thinking," he said, swallowing hard, "that I'd hate to be in that Chinee boy's place in the galley—and now I'm there! By golly, I'll be working with a cannibal!"

"You're almost seventeen, aren't you, Tod? Old enough, surely, to look out for yourself. Oh, well, if you're afraid——"

"I'm not. I'll go."

"Then go down immediately to the Seamen's Bureau and sign on. You'll see Captain Ramsey there. And listen—tell him you'll have to get your clothes, so you can't come aboard till after dark."

"So I won't——"

"Yes, so you won't see Mr. Swickard again. He mustn't know. And he won't, for he leaves to-night for New York. Now, go straight to the Seamen's Bureau at Pier 1."

Tod hesitated a moment. "You're the real stuff," he stammered at last. "I—I can't begin to thank you."

"You needn't bother," she answered. "Good-bye, Tod Moran, cabin boy."

He turned away into the fog. A hand reached out and grasped his own as she added: "Good-bye, Tod Moran—cook's help!"

III : S. S. "ARABY"

AT THE Seamen's Bureau, Tod was signed on the ship's articles as mess boy of the S. S. *Araby* of San Francisco.

"Report on board at once," said Captain Ramsey. "The mate will give you your orders."

"Yes, sir," answered Tod. "But my clothes—I'll have to get them. It'll be evening before I can get back."

Tod gave the captain a searching look. Somehow, he was disappointed. The commander of the *Araby* was a tall, thin, bleary-eyed man of middle age, certainly not the usual forceful personality that Tod imagined should pace a bridge at sea. He had evidently been drinking, too, for he lurched slightly as he turned away with a gruff, "All right," thrown over his shoulder.

Tod, aglow with joy and expectation, left the office. He had done it! He was a sailor on an ocean tramp. All those rose-tinted dreams of high adventure, those glorious visions of his youth, were about to be realized. No longer need he sit in his firelit room and improvise pictures of Tod Moran standing on the rolling bridge of a liner as it steamed across wintry seas; no longer need he conjure up mythical fancies of Southern isles rising, palm-covered, from the trembling blue of tropic seas. Now he was going there. By golly—by golly! He was a sailor!

Outside, several men lolled about the dock. They strolled his way as he went whistling toward the Ferry Building.

"Got a berth?" queried a grizzled seaman.

"Yes," Tod answered gaily. "I sail to-morrow."

"What on?"

"The *Araby*."

A series of laughs rose from the little group gathering about him.

"The *Araby!* That tub? Oh, Gawd!"

"Poor kid—he's done for."

Tod surveyed them in surprise. "Why, what's wrong?" he asked. "Isn't she a good ship?"

"Good? Listen to 'im!" jeered a voice. "Say, that old tramp's done for. She'll never make this port again —or any other neither. We've all turned down berths on her. Her boilers are liable to blow up at any old time, and as for her hull—well, it's rotten."

"Ain't that hard luck fer yuh!" chimed in another. "And him just a kid, too. He'll never see Frisco no more. Too bad."

Tod tried to smile at the sad faces. "Aw, she looks like a fine ship. She's not that bad, is she?"

"She ain't? Say, they can't never get a crew for her. Always changing mates and skippers, too. Just you wait till she hits a swell—you'll know then as how we warned you. Well, so long. Too bad. Too bad."

Tod hurried away from their commiserating voices. He pulled his coat collar up. Gosh, what a fog! Cold, too. So the *Araby* was a rotten tub! And her captain smelled of too much liquor. And her cook was a tattooed savage. Where were his visions now?

About noon the fog lifted, and with it Tod's spirits rose. He strolled through Sailor Town, then took a street car to the Cliff House where he watched the seals playing round on the rocks. At four o'clock he saw the mist sweeping in from the sea and, when he returned to the Embarcadero, the city was again enveloped in its thick gray blanket.

He ate his supper in a chop house frequented by the riffraff of the water front. Yarns of ships and shipping were tossed along the counter with the food. One old sailor had been on the beach in Singapore for six months. "Keep away from that blasted port, kid!" Another had been stranded on a South Sea Island and was sorry he ever left. "A white man's a man there; here he's only a dog!" Tod ate more than was good for him of the cold, greasy food.

When he came out, the lamplighter had already made his rounds; along the water front the flickering lights tried in vain to pierce the thick damp atmosphere. Tod picked up his suitcase and the blankets he had purchased and trudged slowly along the docks to Pier 43. The wharf office was silent and dark, but a light burned at the gangway. With a scuffling sound, Tod dragged his dunnage across to the deck of the *Araby*, whose dim superstructure he could vaguely make out.

He paused as a figure detached itself from the gloom near the forward hatch and came toward him.

"Who's there?" It was the watchman's voice.

"I'm the new mess boy," Tod answered. "Captain Ramsey told me to report to the mate."

The watchman snickered. "The chief mate ain't here. He's gettin' drunk, most probably, like the rest of this blasted crew. The third mate's the only officer aboard. They makes me stand watch—and this the last night in port!" He swore softly.

"What'd I better do?" Tod asked.

"Do? Oh, Gawd! Are you a green one?" He came closer to view the boy. "Well, you don't look so bad. Take your things and throw 'em in a bunk in the seamen's fo'c'sle. Don't get the one on the port bow—that belongs to the Black Gang." He motioned the boy forward.

Tod hesitated. "The port bow?"

"Oh, what a lubber!" The watchman sighed deeply. "The port's the left side goin' for'ard, and the sta'b'rd's the right."

With tired arms, Tod dragged his things toward the ship's bows. Suddenly, he was brought up against an iron wall in which he glimpsed two doors. The one to the right he swung back on creaking hinges. All was silent and dim within the forecastle. He threw his blankets below, then made his way down the three iron steps. He found himself in a small triangular compartment, tiered on each side with a double row of bunks. A single electric bulb shed its dim rays upon a littered table fastened to the floor in the centre, upon piles of clothing strewn about. A long guttural snore from a bunk on his right told Tod that at least one of the crew was aboard. Above him a frowsy head looked out and a sleepy voice with a cockney accent said, "Hallo, mitey," and vanished.

Tod, making the rounds of the bunks, discovered that these two were all of the crew in evidence. Upon nearly every mattress, however, sprawled a blue dunnage bag; evidently, in this way, the seamen claimed their beds. Tod found an empty one near the peak, a top bunk, and piled his blankets upon it.

"Better make your bed, mitey," said the cockney voice across the top row. "Yer don't 'ave no servants on this bloomin' ship, y'know." He pointed to the straw mattress. "Ye'll be a lucky bloke if that donkey's breakfast ain't got bloomin' livestock in it."

Tod laughed. He pulled aside the greasy brown light-curtain on its piece of string, whipped the straw mattress into shape, and spread his blankets on it. "Why aren't you ashore?" he asked in a friendly tone. "Everybody else seems to be." He glanced up at the man who was leaning on one elbow, smoking a cigarette.

"Blimey, ain't this luck?" returned the other. "My duds all pawned and not a blarsted penny left to my nime. And me from Lunnon for th' fust time! Say, ye ain't got an extra blanket, 'ave yer?" The little cockney smiled pleasantly.

"I'm rather short myself," Tod answered. "It took all my cash to get these."

"That's all right, mitey. Wot boats 'ave ye bin in?"

"This is my first."

"Ye' fust? Oh, well—ye'll l'arn—ye'll l'arn. This bloomin' boat ain't so bad. Blimey, no! I took a pier-head jump wunst into a windjammer and came round the Horn in a 'owlin' gale. But I left 'er at Valparaiso— 'it the chief mite over the 'ead with th' p'int ov a marlin-spike and——"

"Shut up, Toppy! Can that stuff!" a voice suddenly broke in.

Tod turned to see the seaman roll over in his bunk.

The little cockney threw his cigarette stub to the floor, dangerously near a pair of grimy socks. "That's all right, mitey," he went on, unperturbed. "Ye drunk too much ov that bloomin' stuff—that's why ye've got a 'eadache. Go t' sleep!" He showed his yellow fangs in a wide grin.

"Go t' sleep yerself, yer scurvy limejuicer," came a muffled reply.

At the words, a smooth flow of invective came from Toppy's lips. Tod was appalled by the language. It was his first contact with a cockney sailor, and the oaths, low and obscene, disconcerted him.

Presently he climbed to the deck; he wanted to look over this ocean tramp which was to be his abode, per-haps, for months to come. The watchman was seated upon the forward hatch, smoking a pipe.

"Well, did yer get a bunk?" he greeted.

"Sure," Tod answered. "I'm all ready for work."

The watchman chuckled. "Don't be in a hurry, kid," he advised. "You'll git enough o' that before we hit the Caribbean.—Now, I wonder what that is."

He went toward the gangway as voices from the dock struck their ears. Two more of the *Araby's* crew were coming aboard, arm in arm and singing boisterously. They stumbled across the deck and disappeared into the forecastle.

"Well, let 'em enjoy themselves to-night," said the watchman philosophically; "something tells me that they won't enjoy this passage, they won't. No, sir!"

He seated himself again and conversed with Tod in low tones. He was entered on the ship's articles as John Nelson of Copenhagen, but he intimated that that wasn't his real name. He only went to sea when he had to—now and then. He hated the blasted sea.

"What?" said Tod. "I thought sailors loved the sea."

The old seaman took his pipe from his mouth and laughed uproariously. "Love it! Blast my hide! Say, kid, somebody's been filling you with opium. They all hates it. Hates it! I've been on barks and steamers for thirty years, and I ain't yet ever heard a feller say he liked it. No, sir, not one!"

He puffed slowly, then went on. "You never have a home; you travel around the globe, but you only see the dirty foreign ports with their water fronts all alike. This ain't the life for a feller. No; a farm's the place he orta be. Yes, sir, sometime I'm goin' ter quit it fer good and buy a nice little chicken farm in the hills where I can't never see the old ocean. Yes, sir, I am."

A step and a low laugh sounded behind them in the gloom. "Who're you giving advice to now, Nelson?" said a voice.

"Just this kid, sir—the new mess boy," replied the man.

From his tone and the way he jerked himself erect, Tod knew that it must be one of the ship's officers, the third mate, probably, whom the watchman addressed. Tod sprang to his feet also.

"You'll never leave the sea, Nelson, you know you won't. Yes, you think you hate it all right, but you'll never be able to leave.—Captain come aboard yet, Nelson?"

"No, sir. The chief engineer is in his room, sir, that's all."

The third mate turned to Tod. "This your first trip?"

"Yes, sir."

In the dim light Tod could see that the third officer of the *Araby* was little more than a youth himself, certainly not more than twenty-three or -four.

"Well, come with me," went on the third mate. "We'll have a look-see round the deck. It wasn't so very long ago that I made my first voyage myself."

In straightforward tones, the boy was given his orders. He was to rise at eight bells of the middle watch—four o'clock in the morning—and report to the galley amidships. Later, he must wait on the officers in the cabin aft. Not a hard job, but he must be alert.

Tod's depression left him as he listened to the even tones of the young officer. It wasn't so bad after all.

When he returned to the forward main deck, he had gone over the *Araby*, superficially, at least. She was a

three-thousand-ton cargo carrier of ancient build with
derrick supports fore and aft and a single funnel. In
the amidships section she carried the engineers' cabin
and the cook's galley, with the latter opening in the
alleyways next to the engine-room doorways. Above this
was the boat deck. Aft was the poop, containing the master's and the first mate's quarters and the officers' saloon. Tod would doubtless get to know well these quarters later on.

He seated himself again upon the hatch. The night
was cold and wet, but he did not care to descend to the
stuffy forecastle and try to sleep. As the hours wore on,
the crew returned in little groups. Most of them stumbled
up the gangway and lurched across the deck to the forecastle. At eleven, the second mate came aboard. At midnight, the captain and the first mate arrived.

The watchman heard their voices on the pier. "That's
them," he whispered to Tod, "and both filled to the
scuppers with booze."

The gangway creaked as the two men stumbled across.
"Watchman!" It was the captain's voice.

"Yes, sir."

"Third mate aboard?"

"Yes, sir."

"Second mate aboard?"

"Yes, sir."

A pause ensued as Captain Ramsey unbuttoned his
pilot coat, pushed back his cap from his red-rimmed
eyes, and grasped the first mate for support. "Chief
mate aboard?"

"Just come aboard," said the watchman without a
blink.

The first mate, a gorilla-like man with a powerful chest and long arms, lurched to the rail and left the captain without support. "Can't ye see me here, sir?" he queried in hurt tones through his short black beard. "How'd ye ever git here if I hadn't brought yuh!"

"Th's a' right, Mr. Hawkes," hiccoughed the captain. "No harm intended. 'Pologize, Mr. Hawkes. Where's my cabin on this ship?"

"Aft, sir," said the watchman. "Here's the cabin boy, sir. Let him help you."

"Yeh, boy—give me a hand. I wish this was a bark. It was a sad day—when I left the sea—to take a berth in a steamer."

The watchman whispered into Tod's startled ear: "Get 'em to their cabins, kid. You'll have to do it in every port, I'm thinking."

"This way, sir," said Tod.

With the thin, swaying captain on one arm and the heavy-set first mate on the other, Tod went along the port alleyway, past the after hatches, to the poop. In the officers' saloon, where electric globes burned in a brass lamp overhead, the two men dropped into old red plush seats.

Tod, wiping the sweat from his brow, was immediately struck by the strange marine odour of the place. Its walls, at some remote time, had been painted white; it possessed a skylight that could only dimly have let in the light of day. The captain, too, appeared to fit into the shadowy contours of the cabin. His gray wisps of hair dropped over his forehead; his weak mouth hung half open. The chief mate had risen and gazed with apparent scorn at his superior officer. He crossed to the

table and steadied himself with a hairy paw upon the
green baize cover. His round bearded face, flushed with
liquor, had lost its look of friendliness. Upon his temple
Tod saw a scar which, extending to his cheek, drew down
as his dark eyes squinted in a manner that made the
boy step backward.

"I ain't goin' ter eat ye," grunted the mate, his thick
lower lip jutting outward. "Gi' me a hand, here. We
got t' git the Old Man t' bed." He jerked his head toward
a door behind him.

Tod opened the door. The light from the saloon lamp
showed him a comfortable cabin containing a bed, a
chair, and a desk. Together, he and the mate half lifted
the captain within, laid him on his bed, and undressed
him.

"Now we'll tuck him in nice," said the mate with a
grin. "Nighty-night, Captain."

He waved Tod out and stepped into the saloon, closing the door sharply behind them.

"Is that all?" asked Tod. "I'm tired out—think I'll
turn in."

From his position near the table the mate whirled.
His thick lips writhed in anger; his eyes narrowed to
points of glinting fire. "Think you'll turn in, do you?"
he blurted. "You wait till I tell ye to."

His long arm reached forth and grasped Tod's shoulder in a grip of iron. Slowly, deliberately, the mate
shook the boy, shook him till his teeth chattered and his
eyes closed.

"Speak to the first officer like that, will ye! I'll learn
ye, ye wharf rat! Be 'spectful to yer officer. Git!"

He flung Tod from him with a sudden movement, and

the boy went crashing against the cabin wall. The mate stood there with chin shot forward; the scar on his temple flamed crimson. Tod picked himself up.

"Don't speak till ye're spoken to—understan'? And call me 'sir.' Ye got to start right on this ship, or I'll throw ye overboard." He grinned broadly. "We'll lick ye into shape—the cook and I. Yeh, if the cook don't do it, I will. Now go crawl into yer donkey's breakfast, little boy."

The new mess boy of the S. S. *Araby* was learning. "Yes, sir," he stammered as he let himself out the door. "Yes, sir."

IV   THE CABIN AFT

T EIGHT bells, Tod was roused by the call of the watch. He lay in his bunk for a moment listening to the grumbles of the men as they turned out. The electric globe burned dimly above the table; a lone beam strayed on the wall near his hand. Tod blinked. Something small and brown was moving on the wood of the bunk beside him. He wiped the sleep from his eyes and stared. Yes, there was another of those moving spots. A cockroach! Two of them—no, three. Evidently the men were not to have the forecastle to themselves on this voyage. Well, what was a cockroach anyway! So long as there was nothing worse—— He sat up in bed and began pulling off his pajamas.

Suddenly a yell burst from a tall Swede who was slipping into his dungarees across the way. "Yiminy! Look —the kid's undressed!"

Tod glanced round in surprise. The four men of the watch were eying him with amazed grins.

"Blimey! What's the bloomin' lubber wearin'?" called the little cockney. "Oh, Gord! Strike me bline if he ain't sleepin' in a suit!"

Tod's cheeks reddened as he slipped into his shirt. One glance told him that all the seamen had slept in their underwear.

"Aw, leave the kid alone, ye blasted limejuicer!" said Nelson the Dane. "Ain't he got a right to wear 'em if he wants to? You guys don't know no better. Ye're too fresh, anyway. He'll larn. Yes, he'll larn."

Tod quickly finished dressing, his mouth a hard thin line. He vowed that at the first opportunity he would toss the offending garments overboard. A forecastle was no place for pajamas!

He followed the men up the three steps to the deck. A chill breeze had sprung up; the sky was strewn with a mass of quivering stars. The water front lay silent and black about him. Aft a winch whirred noisily where the boatswain loaded a few belated boxes.

"By sunrise we'll be sailing," thought Tod, pausing to look about.

How little he knew that morning of the ways of ocean tramps! Unlike the great passenger greyhounds that ply regularly across the lanes of the sea as promptly as the overland express trains, the tramp freighter, rusty and woebegone of aspect, comes and goes like a will-o'-the-wisp, sailing days and even weeks after its scheduled departure. It follows not the well-charted lanes of travel, but takes to the open sea, filling its holds with cargo disdained by the larger ships, and taking it to remote ports of the world seldom visited by its luxurious sisters.

The crews, too, are men of a different stamp. Their seamanship has been learned before the mast, in the rigging of windjammers rounding the Horn, where life is cheap and the food sea biscuits and salt horse. They know the far ports of the world as a cockney knows the streets of London; they look with contempt upon those well-fed seamen who are familiar only with their regular ports of call.

As Tod, this early morning, crossed the deck to the port alleyway leading to the galley, his steps faltered in trepidation. After his encounter with the first mate the night before, he was now prepared for any eventuality when he became mess boy to the strange being who was cook aboard the *Araby*. He was in for it now!

The galley door was open; a light burning within showed a gigantic shadow passing across the doorway. Tod stopped on the threshold. The Tattooed Man bent above the ship's range making the fire. He was clothed in blue pants and a jumper, and when he turned, the boy saw that it lay open upon his shaggy, powerful chest.

" 'Bout time ye're here," he greeted. "After this ye start the fire—see?" He closed the lid with a bang.

"Yes, sir," Tod said meekly.

The cook flushed. In amazement, Tod saw the red creep up the broad neck to his cheeks. The light-blue eyes above the high cheek bones, which gave the man a strange Tartar look, shone pale and stricken in the light.

"Gut me, if I'll have you call me 'sir,' " he growled. He swung about and rattled the pots on the stove. "I'm the cook—and a damned good cook too!"

Tod blinked. The words were so different from what he had expected. "What'll I do?" he asked. "I'm new at this game, but I want to begin right. You tell me where to start and I'll light in."

The Tattooed Man, with one muscular arm on the drain of the trough, turned and looked the boy steadily in the eye. "Sufferin' tripe! Ain't you never been on a ship before?"

Tod shook his head.

The cook heaved a deep sigh. "Gut me, if I don't have the worst luck! Well, you don't look quite so bad as the Chink, anyway. Here—put on the Java."

Tod gave him a questioning glance. "Java?"

"Sufferin' fish hooks," exclaimed the cook. "Where was you raised—on a cow farm?" He looked the boy up and down. "H—m! A regular dude, a swell, a maca-roni. What's your name?"

"Joseph Todhunter Mor——" Tod stopped. Did he want to tell his name?

"H—m! Well, Joe Macaroni, you got t' work on this here job. Dive in!"

As Tod worked there in the close quarters of the galley, getting the watch's breakfast for six o'clock, he cast surreptitious glances at the cook. He wondered what story lay back of this strange figure. His age, Tod reflected, might be anywhere from twenty-five to thirty-five; certainly he had not always cooked, for his great body was brawn and muscle, without an ounce of fat upon it. This Tod could see when the heat of the stove made the man throw off his jumper to reveal the dragons upon his herculean frame. Between the faint red-and-blue figures, the skin gleamed satin-white. He seemed out of place there, dexterously lifting a kettle or a pan with his enormous biceps; rather should he have been climbing some ship's rigging in tropic waters, his two hundred thirty or so pounds of solid healthy flesh standing out against a Southern sky. His tawny hair was cut short. His eyes, Tod felt, were clear and strong—and hard.

At four bells, the crew brought their mess gear to the galley door to receive their hand-out. Only in rough weather, the cook informed him, was chow taken to them in the forecastle. At seven o'clock, Tod, in a clean white coat, served breakfast to the officers in the cabin aft. He covered the green baize table with a red-and-white cloth, set the plates against the fiddle, which in rough weather served to keep the dishes off the floor, and on the stroke of seven set a covered dish of hot cereal before the captain's place.

The commander of the *Araby*, clad in officer's blue serge, was seated in one of the five permanently fixed swivel chairs; he glanced at the new boy as if he had never seen him before, and truth to tell, Tod was ready to admit that their meeting of the previous night had

probably been forgotten. The black-bearded first mate,
upon the captain's right, watched him with dark eyes
beneath dark brows, but said no word. The chief engineer, upon the left, was a pleasant, rosy-cheeked Scotchman who hailed from Glasgow and wanted everyone
to know it. Being deaf, he talked in a loud high voice.

The conversation that was tossed across the table between hasty gulps of coffee was scarcely the sort that
Tod's firelit dreams had led him to expect upon a glorious ship in harbour. When the captain and mate cou-
pled freights and cargoes and tonnage with the name
of some glamorous port beyond the horizon, they did
so in terms of dollars and cents. Confronted thus with
sordid reality, the new mess boy found it a moment of
corroding disillusion.

He was pouring the steaming coffee with a listless
hand when a startled oath from the first mate brought
him to a halt. "What's this?" shouted the mate between
his beard. "Blast my hide—it's a cockroach!" The hairy
paw of the man held up the offending insect in his spoon.
Tod saw his beaked nose, like a bird of prey, hook down
over his snarling lips.

Tod swallowed, his knees trembled. The first mate was
staring at him with his evil face twisted into the mask
of a Chinese idol. "Captain, what sort o' cook has we
got this trip, I asks yer. Look, do we eat this every day?"

Captain Ramsey wiped his mouth with the back of his
hand. "Mr. Hawkes," he returned solemnly, "I ain't
never seen a ship without 'em. They're like rats—and
I've heard it said they leave a sinking ship, too."

"Wull ye no' eat them with th' porridge, Mr.
Hawkes?" grinned the chief engineer. "Now, well I

remember, whin I was in the *Mary McKinnon*——"

Tod did not hear more of the chief engineer's story. The first mate had reached out his arm and seized him by the tender flesh of his waist. The big fingers, closed on the boy's slim body, brought forth excruciating pain.

"Serve 'em with our meals, do you!" he hissed. "What'd I tell yer last night?"

Tod's teeth closed over his lips to keep back a cry. A hand went to his head as if he would ward off an impending blow. The other held the handle of the steaming coffee-pot. He saw the dreadful face of the mate close to his; he jerked back, at the same moment tipping the coffee-pot's boiling contents on the mate's thick legs.

With an oath, the man was on his feet. His arm shot back for a blow.

"That'll do, Mr. Hawkes," said the captain. The chief engineer had risen; he glanced thankfully at the master. "Sit down," went on the captain. "Doesn't pay to get too touchy, Mr. Hawkes."

The Scotchman smiled grimly. "Mon, d'ye think this is a win'jammer?"

"It's as bad," snapped the first officer as he took his seat. "I'll teach the kid to treat the officers' mess like this, I will."

Tod stumbled to the door; the blood had left his face; his eyes, beneath the shaded lights that burned above the table, were steel gray with hatred.

"Take the stuff away," said the captain. "And tell the cook to be more careful after this."

"Yes, sir." Tod gathered up the dishes and almost ran from the cabin.

In the galley, the Tattooed Man was flinging slices of

bacon on to a platter. "Well, Joe Macaroni," he boomed in his deep rich tones, "how you gettin' along?"

"Not very well," Tod gulped as he rubbed his side. "There was a roach in the mush."

"The deuce there was! Well, we'll have to be more careful, won't we." He laughed deep in his throat.

The new mess boy sighed. Grimly he went about the remainder of the meal; but it passed without mishap. He cleared off the table in the saloon, then made up the cabin of the captain. It was roomy and comfortable, although the chair and desk were of ancient make. A porthole opened starboard and another aft. A calendar hung on the wall; a picture of a small girl lay in a frame on the desk. Tod closed the door with the feeling that the master of the *Araby* was not a bad man at heart; he was weak, perhaps, and inclined to lean too much upon his first officer.

In the cabin opposite, he made the bed with the greatest care. The first mate, he knew, would only await an opportunity to vent his rage upon him. He therefore must not give the man a chance.

Day was just breaking, but there was no promise of the sun. In the gray light Tod straightened up the little cabin. Upon the walls he saw several pictures cut from a pink weekly, and a photograph of a scantily arrayed Spanish woman with tantalizing eyes, signed: To my Sweetheart—Jerry; from Lola. Other photographs, even more interesting, adorned the chest of drawers; here, at least, Mr. Hawkes rose to Tod's idea of a true sailor.

Through the port he saw that the streets were again busy with their traffic. The trucks were covered as if for rain. "Golly, I hope not," thought Tod.

As he made his way back across the after deck, he was met by a burly longshoreman. "Are yuh the mess boy?" he asked.

At the boy's nod of assent he brought forth a white envelope which he carefully handed over. "She said to give it only to you. Now, yer sure it's for yuh?"

Tod smiled. "Yes, see? It's addressed to me: Tod Moran, mess boy of the steamship *Araby*. I think I know who it's from."

He glanced about him quickly. Forward, the carpenter was busy battening down the hatch. Above him, amidships, the youthful wireless operator was entering his cabin. Tod took the letter to the port alleyway and ripped it open.

It was from Sheila Murray, as he had thought, and read:

DEAR TOD:
Just a line to wish you the best of luck upon your trip. Mr. Swickard left last night for New York, supposedly; but the rumour has leaked out that he is going to France. Can Neil, in truth, be there?

Are you making friends with Mr. Hawkes, the First Mate? He was on the *Panama* with Neil, you know. Find out all you can from him. I won't try to give you advice; you know what we want—you and I.

Ever your friend,
SHEILA MURRAY.

Tod reread the letter twice, then entered the galley to wash the dishes in the trough. Somehow, those written words seemed to keep him in touch with friends. Without his brother, he was alone, and now he knew that Sheila loved his brother, too. He leaned against the galley doorway. The cook had disappeared into his narrow cabin across the alleyway.

Suddenly shouts struck his ears. He listened. It was the captain's voice. "Let go aft!"

Tod's heart jumped. He dropped the dish rag into the trough and ran to the forward deck. The *Araby* was slipping away from her moorings.

V: OUTWARD BOUND

L ET go for'rd, Mr. Hawkes," called Captain Ramsey from the bridge.

On the forecastle head, the chief mate lifted his hand in acknowledgment of the order. At once the single dock-line slackened; the capstan whirled; the longshoremen on the pier lifted the line off the bollard, and the capstan drum began to wind in the hawser through the chock.

Tod, leaning over the forward rail, suddenly felt the ship tremble under the first thresh of the propeller. She was slipping astern, out of the dock to the bay. A deafening blast from her whistle sent up a cloud of steam to mingle with the black smoke from her funnel; the bay craft were warned that the freighter *Araby* was leaving her slip.

Tod glanced up at the bridge where the bar pilot stood by the rail stanchions, Captain Ramsey on his right. The boy heard the pilot's hoarse voice as he gave his orders. Near him he saw the young third mate standing at the engine-room telegraph, calmly moving the indicator at each command. In the wheel house the quartermaster stood at the helm.

The little freighter backed slowly out into the bay, stopped, and swung ahead, her bows pointed toward the Golden Gate. Against the gray sky overhead, the gulls screamed and wheeled. A breath of moisture-laden air struck Tod's cheek. On the port beam, the docks slipped past; for a moment Fishermen's Wharf, with its lateen-rigged sloops, lay like a bit of Italy at the foot of Russian Hill; then it was gone, and Fort Mason took its place. Alcatraz Island was left behind; ahead lay the Golden Gate.

The grizzled boatswain, now that the decks were cleared, the derrick booms lashed, and the hatches battened down, crossed to the rail at the boy's right hand; his gaze drifted toward the black sky outside the headlands. "The barometer's falling. Dirty weather ahead," he announced. "February's a bad month for a passage south."

Tod's eyes glowed with expectation. "Think we'll hit a storm?" he asked, eagerness in his voice.

"Running right into one," returned the boatswain calmly. "Just wait." With this parting shot he passed forward to the hatch, inspected its canvas covering, and disappeared into the seamen's forecastle.

Tod stood a moment, pondering. Neil's first ship had hit a rock outside the Columbia River bar, and his brother's story, told with flashes of colour, had ever remained in the boy's memory as an experience intense and thrilling, one to be treasured always as something infinitely precious. Now the *Araby* was ploughing ahead into a storm. This was life—this was living!

Rousing himself from his meditation, he returned by way of the port alleyway to the galley. A door opposite was open, and Tod saw the cook's great body lying inert upon his bunk.

"Peel the spuds," he grunted, as he looked up from a book upon which Tod saw the word "Astronomy."

Tod washed a few pots in the trough, and taking a basket, filled it with potatoes from the locker. Then he seated himself upon a stool and began running his knife round a potato. Through the porthole he saw headlands slipping by. He could feel the pulse of the engines.

"It's great to be at sea," Tod hazarded. "It's wonderful, isn't it, Mr. Jarvis?"

"Huh!" grunted the Tattooed Man from his berth. "Just you wait, kid. You'll see. Wonderful? Sufferin' catfish!"

Tod rose and renewed the fire in the range. The galley was hot; he wiped the sweat from his forehead. The ship rolled as she met the swells coming in from sea.

He felt he must have a breath of air. He went on deck. They had passed through the Gate, and the ship lay quiet on the bosom of the ocean. The *Araby,* safely across the bar, was dropping her pilot. Tod watched him descend the accommodation ladder to a waiting skiff, which was rowed by two seamen to the pilot schooner standing off to port. From the deck, the pilot raised his hand in a farewell salutation; the schooner's auxiliary engines drove her nose through the waves toward a cargo liner approaching harbour.

Tod climbed the ladder to the forecastle head. Stepping over the chain cables, he passed round the windlass and leaned over the rail.

The blood seemed to sing through his veins with the rhythm of the ship's vibration. At sea! By golly, he was at sea. On the Pacific in the freighter *Araby*. And Panama the first landfall.

The potatoes in the galley forgotten, Tod stared about him in ecstasy. On the port beam, the land was a dark smudge against a threatening sky. A wind had set in from the southwest and increased in violence with every turn of the ship's propeller. The *Araby*, rising and falling as she plunged on through the heavy swells, headed south toward warmer climes. To starboard the red-hulled lightship lifted and fell astern. Ahead lay a vast expanse of heaving ocean, with the wind beating the dark green waves into whitecaps. To Tod's ears came the mutter of seamen in the forecastle, and the monotonous swish of the water about the steamer's bows. In the slip at San Francisco, the three-thousand-ton freighter had appeared, to his unaccustomed eyes, a veritable leviathan of the deep; here on the lonely sea she was no more than a toy boat adrift on a vast immensity.

"Where's that kid?"

Tod looked aft in terror. He had forgotten the potatoes. And dinner was not far off. Conscious that the ship was beginning to roll as well as to plunge, he swung down the companion rail to the deck. The giant cook was standing in the port alleyway, his face contorted into an angry grimace. Tod felt his way along the bulwarks. His head felt slightly dizzy; sweat lay damp on his brow. It was almost chill here in the wind; then why the strange warmth in his face, that parched feeling in his mouth? The sense of ecstasy left him.

"Run away, did yer?" shouted the cook. "Yeh, that's

a blasted queer way to begin a passage. Git busy! See?"

Tod swallowed. His stomach felt as if it were whirling around. "I forgot," he began. "I'll——"

"Forgot!" bellowed the Tattooed Man. "I'll teach yuh not to forget." He stretched forth an arm in a furious gesture of rage.

Tod slid past him down the alleyway to the galley.

"Ten minutes yer got to finish in. See?" went on the cook from the doorway behind him. "Just fer that you can wash every blamed pan to-day!"

"I'll be glad to," Tod said in a conciliating tone. But as his mind turned to thoughts of the greasy water in the trough his hand went to his head in sudden horror.

How the ship was wallowing! She plunged and rolled in a strange corkscrew manner that made the tiny walls of the galley swim wildly about him.

"What's th' matter?" the cook jibed. "Sick?"

Tod smiled wanly. "Oh, no! Only I don't feel very well."

The Tattooed Man's white teeth flashed in a wide grin. "Sufferin' halibut!" he murmured. "Our little Joe Macaroni is seasick!"

"No, I'm not," Tod denied valiantly. "Only—this sea. It's sort of rough, isn't it?"

"Rough? Naw, this is only small rolls. Just wait'll we hit a real nor'wester, and then we'll get dirty weather. Git busy, see?"

The floor of the galley heaved as a shudder went through the ship. Spume flew like rain past the port-holes. The copper pots on the wall tolled dismally. The pan of potatoes slid slowly across the floor, and Tod, reaching to grasp the runaway, felt his knees tremble.

"Yeh," grunted the cook, "that's a big one. Kind of got yuh, did it?"

Tod in silence admitted that it had. The walls of the galley careened appallingly; the floor tilted up and down every moment; the potatoes became a blurred mass in a swimming pan. His stomach felt queer, his head hot. He gasped.

Nausea gripped him.

The Tattooed Man gazed at him in scorn. "Git, you landlubber," he bellowed. "You're sick. You won't be worth the price of a herring till it's over. Now, git."

Tod went. He grasped the door for support and stumbled down the alleyway to the forward deck, where the men on watch, with swabs and holystone, sent buckets of sea water sluicing his way. Indifferent to the amused, contemptuous glances, he lurched to the rail. Here the biting wind met his cheek with a welcome caress.

At sea. At sea in the tramp steamer *Araby*. The irony of the thought burned in his brain. He had no dreams of high adventure now; other matters required his attention.

A few minutes later he crawled weakly along the bulwarks toward the seamen's forecastle. He wanted his bunk. He wanted it more than all the rosy visions of his mind. It had become a haven of rest in a world cruel and heartless, a world of mountainous seas whose white crests foamed high above the forecastle head.

From stem to stern the *Araby* was lashed by heavy sprays. She rose on a swell, then plunged. By golly— by golly, was she never coming up? Yes; she shuddered; she rose with a brave yet sluggish motion. The flood poured past.

Tod reached the iron wall of the forecastle head; it was cold and clammy to his touch. It was sheltered here by two short wings which housed the boatswain and Chips the carpenter on the port side, and the wash-room on the starboard. He breathed easier; he felt his way past the firemen's forecastle to the second doorway. Down the three steps of the ladder he half fell to the thick stuffy atmosphere of the seamen's quarters. He dimly saw the members of the watch below at rest after their weary morning, playing cards, reading, unpacking their duffel bags; their figures were blurred in a blue haze of cheap tobacco smoke that hung stagnant in the air.

"Blimey, the kid's sick." It was the cockney's taunting voice.

"Aye, he looks green as er lizard."

Amid laughs and jeers, Tod climbed up to his bunk. He dropped flat on his back. Ah, this was better; this was heaven after the warm odours of cooking in the galley. Just to rest. Let the crew rave; he didn't care.

"Ain't our new cabin boy cute, now, mitey," went on Toppy. "I bet the bloomin' cook is 'appy, too. And what'll our chow be like, I ask yer, with the kid gone. He'll never get well. Blimey, we'll 'ave t' toss him over ter th' fishes."

"Shut yer jaw!" cut in Nelson the Dane. "Leave the kid alone."

"Look 'ere, now," said Toppy aggrieved. "Cawn't I even open me mouth on this bloomin' ship? A bloke like you ain't got no right——"

"Aw, hold yer jaw or I'll twist yer blasted neck off."

"Yah, dat's ri'," drawled Swede Jorgenson.

The cockney spat viciously. "Th' kid's a toff, that's what 'e is. He ain't got the guts——"

Tod saw a shoe cut the blue fog of smoke. It crashed against a bunk and brought a yell of rage from Toppy. Above the muttered imprecations Tod heard a boatswain's pipe sound above.

"All hands on deck!"

The cry came down from the doorway like a sudden pistol shot. With muttered curses the men pulled on their shoes.

"Didn't I tell yer this ship wasn't no good? She can't stand even a sou'wester, she can't."

"Yes, nice way to begin a passage. She'll knock to pieces in a sea. Sorry I ever signed on."

Grumbling still, they climbed the steps to deck.

"Good-bye, kid," yelled Toppy from the entrance. "An' look 'ere, if the bloomin' ship starts to sink, I'll call yer. It ain't nice ter drown down there. No, it ain't nice."

Tod heard him laugh as he closed the iron door.

The boy lay silent. The deserted forecastle was dark with shadows. To his right a twilight of powdered blue pressed against the glass of the portholes, like three round eyes, faintly luminous, peering within. Close at hand he heard the seas pounding on the bows, and the whistle of the gale outside. Beneath him the bunk rose with a great swinging movement, quivered for a moment, then plunged down into what seemed a black abyss. He closed his eyes. Let her sink; he didn't care. Anything to end this awful misery.

But it wasn't fair. This was his first voyage, his first day out, and they had to hit a storm. Sheila Murray had put him aboard this ancient tramp with its strange crew of men and its strange officers. Their figures passed like a dream across his vision: the weak captain, the burly first mate, the youthful third officer, the Tattooed Man in the galley. And his forecastle mates. Sheila Murray— Neil! He had almost forgotten his brother.

No, it wasn't so bad. He'd do anything for Neil. He had told Sheila Murray that. Yes, if he had it to do over, he'd ship again on the old tramp. True, this was not the sea that he had dreamed of. All those books he had read had lied. Yes, lied. They hadn't told the truth. None of them had been like this. And that book he'd read on the train—"The Lookout: A Romance of the Sea." Rotten stuff! He'd toss it overside.

Well, to-morrow he'd get his sea legs. He'd work. He'd show them. What was it that Toppy had said in his elegant language—he didn't have the guts? He had. Just wait. He'd be tough; he'd be hard-boiled. He'd swear too, by golly!

The plunging and rolling of the ship increased, but his mind cleared. He was sick, deathly sick. He admitted that, even as his mouth became a straight determined line in his flushed face. Romance? No, not this. He almost smiled. This was the real stuff.

Presently he became aware that a hand was dragging at the door. In the gloom he saw the Swede, huge and fair with his child-like face, descend the steps.

"The cook sent yuh this lemon," he began in his slow deep voice as his dog-like eyes searched Tod's face. "He wants t' know as how ye feel. He says, 'Ask Joe Macaroni if he still thinks the sea is wonderful.' "

Tod rose on one elbow. His white face screwed into

a smile. "Tell him," he answered slowly, "that I think
it's great. It *is* wonderful. I wouldn't be back in Frisco
for all the money in the world. Blimey, no. This bloke
won't be a lubber very long."

Jorgenson put up his hand and touched Tod's moist
hot brow. "Now, matey, yoost lay down. Yah, you got
fever. I'll tell the cook you be on deck in couple o'
days."

"Couple of days! Say, I'll be serving breakfast in the
cabin to-morrow morning."

"Yah—yah." The Swede turned and climbed the
steps. "I'll tell him you said it ain't so bad."

"Bad?" Tod shouted after him. "You tell the bloomin'
cook it's great. By golly, this is the best little freighter
that ever hit the Pacific!"

As Jorgenson let himself out, Tod heard the whine
of wind in the rigging, and the beat of rain on deck.
With a frantic movement he picked up the lemon and bit
into its acid centre.

VI : MAN OVERBOARD!

POINT CONCEPTION lay astern and the Santa Barbara
Islands on the starboard beam when, for the second
time since leaving San Francisco, night overtook the
freighter *Araby*. In the heavy seas, the steamer's eleven
knots an hour had become only nine.

Tod lay in his bunk, his tired eyes closed. Although
the violent nausea of the day before had left him, he had
not yet gained his sea legs. It had been a fatiguing day

for him, for he had gone doggedly through his work without a murmur. Eight bells had just rung; he was free now until ten o'clock, when it was his nightly duty to take hot coffee and sandwiches to the officers in the cabin aft.

The forecastle was rank with tobacco smoke. Regardless of the clamour and fury of the wind without, the men in their watch below talked in fitful spasms from their tiers of bunks, or read paper-covered books by the light of two electric bulbs which were fastened in the deck head above table and doorway. Directly below Tod, Red Mitchell, a small young coal passer of uncertain age and antecedents, who bunked in the firemen's forecastle, was conversing in low tones with Swede Jorgenson across the way.

"I tell you I don't like this ship," Red complained. "For one thing, she's too old; she ain't safe. She's rotten. She ought to be tied up at Benicia. And for another, the Old Man's no good. Ain't I right, now?"

Swede Jorgenson nodded slowly.

"But it ain't only the skipper," went on the querulous voice of the visitor; "it's the whole cabin aft. If you asks me—why, they're all three sheets in the wind. 'Specially that bucko mate—that bully Hawkes. Ain't I right, now?"

Jorgenson, in the act of pulling off a soiled singlet and donning another, grunted an agreement.

"This outfit's a cheap un—ain't even a steward. And the grub's no good, either. Gotter match, Swede? Yeh, what'll they give us to eat after we hit Panama? Wormy biscuits and maggots in the prunes. Oh, I know. I've been on these tramps before, blast 'em. Hanged if I know why I signed on this one."

"Yah—but she ain'd so bad," commented Jorgenson, as he rolled into his bunk. He spoke slowly, resting between his words, as if his brains were not equal to the size of his huge body. "She might sink—yah?"

"Sure she might. And burn, too. Yuh orta see the rotten dust in the bunkers they call coal. Just th' kind t' smoke 'n' blow up."

"Do you think there's a Jonah on her?" Jorgenson whispered.

Red Mitchell lowered his voice. "Mebbe there is, and mebbe there ain't. I'm wondering, that's all. Now that cook—he's a funny one. What's he up to on this old tub? He ain't a real cook. Ain't I right, now?"

Swede Jorgenson sighed as if too much thought might bring on a headache. "Yah," he grunted, pulled his light-curtain, and began to snore softly.

Tod turned in his bunk, listening to the talk of the men above the muffled roar of the crashing seas without. What a night! He'd have to watch his step when he took the coffee to the officers' saloon.

At nine-thirty he slipped on his shoes and made his way to deck. The night was alive with the shrieks of the gale. Low in the east a single star rushed up as the ship plunged. Across a slanting deck the boy lurched. The icy wind flung him down the alleyway to the galley door. Once within, the warmth soothed him. He stirred the fire in the range, put the coffee on to boil, and began cutting thin slices of bread and cheese.

Abruptly, he became aware that voices were coming in loud tones from the cook's cabin across the alleyway. Then, in a lull in the wind, a name struck him into attention. The *Panama*.

He waited, athrob with hope. The voice was now unmistakable. It was that of the mate, Mr. Hawkes. Tod caught his words:

"The *Panama* put in . . . Bordeaux. . . . He got wise, I tell yeh. . . . You're a fool. . . . Now, listen." The mate's voice was lost as the wind whined down the alleyway.

What did it mean? The *Panama* put in at Bordeaux. Mr. Swickard had admitted that Neil had left at that port. Who had "got wise"? Were the two men discussing his brother? Did they know the truth of what lay back of Neil's sudden departure from the ship? Tod smiled grimly. If they did, he, Tod Moran, would find out. The veil of untruth which shrouded the dealings of the European-Pacific Steamship Company must be torn aside. Yes, even though the way was blocked by such forbidding figures as Mr. Hawkes and the Tattooed Man.

Tod could now hear only a sibilant murmur behind the door of the cook's cabin. He grasped the swinging handle of the coffee-pot and felt his way through the stinging blackness to the cabin aft.

Across the green baize of the table the commander of the *Araby* faced the chief engineer. The Scotchman was dealing cards for a game of coon-can. "Well, lad," he greeted Tod, "I was just thinkin' I'd no' be sorry fur a hot gless." His pink face dropped into a frown as a plunge of the ship's bows sent the screw racing furiously beneath them.

Captain Ramsey nodded over his cards. "Thick weather, to-night," he muttered. "Boy, you'd better take a hot cup up to Mr. Burton on the bridge. He'll need it."

"Yes, sir," Tod answered.

The bridge! Athrill with joy, he returned to the galley.

For two days he had glimpsed the officers pacing the Olympian heights of the bridge, that shrine upon which no seaman dared venture. Now he, the mess boy, was ordered above. He began to whistle a tune.

The song died on his lips, however, as the impression seized him that someone had entered the room. He whirled. Mr. Hawkes stood close beside him.

Beneath lowered lids, the first mate regarded him steadily. "What 'er you doin' here?" he boomed. "Why ain't the little boy in bed yet? Was you listenin' to us —yeh?"

Tod flushed. "No, sir," he replied. "Captain Ramsey ordered me to take coffee to Mr. Burton on the bridge."

The mate turned with a laugh to the Tattooed Man, who stood in his cabin doorway. "Look, cooky, he's larning. See how he answers? Yeah, we'll larn him, cooky— you and me."

The cook grinned broadly. His strange Tartar eyes gleamed above his broad cheek bones. "Oh, Joe Macaroni ain't so bad," he chuckled, as he crossed to the galley. "I've seen 'em worse."

"Look here, cooky," pursued the mate. "You don't make him work enough. Why don't he clean the place of these cockroaches?"

"Are you trying to insult me, Mr. Hawkes?" grinned the cook. "Do you mean to say that there's a single roach in this here galley?"

"I do, Mr. Jarvis. I do."

"Then we'll have the kid get rid of them." He turned to Tod and the smile left his face. "Kid, clean up this place—and don't ever let me see another cockroach here. Understand?"

Tod stared. Were the men drunk? Were they making sport of him? "But how can I?" he blurted. "It isn't only the galley. The whole ship is——"

"What!" roared the mate. "Talk back to your boss, do you? Do you allow that, cooky?"

"Gut me, if I do!" The Tattooed Man's face became grim and hard. "Come here, kid."

Nonplussed, Tod approached him. Under Mr. Hawkes's watchful gaze the cook waited until the boy stood within arm's length. Tod saw that his shirt lay open upon his deep chest, that his breath came quickly as he drew his arm back for a blow. Hate, blind hate, burned in his eyes. "Yeh think I can't even boss a mess boy?" he hissed. "Well, I'll show yeh. I've knocked men down in my day —men, you understand?"

For the length of a dozen heartbeats, Tod stood waiting for the blow. He was not surprised. No, he told himself, he would not be surprised at anything that happened upon this ship. Why was the Tattooed Man waiting? Why didn't he strike?

Steadily Tod returned the burning gaze of the cook. He never took his eyes from the other's face. Then, as he watched, he saw the features suddenly soften. The cook laughed shortly. "Sufferin' mackerel! If I hit the kid, he'll never get the coffee up to the bridge."

Behind Tod the mate grunted. "He'll never git it there, anyway, in this gale. The lubber'll probably get swept off the ladder." He went out chuckling. "He's larnin', Tom. He's larnin' all right."

The boy stepped back to the stove and took up the coffee-pot. "Yeh, that's right," commented the Tattooed Man; "better hurry along with the Java."

Tod did not answer. At the door he paused as the cook resumed: "Watch your step going up that ladder. I don't want to lose the only mess boy aboard."

Tod gave him a quick sweeping glance. He couldn't understand the man. In a fury of anger one moment; calm and human the next. Baffled, he slipped out the door.

Sudden booming gusts of wind hummed down the alleyway. The ferocity of the gale sent him reeling against the boat-deck ladder. He stopped in consternation, gazing about him. Spindrift hazed across the deck. The ship, as she plunged, seemed to sink beneath him; giant waves towered against the black sky. A sea crashed over amidships with a terrible bellowing roar. Tod clung to the ladder with the coffee-pot swinging in his hand. Salt water swirled and hissed about him. It was in his eyes, his nose, his mouth. Masses of sea foam, cold and clammy, darted about his feet.

Was the *Araby* sinking? Would she weather this storm? Tod waited, expecting to hear a call for all hands on deck. Nothing happened. The wind continued to scream through the rigging; the ship rose gallantly on the waves, plunged on through the night. The boy sighed. Well, he'd get used to this, he supposed. Evidently there was nothing to worry about.

He hoped another wave like that last one wouldn't hit her just now. If it did—he'd surely be washed overboard. And on such a night as this, what chance did a man have lost in that dark and heaving obscurity? None. The slanting deck sent him lurching up two steps of the companion. There he paused, amazed, unmindful of the biting wind that stung his face.

The black figures of two men blocked his way. Tod discerned white sweat rags round their necks.

"Who's that?" yelled a voice above the whine of the gale.

"The mess boy," Tod shrieked in reply. "I'm taking coffee up to the bridge."

"Drat those officers," went on the voice. "I wish they'd —have to shovel coal—with me down in the stokehole."

"Are you—a fireman?"

"Yep. Just came up the fiddley—to get a breath of fresh air. Now, you'd never guess it was hot as hell down there, would you?"

"Phew! That was a bad comber," said another voice. "Ain't I right now? A bad un—that was!"

Tod grasped the icy hand rail as a heavy sea rolled over the starboard bow and fell crashing into the waist. The *Araby* shuddered beneath the shock. The dull thunder of the seas was like the mighty booming of a drum. At the next lull in the wind, he went upward, past the stokers, to the boat deck. There another companionway led up to the bridge.

At the top Tod paused, one numb hand gripping a rail stanchion for support, the other holding the coffee-pot. Mr. Burton, the young third mate, whom Tod had hardly glimpsed since the evening in port when he had given Tod his orders, stood in the lee of the weather cloth, his figure swathed in an oilskin coat. "Java?" he queried; "that's thoughtful of the skipper. Thanks."

He stood with his black rubber boots planted wide apart, drinking the hot fluid. Beneath the brim of his dripping sou'wester, his eyes glowed keenly. Tod glanced round. In the wheel-house the grizzled quartermaster at the helm steered with both hands gripping the spokes; his unshaven cheeks stood out in the oval glow of the binnacle light.

"Dirty weather," commented the third mate heartily. "But it was worse than this—one passage I made on the *Panama*."

At the word, Tod twisted about till he faced the man. He tried to keep the eagerness from his voice as he asked: "You were on the *Panama*, Mr. Burton?"

The third mate raised his voice above a sudden whistle of the wind. "Yes, a year ago. Better ship than this."

"Did you know the purser—Neil Moran?"

The third mate grasped the rail and walked up the slant to the shelter of the weather cloth. "Sure I knew him," he called. "Jolly chap, too."

Tod passed the wheel-house windows in short quick steps. In the green glow of the starboard light he stopped. "Do you know what became of him, Mr. Burton?" he cried. "He was a—a—friend of mine."

The kindly face of the youthful third officer stared out into the darkness. "No, you see I left the *Panama* about a year ago. I heard that Moran got into trouble. Don't know why, I'm sure. Ask Mr. Hawkes. He ought to know. He went out with her on the last trip."

Tod tried to quell the disappointment that leapt into his consciousness. Ask Mr. Hawkes. Make a friend of Mr. Hawkes. Yes, it sounded so easy, so simple.

His bitter meditations were interrupted by the third mate speaking at the wheel-house window. "She seems to be riding easier, quartermaster."

"Aye, sir. She does," replied the man at the wheel.

Mr. Burton walked the length of the bridge, then turned back to Tod. "What is your name, boy?" he abruptly asked.

"Tod Moran, sir."

"Ah—then Neil is a relation?"

Tod nodded in the gloom.

The third mate contemplated the boy with deep thoughtfulness. "You don't believe that story about him? No, of course not. Well—neither do I. Look here, now, you'd better keep quiet on this tramp." He stopped short, and his gaze went to the ladder. "Hush. The Old Man."

In the darkness Tod saw Captain Ramsey, his cap low over his eyes, climb to the bridge. "A dirty night," he remarked, turning up his coat collar. "How far has she logged since noon, Mr. Burton?"

"Ninety-two miles, sir."

"Not so bad," the master conceded in a thick slow voice. "No, not so bad for an old tin can like this." He peered over the canvas wind-dodger into the night. "Mr. Burton," he called, "better tell the chief engineer to keep her down to sixty revolutions. If the gale gets worse—I'll be on the settee in the chart room."

The captain lurched up the slanting deck and disappeared down the companion steps toward the chart room under the bridge. Tod picked up his coffee-pot. He paused as he became aware that another wave had crashed into the waist of the ship. The steamer quivered under the impact of the blow. He grasped a rail stanchion and peered down into the moving blackness. Stinging salt spray filled his eyes. Then, above the furious clamour of the night, he heard a voice, small and distant, shouting.

Tod strained his eyes into the darkness. The third mate muttered at his elbow: "What's that? It can't be!"

Again came the cry. Tod started. His hands closed on the rail in a vise-like grip. High above the exultant scream of the gale a voice sang out the dreaded words:

"Man overboard!"

VII : THE LIFEBOAT

"MAN OVERBOARD!"

The words electrified the third mate into action. "Which side?" he shouted.

The lookout's cry came back on the wind: "Port."

"Hard a-starboard, quartermaster!" the third mate ordered. Already he had sprung to the engine-room telegraph. The indicator curved to the word: *Stop*.

"Quartermaster, put the helm down hard. Moran, call the cap'n—quick!"

Tod, dropping the coffee-pot, slid down the companion to the chart room. "Captain Ramsey! Captain Ramsey, man overboard!" He dragged at the door with all his weight, bracing himself against the wind that fought like an enemy to keep it closed.

Slowly the door opened. Tod stumbled across the brass-shod storm step. "Cap'n—man overboard!"

The commander of the *Araby* rose sleepily from a couch and switched on the electric globes in the deck head. "What's that? Overboard?" He swore beneath his breath.

He yawned, stretched, swayed slightly, and reached for his cap. "Rotten luck," he growled, "on a night like this." He glanced at a chronometer on the wall, and Tod saw that the hands pointed to eleven o'clock.

Abruptly the captain lifted his head. Tod became aware that the faint pulsating tremor of the ship's propeller had ceased. So used to that regular vibration had he become that this cessation seemed to leave a void in his little world. He was appalled. The great iron heart of the *Araby* had stopped beating.

Captain Ramsey jammed the cap over his eyes. "What's that young rascal Burton doing?" he snapped. "Stopping her?"

"He's bringing her about," Tod exclaimed. "Putting out a boat, I guess——"

"Manning a boat? Where'd he get the orders, I'd like to know. Hawkes told me I'd have to watch that young feller. I'm the cap'n of this ship, I'll let him know." A gust of wind whirled into the room as he opened the door.

Once more on the bridge, Tod hung over the rail. He could see the door of the two forecastles open and the men streaming up on deck. Behind him Captain Ramsey was shouting at his third officer.

"Who was it, I ask you?"

"A fireman, sir. He was sitting on the ladder. A big sea—it got him. Red Mitchell gave the alarm. The bos'n threw over two life buoys."

"Humph. A stoker. Who told you to stop the engines for a stokehole rat?"

The third mate's voice was hoarse with anger and amazement. "I didn't want the man cut by the propeller, sir."

"Oh, yuh didn't." The captain grasped the bridge rail as the ship wallowed in the trough of the sea. "Don't you know that the ship won't have steerage way? Telegraph slow ahead, Mr. Burton."

"Very good, sir." Reluctantly, the third mate crossed to the engine-room telegraph and swung up the indicator. Almost immediately, Tod felt the regular rhythm of the ship's propeller.

He peered down from the height. His heart thumped madly. Out in that black sea a man was tossing, clinging, perhaps, to a life buoy, lost in the heaving fury of the waves. Would he be saved? Was he lifting brine-filled eyes toward the lights of the ship, his ship that was now slowly moving away from him? And he, Tod Moran, had spoken to him there in the blackness of the bridge ladder. He had been only a shadow, a voice in the night; and now he was gone. He was being left behind. His cries for help were drowned by the gale. Tod shuddered and, with his face distraught with hatred, turned to the captain.

That man was shouting angrily at the third mate. "Oh, you ordered a boat got ready, did you?"

"Yes, Captain. The port whaleboat. But I told the bos'n not to cast adrift until you came, sir."

Captain Ramsey laughed deep in his throat. "Well, I'll see that no more men are lost to-night." He spun about and descended the companion to the boat deck. Tod went carefully after him.

On the boat deck in the pale gleam of a searchlight a little group of men stood by the port whaleboat which swung on its davits, cover off. Tod stumbled to a sheltered spot abaft the warm funnel, where he gripped the handles of a cabin ventilator. He saw the thick form of the first mate standing against the inboard gunwale of the lifeboat.

"This is murder, Cap'n," Mr. Hawkes protested in a loud voice. "Ye can't keep no boat afloat in this sea."

"I know it, Mr. Hawkes. Put her back in the chocks, men."

"Yeh, that's better," commented Red Mitchell with his whining accents. "The Old Man ain't got no business to send me out tonight. I ain't no sailor; I'm a fireman. Ain't I right, now?"

"I ain't goin' out in no bloomin' boat, either,"

blurted out a cockney voice. "Serves the blarsted fire-man right——"

"Yeah, I told the blamed fool to hold tight—and he didn't. Sitting right below me, he was——"

"Shut up!" snapped the boatswain. "Who's askin' a coal-passer to go, anyway."

They set about covering the boat and lashing it to its cradle. Tod, clinging to the ventilator, heard a low murmur of discontent from the group of firemen who stood watching the scene. Suddenly, a tall figure loomed up beside him. It was the Tattooed Man.

"Cowards!" he said.

At his approach Captain Ramsey whirled. "What's that? The cook?"

"What're you doin' here, cooky?" laughed the first mate. "This ain't the galley."

The cook stepped forward into the full glare of the searchlight, and faced the officers of the *Araby*. Tod could hardly restrain a gasp of admiration. The man, now that he was out of the galley, seemed to have dropped the vestments of a cook. With his eyes glowing like burning coals, his mouth drawn into a straight line, and his fists clenched, he appeared every inch a seaman. His blue jeans bulged over his enormous thighs; his white singlet, taut across his deep chest, showed the quivering dragon heads near his thick neck and the gleaming stars on the great biceps of his arms.

"Captain Ramsey," he said, "you've never asked me about my past, and I've never told you. But I've not always been a cook." He paused and glanced round the little group of surprised seamen. "You say a boat can't live in this sea. Gut me, if I don't say it can! I've cast adrift on Skagerrack in a worse sea than this. Let me take out the boat. I'll ask for volunteers. We'll save that man."

A murmur of approbation went round the circle. But the mate cut it short. "What's got into him?" he growled to the captain. "Has he gone plumb crazy, now? Who does he think is captain on this here steamer?"

Captain Ramsey's lips twitched nervously. "I've said we'll not take the risk. Yes, I'm captain here." He repeated the first mate's words as if he had need to justify his position.

"Look—the men are willing to go, sir," went on the Tattooed Man in his deep quick voice. "I heard that fellow scream when he went overboard. If you had heard—— Let me go, sir! The gale's falling off."

"You'd never find him." The captain was relenting. His eyes searched the dark seas that beat outside the circle of light. "We should have had a Holmes light, Mr. Hawkes, then in this blackness we could make out his position."

"A Holmes light on the *Araby?*" Mr. Hawkes chuckled in his beard. "Yes, this is a great ship all right—where no one obeys the skipper." He said the last phrase softly with a glance from the corners of his eyes to see how the shot told. "Why don't the cook go back to the galley— where he belongs?"·

The wavering captain of the *Araby* bit his lip. Crimson crept up his cheeks. His glance, straying across the group of firemen, settled upon the first mate. "Hawkes," he scowled, "you forget yourself. Perhaps the cook is also a—a man."

Tod stared. What had happened? Had the commander

that lay submerged in the depths of his weak nature come to the surface? The boy wondered as he perceived Captain Ramsey draw his frail lean body erect. The gray eyes glowed sombrely in his pallid face; his voice grew deeper, fuller.

"Very well, Mr. Jarvis. The boat is yours."

The wind, whistling through the rigging, carried aft the reply of the Tattooed Man. "Volunteers!" he boomed. "Volunteers to go in the boat!"

A sigh went up from the waiting men. Swaying to meet the roll of the ship, they looked hopefully across the windswept deck.

"Step forward, boys!" cried the boatswain. "Of course we go."

Above the drumming of the seas came Swede Jorgenson's voice: "Yah, we go."

"Blimey, I'm goin' too!"

At once Tom Jarvis broke in. "I want the six best oarsmen here. You, Jorgenson! You, Toppy! Bos'n, take your place in the stern."

Red Mitchell slipped back into the shadow. The cook's eyes passed over him as he chose his men. In a moment, the six had taken their places in the lifeboat.

"Put on the life belts, lads!" called Jarvis. "Wait—we want someone to bail."

As his eyes swept the group, Tod sprang forward. "Let me!" he beseeched in a voice vibrant with earnestness. "I can bail."

Jarvis nodded curtly. "Get in!"

With pounding heart Tod clambered over the gunwale into the swaying boat. Toppy pulled him down into a seat beside him. "Put this blarsted life belt on, kid," he said quickly. "And here's yer bucket. You got work ahead."

The whaleboat, already lifted sufficiently to clear the cradles, was now swung out on its davits by the men on deck, till it hung clear of the side, ready for lowering. With the weather on the starboard beam, the *Araby* now had a perceptible list to port. Tod pulled his cap low over his eyes and fastened the belt about his waist. He was dimly aware that the Tattooed Man was taking his place in the sternsheets, an ax in his hand for emergency.

"Lower away together!"

Nelson stood at the ropes of the after fall, another seaman at the forward, both in readiness to cast adrift when the boat struck the water. Tod dropped on his knees to the rounding bottom, one hand clasping the gunwale, while Toppy and the men in the waist thwarts held the boat away from the side of the ship.

The glow of the searchlight vanished above. The boat floated in a void. Night, mysterious and evil, encompassed them. Below, the boy heard the foaming waves leaping hungrily toward them out of the darkness, drawing nearer, ever nearer.

In the stern the shadowy form of the Tattooed Man was barely visible. Abruptly his voice thundered out above the roar of wind and wave:

"Ready, lads. Let go the after fall . . . Cast adrift!"

Water swished greedily about the sides of the boat. Tod saw the cook throw his weight against the long sweep oar in its crutch at the stern, and swing the stem of the boat out toward that wintry flood of wind and sea. The round lights of the *Araby* slowly forged ahead.

"Pull like the devil!" sang out the voice of their leader.

The whaleboat, of the New Bedford type, light and seaworthy with its airtight tanks, rode the waves buoyantly. In the bow a hurricane lantern with a leaping flame made a pinpoint of light in the surrounding blackness. Crouched in the bottom of the tossing boat was Tod, bucket in hand. In front and behind him the men pulled at their oars, the muscles of their backs and legs working with the easy precision of experienced oarsmen. The boat rose swiftly on a wave, then fell with sickening suddenness into the trough. For a second two oars swung wildly in the air, while the foam settled and swirled about the frail sides of the craft.

Of a sudden a shadowy wave, mountain high, bore down upon them. Gallantly their fragile boat rose to meet it. As they lay poised above a hollow trough an icy spray descended upon them. Down the incline they plunged. Tod dipped his bucket in the slushing bilge and flung the water overside. The snowy foam swirled past. The water, perishing cold, numbed his hands. His legs grew chilled and cramped. Salt brine stung his eyes into wakefulness. The men dragged at their oars in silent, steady movements. Their commander in the stern cheered them on with a voice of thunder that was carried away on the shrieking wind.

Back in the wake of the ship went the lifeboat. The *Araby*, Tod saw, was a cluster of lights swinging round in a circle toward the point where the stoker had been lost overboard. Behind her, off to the south and west, there were intermittent flashes of lightning.

In a hollow depression of the towering waves Tom Jarvis yelled to the boatswain in the bow. "About there, bos'n?"

"Almost, sir."

"Think the stoker—got a life buoy?"

"I'm sure—he did! I threw two—from the poop." His voice was lost in the hum of the gale.

Overhead, a moon, cold and gray, appeared behind scudding clouds. It fitfully lighted the heaving ocean. The spray flashed in silver sheets across Tod's vision. The bitter wind stung his face; the spume rattled like shot against his life belt. Still he grasped his bucket, bailing, bailing.

It seemed hours to him before he heard the boatswain's triumphant cry: "To port—to port! There it is!"

As the boat hovered for an instant above a cavernous hollow, Tod glimpsed a white object swaying in the foam.

"Pull, lads, pull!" Jarvis flung his great weight against the steering oar. The boat careened perilously to the right.

Tod strained his eyes through the gloom. Down the slant flew the boat. Unexpectedly, a white life ring grated softly alongside.

"God! It's empty!"

Nelson the Dane caught the ring and lifted it, dripping, inboard. It fell to the bottom with a deadening thud. The men made no sound.

The Tattooed Man flung out an arm. "Where's the other?" he boomed. "Bos'n, look sharp. Pull, lads; we'll get him yet!"

Again the blades of the oars dipped rhythmically. Again the boat rose on the waves and fell, while the wind howled past them across that dark immensity of moving ocean.

Tod glanced round. Fired by the thought of the proximity of the second life buoy, he tried to pierce that wall of encircling gloom. The waves dissolved in the night. An occasional crest of white and green appeared for a second, only to melt again into oblivion. The whine of the wind decreased. The Tattooed Man sent a gull-like cry flying over the water; but no answer came out of the profound darkness.

The moon suddenly slid from behind a scurrying cloud. Tod's heart leaped. The pale light revealed to port and incredibly near them the half-submerged circle of the second life buoy.

"Pull, lads!" yelled Jarvis exultantly. "He's there!"

The boat quivered under the strain of the oars. The men were aflame with hope. Tod's hands gripped the gunwale. He hardly breathed as he watched that white circle draw near.

Clinging to it was a man. One arm was thrown over the ring; his head was swaying listlessly against a sodden shoulder.

The boatswain reached him first. Stretching forth an arm he pulled the ring toward the boat. He grasped the man below the arms. Jorgenson, leaning over the gunwale, put a hand under the soggy knees, and together they lifted the inert, dripping body of the stoker into the boat. The wan light showed a face blue with cold and exhaustion. The eyes were half open, the teeth chattering.

"Wave your light, bose," called Jarvis. "We must make the ship—quick!"

Swaying in the stem, the boatswain swung aloft his lantern in a wide arc against the sky. A moment later four short blasts of the ship's whistle came back on the wind. The *Araby* had seen.

Jorgenson, in his slow, placid way, was working over the stoker. Tod dropped the bucket and, taking hold of a limp hand, began rubbing it quickly. It was cold, clammy cold, as if all life had departed.

"Oh, Gord! We're too late!" wailed Toppy. "He's a goner."

"Shut up!" snapped Jarvis from the sternsheets. "Don't begin that—till we get aboard. Look out, boys! We're a-swinging round."

The little cockney dragged at his oar. "Blimey!" he said in Tod's ear. "Ain't we the blarsted fools? We come out—in this whoopin' gale—to save this blighter!"

"But he's a man, isn't he?"

"Naw! He's a stokehole rat." Toppy spat viciously into the heaving, moonlit sea. "And that cook," he whispered as he leaned over his oar, "he's stark, starin' mad!"

Tod raised his eyes to the man in the stern. It was a Viking who stood there with his feet planted wide apart, his hands gripping the sweep, his head thrown back, and the wind whipping his closely cropped hair. Beneath the straight white brow the pits of his eyes stared out across the waves as though he were peering into another world.

Yes, he was mad, thought Tod—mad like Leif the Lucky when he stood at the helm and sailed to the unknown West, mad like Magellan when he ordered spread canvas and navigated the perilous straits. Courage, fearless, intrepid, steered the fragile boat that night.

And in the heart of a boy, a lubber reared on inland soil, it struck a warm responsive chord that came down to him, like an echo of a song, through the bitter, gallant ages.

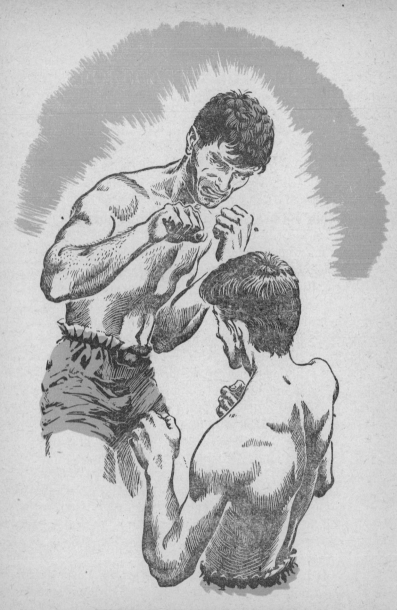

HIS MOUTH CONTORTED IN A SNARL . . .

PART TWO

THE FIGHT IN THE FORECASTLE

Wireless Report:
8 pm March 7
Araby—San Francisco for Balboa
2538 miles south of S. F.

San Francisco *Chronicle*

I : SOUTHERN WATERS

IN A SLOW monotony of daily routine the freighter *Araby*, that time-worn little vessel, steamed steadily down the Latitudes. The storm vanished astern, with only the heaving ocean left as evidence of a passing fury. When Lower California rose mistily to port as a thin gray line, the swells had become an almost imperceptible undulation, and the sky a clear translucent blue. The ship's course veered east; Mexico lay off toward the blazing dawn across a sea of molten gold.

Tod often stole moments to hang listlessly over the forward rail, where he watched the *Araby's* blunt bows cut the water into white masses of foam. At such times, he had the feeling of being in a dream. Pictures arose which were unconsciously put away in the lavender of his memory, pictures of ships coming up over the horizon from the south—lumber schooners bound under sail for Columbia River ports, long oil-tankers returning home from Europe, great cargo liners out of New York for San Francisco with a ribbon of smoke trailing behind them.

One morning, off Tehuantepec, he glimpsed his first flying fish. They splashed, a gleam of leaping silver, in a broad arc above the sea, then sank again into those fairy depths. White gulls placidly circled overhead, awakening to swoop and shriek when the waste from the galley was thrown overside. Once he saw a whale spout close by; and off Salvador, one late afternoon, the ship ran into a school of porpoises. Tod thought how like seals the lean black bodies appeared as they dived in small half circles in and out of the water.

The past fell away in the wake of the ship. Only the life on board mattered. But if the ship seemed trailing through a dream world of peace and beauty, that only served to accentuate the stark reality of the life on deck.

Murmurs of discontent rose with the heat from the engine-room skylight. The Black Gang was not satisfied with the events of that night of storm. Though the stoker had been saved from the sea, he apparently was not to be saved from the effects of his hour of exposure in the numbing water. He lay in his bunk fighting pneumonia, while the two forecastles took on a strange subdued air. The heightening tension might have been relieved by a sick-bay; but there was none aboard the *Araby*. The deck crew silently came and went; the stokers drifted in from their inferno in the bowels of the ship, paused a second to glance at their muttering and tossing comrade, and cursed softly under their breath. Captain Ramsey, acting as ship's doctor, made daily ineffectual visits, but the man barely rallied. The spark of life threatened to grow dim at any moment and flicker out like a candle flame into the void.

During daylight, Tod seldom went forward. Depression had crept like a fog into his mind. From four in the morning until eight at night, he remained at the work that seemed never ended, with an hour or two of stolen rest in the afternoon. He would slip up to the boat deck and throw himself down in the shade of a lifeboat, where the warm breeze coming up from the south would fan his mind into forgetfulness.

He awoke there one afternoon to find the Tattooed Man reclining against the chocks with his feet hanging precariously over the edge of the deck. In blue jeans and singlet he was reading a book, his large carved pipe in his mouth. Tod, silently regarding him with growing incredulity, noted how his flexed arm showed the knotted cords standing out. What a man! thought Tod. How could he lie there in contentment, slowly turning the pages, puffing on his pipe? How could he endure this ship without a murmur, without a word against the officers who commanded it? Who was he? What had he been before he stepped aboard the *Araby?*

The boy had pondered the question often; but never could he come to any satisfactory explanation. He admired Jarvis greatly, he admired the litheness of his huge body and the mind that appeared equal to any eventuality; above all, he admired the spirit that animated the

man. Yet he was not a friend. About the cook there was
a wall of cold reserve which Tod had never penetrated.
It was there, palpable as a mist, and it served as well to
hold back any confidences that the boy may have desired
to make to the older man.

If he might only talk to him of Neil! If he could only
get someone's advice! Not a word had he learned of Neil's
whereabouts, not a word of the mystery of his brother's
disappearance; and here he was with the passage of Panama almost completed. Then, too, there was a suspicion
still tapping at the threshold of the boy's consciousness
that the cook was somehow in league with the first mate.

Were not Jasper Swickard and Mr. Hawkes his enemies,
Neil's enemies? And were not Hawkes and Jarvis obviously friends? Yes, a suspicion was tapping, tapping at
his mind, slowly gathering, taking form. It flashed suddenly clear as crystal. Tom Jarvis's job as cook aboard
the *Araby* was a blind. If a blind, then why was it not
another link in the schemes of the company, schemes
which had sent his brother as a fugitive in a foreign land?

Tod drew a deep breath, and immediately he was aware
that the Tattooed Man had put down his book and was
surveying him out of those strange Tartar eyes.

"Awake, Joe Macaroni?" he said in a voice that vibrated above the hiss of the ship's funnel. "It's gettin' too
hot to sleep daytimes."

"Yes," Tod admitted; "but I can't sleep in the fo'c's'le
with the stoker moaning right next door." He rose to a
sitting position and faced the open sea.

"Why don't you read, then?" went on the cook. "Say—
this is a fine story you gave me. It's a peach!"

Tod glanced at the title: "The Lookout: A Romance of

the Sea." With a snort of disgust he gripped his knees
with both hands. All the rebellion of the last week came
to his lips in a rush of words.

"Lies! All lies!" he retorted gruffly. "A romance of
the sea. Oh, I know that book and all its kind. I've read
them—and not one bit of truth in the whole lot."

The cook raised his eyebrows slightly as he regarded
the boy. "Lies?" he said serenely. "How come? What's
got into you lately?"

Somewhat sheepishly Tod moved his foot along the
deck. "Oh, I don't know," he murmured vaguely; "but
all that stuff is—bunk! Romance? Not on your life. Not
on this sea."

Tom Jarvis chuckled softly as he struck a match and
relighted his pipe. "Joe Macaroni," he drawled, "you're
beginning to grow up. I know. I was that way once myself. Pat yourself on the back. By the time this voyage is
over, you'll be a man—almost."

Tod stared moodily out across the vast expanse of
sparkling water.

"I know what's wrong with you," the cook went on.
"You've dreamed dreams of what you think the sea ought
to be. You expect your imaginings to have a marvelous
flowering. Instead, you get—this!" He threw out his arms
in a gesture that seemed to include the sea, the ship, and
the ship's company. "What do you want? A passenger
liner? A nice clean white ship and a nice clean white
crew and a sea that's always kind? Well, you won't get
'em—not in this world."

Tod smiled ruefully. "But everything is so different
from what I was taught to expect."

"It always is, Joe Macaroni. Before a boy grows up,

he has to unlearn all those pretty myths about life and death, which have been taught him by tender-minded ladies of both sexes. I feel sorry for the poor kids. They have to go through hell. . . . Most of them don't, though. Instead, they commit intellectual suicide; they remain simply children." Jarvis fixed his keen glance on Tod and his face softened. "Somehow, I feel you won't do that. You'll kick off those swaddling clothes. . . . But I pity you in the process—I pity you."

He paused, puffed for a second, then went on. "I've watched you, Joe Macaroni, taking good things in for the stoker to eat. But he couldn't eat them because he was dying. . . . Dying? How could that be? you thought. Why was he saved that night if he was only to die there in the stuffy fo'c's'le? That isn't even like those tales of glorious deaths—young men swimming along the pathway of the moon, old men sailing into the sunset. You thought that if death were necessary, at least there was beauty in it. You held on. At the very end, you thought, wouldn't his face light up with a smile? Couldn't one envision his soul going out—across? . . . Instead, you feel his hands grow cold. You see a purple death creep hour by hour up his limbs. You hear the laboured breathing of a body given up to dissolution. Oh, those pretty myths! Where are they? . . . Dying within you, Joe Macaroni, dying in agony, like the stoker."

Tod raised his wistful eyes. "I guess I want too much."

Jarvis nodded. "For a kid of your age, it seems to me that you think an awful lot. But it always pays to take regular observations and not trust to dead reckonings," he advised. "Well, cheer up! Let's get busy. It's almost time to feed the animals."

As the men congregated amidships with their tins for chow, Tod noticed an undercurrent of surly discontent which pervaded their talk. The little group of firemen sat apart. Their voices were low, whispering; their glances toward the deck crew were those of sullen hate. All the mistrust and dislike between the deck and the engine room had been brought to the surface by the illness of the stoker in the forecastle. The deck gang, in their turn, were evidently not willing to assume blame for the man's condition. They met dark looks with darker scowls, and passed on that storm of hatred toward any officer who came within range of their vision.

Toppy's voice drifted in to Tod through the open port. "Lookit those dirty Finns! And they used ter be as friendly as cockroaches!"

"Yeh," replied another voice. "Those guys is a nice lookin' bunch—the scum, the muck, the swine! Ain't I right, now?"

"Aw, pipe down," said Nelson the Dane. "This here tub has got trouble enough on her without you startin' any more."

The cook, in the act of pouring the split-pea soup into a bucket, gave Tod a glance of understanding. His short thick lips were humming a song in an uncertain key.

> "Oh, it's a jolly life, a gay life,
> This life on the o—cean wave. . . ."

Tod was filling a bucket with steaming potatoes for the men, and but for the steam, he would probably have laughed loudly; as it was, he merely grinned and passed the food to the men at the door.

The atmosphere of the little galley was increasingly hot, and stale, too, with the odours of boiled pork and cabbage. As they worked side by side after the evening mess, Tod clearing up while the cook prepared dough on the bread board, the boy pressed the man with questions.

"Tom!"

"Yes?"

"Why does a shark follow a ship?"

"Is this a riddle? No? Well, I suppose because he's hungry. There's always good feedin' round an old tramp what doesn't go too fast."

The boy meditated a moment. "Yes—but the crew says that when a shark follows a ship, it means bad luck— somebody dying soon, that he's waiting for us to throw overboard the stoker's body."

"Cut it, Joe Macaroni. The stoker isn't dead yet." Jarvis turned, his great hands buried in the dough. "So they've been talkin' like that, have they? Well, it's all superstition. It harks back to the savages. You better wad up your ears."

Tod began washing up the dishes in the trough. "I

know it sounds foolish here when the sun hasn't yet gone down; but there in the fo'c's'le at night, with the stoker sick and moaning and breathing hard just the other side of the bulkhead, and the crew all talking—well, it's different then. Toppy was on a windjammer in the Caribbean once that was followed by a shark for three days. The crew knew that one of their messmates was numbered— and he was, too. Off Trinidad, a Portugee went crazy and jumped overboard."

"And did the shark stop following?"

"Yes. Queer, wasn't it?"

The cook grunted scornfully. "Those birds in the fo'c's'le are plumb loony. Superstitions cling to 'em like barnacles to a ship's bottom. Don't listen to 'em. Get me?"

Tod placed a saucer of canned milk on the floor for the ship's cat. "I don't believe them, but they get on a fellow's nerves. They all say that the *Araby* is an unlucky old tub. She's had half a dozen collisions. She went aground in the Columbia River, was sunk there till the war came along, and then reconditioned for supply carrying. Her name's been changed more than once. Toppy says that's bad luck, too."

For the first time since Tod had begun his conversation, the cook appeared interested. He turned and scrutinized the boy narrowly. "Did they say what her old name had been?"

"No; they didn't seem to know."

"H—m. I guess they don't know too blamed much, those guys. Ain't I right, now?" His mimicking voice, so like Red Mitchell's, brought a smile to Tod's lips.

"Of course, Red does rave on a lot," the boy admitted; "but after all, isn't there a lot of truth in what he says? If the officers had acted quick enough that night the stoker could have been rescued in fifteen minutes instead of an hour. He wouldn't be dying now, if it wasn't for the mate."

"Oh, he blames Hawkes, does he? Well, he might be right. But I don't see why Red Mitchell should be growling. I didn't notice him stepping forward as a volunteer for the boat."

"Yes, that's just it. The men guy him for not going along, and now he's sore at you. He thinks you insulted him when you didn't choose him, too."

"That coal-passer—a sailorman! Sufferin' sea gulls!" The Tattooed Man's voice boomed out in mirth.

Night was closing on the freighter when Tod left the galley. The sea was heaving gently, with a breath of air blowing from the starboard bow. Up from the stokehole ventilators came the rattle of the ash buckets; the end of the watch was near. As he crossed the deck, he encountered Nelson going forward.

"Hello, kid," said the old seaman, his weatherbeaten face screwed into a frown. "Have ye seen him yet—the shark? Damn him!"

"No," Tod answered. "Is he there still?"

The old man solemnly nodded his gray head. "Tony the Wop just told me the stoker's about dead. The shark is following, waiting. Sonny, take my word for it, he'll be there till he gets what he wants. . . . Go and see. There ain't no one on the poop now."

Tod turned slowly and, going aft, climbed the ladder to the poop deck. It was dark beneath the awning. Leaning over the taffrail near the line of the patent log, he gave a start at the sound of a metallic click close by. He sighed; it was merely the dial marking off the miles behind them. Above him the luminous tropic sky was faintly studded with stars. On the water below, like a ghostly shadow of the Milky Way, extended the churning wake with its blue flames of phosphorous burning without warmth. He watched the blue iridescent glow intently; but the brooding loneliness of the sea appeared undisturbed.

Suddenly, he recoiled, as a shadow as light as gossamer brushed past his feet. He laughed nervously. It was the ship's cat searching for its nightly feast of flying fish that had fluttered out their life against the deckhouse.

Again he turned to the dim radiance of the wake. Straining his eyes downward, he was aware that an undercurrent of expectancy had quickened his pulse. He drew in his breath sharply. Yes—there it was, almost directly below him. Stealthily gliding along to one side of the creaming foam was a long sinister shadow, its dorsal fin cutting the surface into trembling showers of misty light.

Tod stared, immovable. That lithe, furtive brute, outlined in blue flame as it trailed along behind them, at once became the symbol of all his troubles, all his fears. It was uncanny, this feeling that beat oppressively upon him. Let Tom Jarvis laugh at the sailors' superstition. The men were right. They knew.

He crept away noiselessly. Eight bells was sounding from the bridge and then again, like an echo, from the forecastle head. On the forward deck he met the stokers, their sweat rags about their necks, going toward the fireroom fiddley for their watch below. With a questioning glance, Tod paused. They filed by without a word.

Tod approached a heavy-set Italian who, naked to the waist, stood at the casing, waiting his turn. "How's the patient, Tony?" the boy asked in a low tone. "Any better?"

Tony the Wop drew his mouth into a snarl, as he fixed on Tod a sullen glare. "Better! *Dio cane!* He's dead."

"Dead!"

"Yeh. Five minutes ago."

He turned and, plunging into the fiddley, began his descent to the inferno below deck. The muffled drum of his shoes on the iron ladder echoed like the tumultuous beat of Tod's heart.

II : THE ENMITY OF RED MITCHELL

"NEIL MORAN! NEIL MORAN!" Someone from a great distance was calling the name. "Neil Moran! Neil Moran!"

Tod awoke with a start. It was Sunday and mid-afternoon. Through the open port above his bunk, a light breeze fanned his brow; the air was already redolent with the smell of the tropics. He listened for a moment, wondering. Merging rhythmically into the pulse of the steamer, the ship's bell was sounding the hours; the low swish of the water from the steamer's bows was audible. Then voices near him resumed their conversation and a name seemed to leap toward him through the thick, hot atmosphere of the forecastle.

"Neil Moran. Yeh, that's the guy." It was Red Mitchell of the Black Gang who spoke.

"On the *Panama*, huh? And 'e got the money, did 'e?" asked Toppy.

"Yes; I heard the mate tellin' the skipper 'bout it last

night. The feller got away in Bordeaux—some port!
Went to Paris, I guess."

"The wise bloke! Wot a time 'e'll 'ave in gay Paree!"

Red's voice dropped to a whisper. "Yeh—and d'you
know what Hawkes was wonderin'? Well, if this kid here
is any relation to that guy. His name's Moran, too."

"Blimey! I didn't know that."

Their voices droned on in a steady murmur. Tod, raising himself on one elbow, felt a tightening of his heart.
So Neil's story was known on board the ship! Without
trial, he had been judged and found guilty; he was con-
demned at once as a criminal. The boy's face flushed;
anger surged into his consciousness. He wanted to jump
from his bunk and give Red Mitchell the lie, but caution
told him of its futility. Sheila Murray had implored him
to go, to remain unknown, to get as much information as
possible. And see what had already happened! Hawkes
had probably asked Red to find out if he was any relation to Neil Moran. They wouldn't find out from him! He
wouldn't tell—not yet.

Wiping the sweat from his brow, he rose. The men
were grouped about the forecastle, reading, smoking,
playing cards.

"Where ye goin', mitey?" asked the little Londoner
from his bunk.

"On deck to do some washing," Tod said, momentarily
wondering why only Nelson and the boatswain ever took
the pains to wash their clothes and hang them on the line
stretched between the forecastle bulkheads.

Red Mitchell turned away his face, with its film of coal
dust visible about the ears, and spat on the floor disgust-
edly. "Ain't that like the kid, now?" he whined. "Always

tryin' t' git away from us fo'c's'le fellers. What's the matter with him, I asks yuh? He don't talk no more t' us. He don't like our sassiety. Ain't I right, now?"

"Blimey! He thinks 'e's a toff. And 'im—mess boy!"

Tod finished rolling a blanket, then turned. "It's stifling down here," he said, "and a fellow's got to wash up once in a while, hasn't he?"

"Yeh, he don't like our sassiety," went on Red, his little rat-like face screwed into a grin. "He don't talk with no one but the cook."

"And not much with him. We're always too busy to talk in the galley."

"Oh, yuh are! Well, why don't yuh talk to men as does a man's work—not to a ship's cook?"

Tod's eyes kindled. His voice was tremulous with emotion. "He's more of a man than you, Red Mitchell. If you hadn't whined to the mate so much that night of the storm, Jarvis might have saved the stoker in time."

"Oh, is that so!" Red climbed from the bunk and eyed the boy with ferocity. "Mark my words, mister, yuh gotta take that back—see?"

"Blast yer hide, if the kid ain't got guts!" put in Toppy. "Yer know yerself, Red, that the kid ain't far wrong. I arsks yer now, is 'e?" He threw back his head and laughed loudly.

Red Mitchell turned his sullen face upward for a moment. Suppressed anger played about the corners of his wide mouth. "Pipe down, yer lousy lime-juicer!" he snapped. "I'm goin' t' tend t' this kid here, right now."

"Oh, you are!" laughed Toppy. "Well, you better watch out, for you ain't much bigger than 'e is, Red—

and you know you don't always like an even match."

"Shut yer jaw, or yuh'll swaller a fly!" Red whirled and faced Tod. "I'm goin' ter wipe th' dirty floor up with yuh, kid—understan'?" As he spoke, his long pale chin shot forward; the pupils of his eyes narrowed to mere pinpoints.

Tod let his blanket drop back into his bunk. He was in for it now. Why had he been so headstrong! He was dimly aware that Swede Jorgenson across the way was gazing at him in wide-eyed concern; that back by the companion the boatswain and Chips the carpenter were silent with attention. There would be no help from them, Tod knew. They were waiting to see what the new mess boy was made of.

Red Mitchell let a laugh hiss through his teeth. "Ah, so youse is gettin' ready, eh? Well, stamp around like a little sea horse—it won't do yuh no good. I know all about yuh, Mister Moran. And I know all about yer family, too. Thieves! That's what they are. Thieves!"

"You lie, Red Mitchell!" Tod challenged.

"Oh, I did get it right, then, didn't I! Yeh, it hurts, don't it? But yuh know as how it's the truth. Neil Moran —purser on the *Panama*. Jumped ship at Bordeaux because he had to. Oh, yer from a nice family, yuh are, Mister Moran."

"Liar! Coward!" Tod's fist shot forward. It caught his tormentor on the cheek.

Red Mitchell sprang back. Surprise shone in his eyes. His lips snarled over his uneven teeth.

"Attaboy!" yelled a voice. "Wade in, kid!"

"The little devil! Who'd a thunk it!"

A volley of curses came from Red's mouth. Head

down, he rushed blindly like a bull. At the same time his right arm drove forward. Instinctively Tod stepped aside. Red's blow crashed wildly through the air.

Jeers came from the spectators. "Ain't this little red rooster the fighter, though!"

"Blimey, wot a knock-out!"

Tod, balancing upon the balls of his feet, waited, breathless. There was worse coming, he knew. Red was larger, heavier, more powerful than he, himself; but anger for the moment had the better of him. Sheer hate does not help one to fight. "I must keep cool," thought Tod, biting his lips. "He's a coward. I know it. Cool—cool!"

Red rushed upon him again. This time there was no stepping aside. They clenched. Blows from his opponent's right fist, swift, terrific, landed in the small of his back. Red's breath, warm and faintly sour, was on his neck; the red hair brushed his eyes. Tod gasped. His arms were powerless, and those thumping blows came raining upon him in a steady succession.

"Wot's this yer makin', Red! Kidney stew?"

"Yeh, git a knife and cut 'em out."

"Oh, Gord! That coal-passer ain't a fighter—he's a butcher!"

"Hold on there, Red." The boatswain's voice struck Tod's ear as a far-off sound. "Cut it, you fellers. No fightin' in the fo'c's'le! It won't do. Loosen! Quit the clinchin'."

The boatswain put his arms between the two figures who were struggling, swaying across the deck.

"Git away, bose," scowled Red. "You jist leave this to me t' finish."

"No fightin' now, Red. And what's more, the kid's too young to stand up t' ye. It ain't fair."

"Oh, it ain't!" Red loosed his grip on Tod and turned in a frenzy on the boatswain. "Didn't yuh hear the lubber call me a coward? I don't have t' take that—do I, now?"

"Yah, the kid's too young," grunted Jorgenson. "Stop 'em, bose."

Tod gripped the bunk behind him. His head was up, his face white. "Don't stop this on my account, bos'n; I'm not afraid of him. I'm his equal. I know something about boxing, and he doesn't."

"Oh, is zat so!" Red jerked against the boatswain's restraining hand. "I won't take none of his lip, see? Bose, yuh ain't got no right——"

"Yes, that's true," broke in Toppy. He was sitting up in his bunk watching the scene with vast amusement. "Ye cawn't stop the bloomin' fight now, boats. The kid said that bloke was a coward and a liar. Ye gotter let 'em fight it out."

"Not now," said the bos'n, apparently sparring for time.

Toppy nodded. "Aye, not now—but this evening—or to-morrow when all the watch is here. We'll time 'em— we'll give 'em a regular bout with the old Mark o' Queensberry rules. Blimey, that's the thing! Three rounds! It ain't fair ter let the boys miss this."

Red Mitchell cast Toppy a grateful glance. "That's the stuff," he said sourly. "Don't say nothin', bose, t' the mates; and we'll have it out after mess to-morrer. I'll make him swaller his words! Him—mess boy! And brother t' a thief!"

"Shut your mouth!" snapped Tod. "Yes—Neil Moran is my brother—and I'm proud of him, too. Everything you said is a lie. Do you understand? A lie! You're not half the man he is."

"Oh, I ain't, eh? Well, we'll see!"

The stocky, grizzled boatswain put up a soothing hand. "Now, quiet down, you fellers. Maybe after evening mess, to-morrer. But mum's the word. If the after cabin hears of this—good night! Th' mate'll be havin' us walk the plank."

As Red Mitchell was led away, Tod caught a gleam of triumph in the man's evil eyes. Of course! He had made Tod admit that he was Neil Moran's brother. Probably that was just what the mate had put him up to. And he had been successful. Now Hawkes would know. He would be on his guard, careful of any information about the *Panama* leaking out.

With a catch in his throat Tod turned to his bunk. He had failed. Memory bit into his mind. All the plans of Sheila Murray, all his own plans had come to naught, chiefly because he had allowed his temper to become his master. Panic assailed him. Failed! He sat down trembling on his bunk, and trembling, put up his hand to wipe the beads of perspiration from his face. This heat! Worse every hour, and Panama still two days off. Where was Neil? He wasn't guilty. The mate knew it. And Red? Well, Red wasn't worth this failure. What would the girl in San Francisco say when she learned how he had ruined her hopes? And Neil—what would Neil say?

Ruminating, he was suddenly overwhelmed with the immensity of his task. He bit his lip sharply. His thoughts were winging their way out across the sea, searching, questing—crying: "Neil—Neil! Where are you? . . . Where are you?"

III : SHARKS

ANOTHER night dropped astern. The sun rose over the rim of the ocean upon a sea smooth and polished as glass. The humid tropic heat held the ship in its sultry embrace. It seemed incredible to Tod that March could be so hot. Dispensing with his stiff white coat, the boy served breakfast to the officers beneath the awning on the poop. Captain Ramsey appeared in pajamas and slippers, Mr. Hawkes in trousers and singlet.

The two officers were drinking their coffee, facing the faint breath of air coming up from the south, when abruptly they looked up, startled. Tod paused in his work, listening, too. Beneath their feet the rhythmic quiver of the propeller had trembled into silence. The boy felt suddenly imprisoned in the stillness.

"What the deuce is wrong now?" blurted out Captain Ramsey.

"The engines! They've been on the blink all night," said the mate, as he looked questioningly forward. "The chief's been worried sick. He's expecting anything—the boilers to burst, or one o' the cylinder heads to blow off. Ah, here's the second."

The second engineer came hurrying aft. He climbed the ladder to the poop and stopped; his hands, black and greasy, mopped his sweaty brow with a piece of cotton waste. "It's the main steam pipe, sir," he announced. "Broken! It wasn't unexpected."

"It wasn't!" The captain's gaunt, imperturbable face moved in anger. "Doesn't the chief know it's his business to keep the engines going? We're dropping behind our schedule as it is—eight knots!"

"Yes, sir; but it's hard to get a fair head o' steam out o' such boilers."

"Good Lord! What a tub!" remarked the mate, lighting his pipe.

The captain pushed back his chair and rose. "These steamers!" he snorted scornfully. "Now if this was only a four-masted ship, we'd be sailing along with the Trades." He tightened the pajama strings about his thin waist. "How long before you'll have it fixed?"

"By noon—perhaps, sir."

"Very well. I'll be down at once."

Tod watched the commander patter away and disappear into the engine-room entrance. "He'll forget inspection this morning," he thought with glee. "Maybe the galley and fo'c's'le will have a rest, too."

"Kid, come here!"

Tod, who was skirting the saloon skylight with his tray of dishes, spun about. Hawkes was regarding him steadily, his nose hooked down over his wide red mouth.

"Yes, sir." The boy returned to the table and stood silently waiting.

"No fightin' in the fo'c's'le—see?" His eyes gleamed beneath the black gash of his brows. "It'll be the brig fer both of yuh, if I catch ye, see?"

"Yes, sir."

Mr. Hawkes thrust his head forward at the boy. "So you're the brother of that feller Moran of the *Panama.*" The words, loud and gruff, were hardly a question.

"Yes, sir." So Red had told him already!

The mate reflectively scratched his broad chest, where the matted hair showed dark beneath his singlet. "Well, I'm sorry to hear that, kid. I was just beginning t' think you was made of different stuff."

Tod's heart dropped. An obscure dread threatened to rise in a sudden attack and overwhelm him. His gaze fluttered past Mr. Hawkes, past the taffrail, to the sea birds cruising placidly against a burnished sky. Sword thrusts! First by Mr. Swickard, then by Red Mitchell, now by Mr. Hawkes. They thrust deep, then twisted the blade to make him writhe in agony.

His breath came short; his gray eyes were wistful, beseeching, as he turned a stricken face to the man. "It can't be true of Neil. Surely there's some mistake!"

The mate shook his dark head slowly. A grin twitched the bristling muscles of his cheeks. "No—there ain't no mistake. But don't be a silly fool. What if he is yer brother? That don't cut no plum duff."

Tod set his tray on the table and faced the mate across it. "It can't be, Mr. Hawkes. You knew him. What happened?"

"What happened? Don't ye know?" The man leaned forward; his short hairy hands gripped each other. "He stole the ship's money, slipped his cable at Marseilles —cleared for ports unknown."

"At Marseilles? I thought it was Bordeaux."

"Oh, you've heard things, then. Who told you all this?"

Tod's mind flashed back to San Francisco. Should he tell? How much did Hawkes know? Well, he couldn't make things any worse now. His voice, when he spoke, was strange to him, and thin. "I saw the manager in his office."

"Oh, ye did!" The mate surveyed the boy with a perplexed frown. "And what did he say?"

"He was very kind," said Tod, with rising colour. "He told me all he knew. But it is hard, isn't it, to believe that of your brother?"

"H—m! Yes, I s'pose it is." He looked up quickly. "And did Swickard know that ye'd signed aboard this boat?"

"Why—I'm not certain he did. I told him I needed a job badly, though, now that Neil sent nothing to help me at school. The first place I thought of was the European-Pacific Line."

"H—m! Looks kind o' bad for both o' yez, don't it?" Mr. Hawkes showed his dark uneven teeth in a grim smile. "Well, ye can get some good experience on this here ship. How'd ye git along with the cook?"

"Pretty fair."

A hearty guffaw greeted the words. "Oh, that cook! He'll make a steward out o' ye yet."

"Yes, sir." Tod picked up his tray. As he left he was aware that the mate's black eyes were following him with a glance as bright and hard as steel.

When he entered the port alleyway, the hot breath of the galley struck him like the opening of a furnace door. The Tattooed Man, clad only in short rolled pants, was going calmly from shelf to range, from range to bin, opening cans, turning meat, chopping carrots. His great torso glistened with sweat; the dragons on his chest might have just risen from a magic pool.

"Joe Macaroni," said the cook, "go up and trim the ventilators to the wind. It's gettin' as hot as though we was crossin' the Line."

Getting hot! Was worse to come? He climbed the companion, wondering if the cook also had heard of his quarrel with Red Mitchell. Did he know of Neil? Probably not. Just how close an acquaintanceship existed between the cook and the first mate, Tod could not determine. The boy set about his work in the galley with scarcely a word, scarcely a glance toward the man. His mind was busy with thoughts of Neil, of Hawkes, of Red. Whispers of the coming fight were circulating over the ship: at the first opportunity it was to take place in the forecastle. Tod sighed. Each day the obstacles were piling up higher before him; each day his goal receded to a more distant point.

As the sun rose toward the zenith, the heat grew more intense. Tod drooped at his monotonous duties. Was this the life at sea he had dreamed of, the life of a gentleman adventurer? He glanced about him with new eyes. Dirty pots and pans in the trough; a leaky drain below; empty tomato cans on the floor. Odours of salt pork and cabbage. Always cabbage! He smiled wanly to himself. Where were his glorious dreams of high adventure? They had slipped astern with the days—and reality, cruel, malignant, held him in its iron grip. He had discovered the disillusioning fact that even the beautiful deep-sea ships had a commonplace existence, that it was only when seen by firelight upon an enchanted sea of the mind that they appeared romantic.

All morning the old freighter remained quiet on the metallic surface of the sea. The sun poured its scorching rays down pitilessly on the decks. At four bells of the afternoon watch—two o'clock—the boatswain stuck his head into the galley door and announced that the ship wouldn't get under way before night. The Old Man had given the crew leave to swim; so they had brought the gig to the port bow and lowered the Jacob's ladder to it.

"Heigho!" said the cook, with a grin. "That's the stuff. A bath'll do the fo'c's'le good."

"Yes; but how about the sharks?" commented the boatswain, with his solemn, owl-like eyes staring down the alleyway. "The shark won't leave the ship, now that the cap'n is a-takin' the stoker's body to Panama, and they don't bury a man Christian-like there in the Zone: they burns 'em."

"Aw, sharks won't touch a man—if he's a good swimmer."

The boatswain sighed. "They will if they're hungry. And this fellow is. He's been waitin' a week fer a feed."

"All right, bose. Thanks. We may try him out anyway." The cook smiled at the man's departing back. "A swim's just th' thing for us, Joe Macaroni; though we've been swimming all morning here in the galley."

Tod, presently crossing the forward deck to the port bulwarks where the men were making merry, hesitated a second as he saw upon the forecastle head the stocky form of the first mate in low converse with Red Mitchell. Did he imagine that their eyes turned his way, that they stopped talking when he appeared? The mate passed the winch to the rail and, leaning over, watched the men.

Red Mitchell came down the ladder to join the group at the bulwarks.

The boy found a place next to Swede Jorgenson, who was tranquilly viewing the men below as they dove from the gig and swam in circles near the vessel. "Aren't you swimming, Swede?" Tod asked.

"Me? No; I didn't never learn how," answered the big seaman. "I don't like water."

"Humph!" grunted Toppy as he balanced his skinny, dripping body on the bulwarks. "It takes th' blasted cook t' swim on this bloomin' tin can. Lookit 'im now!"

"Yah, he dives like a seal off a rock," said Red Mitchell, taking off his clothes, consisting of shirt and dungarees.

"A seal?" grinned Toppy. "Like a bally painted whale, yer mean."

Leaning overside, Tod glimpsed the cook's stalwart form cleaving the waters with long regular strokes of his arms and legs. Near him other naked forms were scattering sparks of diamonds on the placid surface of the sea. In the captain's gig, directly below Red, several white figures crouched on their gleaming haunches.

"Goin' in, kid?" asked Toppy.

"Sure!" Tod began to divest himself of his clothing, dropping it in a pile on the deck.

"I'll beat yer! Cheerio, old top!" Toppy was gone in a flying dive overside. The sound of a splash drifted up with the yells of the men.

Tod stood poised for a minute on the bulwarks abaft the gig. The intense sunlight hurt his eyes; the deck quivered in the heat. He felt the soft stir of the air about his body. Twenty feet below was the clear blue water breaking in tiny rivulets against the plates of the side.

"Watch out, kid," drawled Jorgenson. "Don't come up under the hull, or the shark'll git yuh."

"Look out below!" called Tod, laughing. Raising his hands to each side, he slowly brought them forward full length, and on tiptoe let himself drop into space. The water plunged toward him, struck. He was racing through the cooling depths of the sea, the water caressing his body. A half dozen flying fish swayed by toward the shadow of the ship. Far above shone a dim azure light. He lifted his head and with a strong stroke, shot himself upward.

Fresh air rushed into his lungs. Treading water, he brushed the hair from his eyes and looked about. Before him lay a glittering expanse of trembling water. The hot hazy sky dipped down to a horizon impossibly near.

"Some dive, Joe Macaroni." Jarvis, swimming up beside him, stopped and trod water. Drops trickled from his hair to the high cheek bones of his face. He grinned in delight. "Got plenty of wind? Then let's swim out a bit. I want t' talk to you."

Behind them they heard the cries of the men. "Hey, Red, don't let the dogfish git yuh! Say, Toppy, 'ave yer got rid o' the cooties?"

With measured strokes they swam out toward the horizon of the tropic sea. At length they turned and rested on their back, luxuriating in the feel of the buoyant water beneath them. The dark outline of the *Araby* stood up a hundred yards distant. Near them, a lazy turtle, undisturbed by their approach, basked in the sun, his shell aglitter, his broad flappers dipped motionless beneath the surface.

"This is sure great," murmured Tod. "I feel like it'd be fine to be one of those turtles there."

"Yes, it'd be fine to have a shell like that to carry round with you; then you wouldn't get hurt so often."

Tod wondered what sort of shell he meant. The cook's blue eyes gazed up into space; the water dripped from his firm jaw; the dragons on his magnificent pectoral muscles lapped at the water greedily.

"Say, Joe Macaroni, I notice you been bunkin' on deck lately."

Tod gave him a quick look. "Yes; it gets so blamed hot below that I take my blankets up to the fo'c's'le head."

"Yeah. Those rats below been botherin' you?"

Tod flushed.

"Oh, they have. Who's it been? Red Mitchell?"

"Not only him. I was so green when I came aboard. A fellow reads those wonderful sea books, and he thinks that all men aboard ship are 'noble, brave men of the sea.'" He spoke bitterly. "You learn better."

The Tattooed Man smiled grimly. "Just wait. I'll fix those fo'c's'le bums. I won't have 'em pulling any stuff on the likes o' you, Joe Macaroni."

"Oh, I've managed to get along."

"Sure you have. But I'm going to fix 'em just the same." He paused a moment to let his anger cool. "If you go fightin', you'll have to watch your step. Red's bigger than you—stronger."

"Yes, but I can knock his block off. He's too fresh."

The Tattooed Man grinned delightedly. "Oh-ho! Well, I hope you fix him good. But what about Hawkes? What you been doing to him?"

"Nothing. Why?"

Jarvis paddled gently with outstretched hands. "Well, when the mate looks at a feller like he looks at you—there's trouble in the air. I'd hate to have you in wrong with him, too. You can't never tell with a guy like that. He'd do anything. I know—see? Anything. . . . Well, let's get back."

Lifting his shoulders out of the water, he dove; his heels flashed for a second in the air. Tod saw him swimming submerged in the clear blue depths. Not to be outdone, he did likewise. He came up sputtering, took a deep breath, and gazed toward the ship. The men were clambering into the gig and up the Jacob's ladder. He heard them shouting, but the words were lost in the distance.

The steam pipes evidently were fixed, he thought. By golly, he'd have to hurry back. He dove again into the pellucid depths.

Below the surface he could see plainly. A school of flying fish went racing by, snapping at the tiny squids near the surface. The little molluscs, only an inch across, apparently made delicious eating. Such an easy way to get a meal! Not a dish or pot to clean up afterward. Then the long slender body of a fish at least nine feet long went vaguely swimming past. The upper lobe of its tail waved mistily. It was after the flying fish, of course. That was its dinner. Better than the squids—larger. No dishes . . .

The great fish swung past again, and he glimpsed green deadly eyes and a wide underslung jaw and mouth. Cold fear clutched his heart. A shark!

With frantic strokes he beat his way to the surface.

His eyes dripped with water. The ship seemed incredibly distant. On deck the men waved and shouted; two seamen climbed the ladder. Only one remained in the ship's gig. It was Toppy, standing up and screaming:

"Sharks! Sharks!"

Tod started toward the ship with all the speed he could muster. Jarvis was waiting for him just ahead. "Hurry up," he said quickly. "It ain't so bad. You don't have to worry. Kick yer feet if the swine comes close. He'll leave you alone."

Even while he spoke, Tod saw coming toward them the whish of a shark's fin. With a little hissing sound it rushed toward them; the gray dorsal fin cut the surface with a knife-like spray. Already Jarvis had seen. He threw his great body to the right between the boy and the approaching shark. In big splashing strokes he swam at Tod's side.

"Kick!" he yelled. "That'll keep him off. The brute must be famished."

Spray rose in a shower of cascades above them. Their arms and legs plunged in and out of the surface. The pursuer turned swiftly; he came driving along even with the cook. Tod, flashing a look across the man at his side, glimpsed a long, dirty gray body, sinister, ugly, murderous.

"You take the ladder," called Jarvis. "I'll get the gig."

In a stirring instant Tod realized that the man was tempting fortune, making for the gig and leaving the Jacob's ladder, which was nearest, to him. The ship was just ahead now, looming up. The ladder dangled maddeningly in the water. Off to the right lay the gig with

Toppy standing upright with an oar in his hands, pushing the boat off the side toward them.

But Tod was already at the rope ladder. Almost overpowered by exhaustion he clung for a moment to the wooden rung swaying in the water. His eyes closed; his breath came quickly. The shouts from above struck his ears like a faint, tumultuous uproar. He pulled himself together and glanced about. Toppy was helping the Tattooed Man into the gig. The shark's fin had disappeared. Where was the beast?

One more breath, he told himself, and then he would climb up. His lungs expanded; he wiped the salt water from his eyes. Suddenly he felt a quick jerk of the ladder. The rung slipped from his hand; it rose swiftly out of reach toward the deck.

A mistake! A mistake! He strained his eyes upward. Among the faces peering, horror-stricken, overside, he saw that of Red Mitchell, triumphant, frightened.

Tod gasped. He was alone in the water with the shark.

The gig! He must make it. He dove, fighting his way through the depths toward the boat. A huge turtle went by with amazing speed; four broad flappers swayed with a rhythmic motion. A flying fish scuttled past. After its prey, the squid? Or was it prey itself of the shark?

Prey! That was what he had become—prey in a shark-infested sea. He breathed out the air in his lungs; the bubbles floated upward. His heart jumped, lost a beat. Coming directly toward him was the long sinister form of the hunter. A cold predatory eye had turned its steadfast gaze on him. Quickly the brute swooped and swung over on its pale gray belly. Its jaw was opening. Its crescent-shaped mouth showed several rows of teeth like saws. Relentless, demon-like, it lunged toward him.

He cut through the surface. Air dashed into his lungs. His feet kicked wildly. He screamed.

Hands reached him. In a flash he was lifted from the water. Exhausted, his breath coming in loud sobs, he sank on a thwart of the gig.

"Hurt?" Jarvis was bending over him.

"No—only scared—I guess."

Toppy grinned in relief. "Blimey, Tom, if yer pictures didn't scare the blarsted shark. He thought as 'ow a two-'eaded dragin was arter 'im!"

From the deck came cries of welcome from the men.

"That'll do," called Mr. Hawkes. "Come aboard at once. We gotta git under way."

"Yes, sir." Toppy threw the oar in the rowlock at the stern-sheets and sculled to the ladder which again hung limp. "Who in 'ell pulled th' bloomin' ladder awiy?" whispered the little Londoner. "Some blighter on deck— blarst 'is 'ide!"

The Tattooed Man, his splendid height and virile strength accentuated by his proximity to the sallow cockney, held the ropes with an iron grip for Tod to ascend. "Yes, who jerked it up?" As the boy passed him, going up, his deep voice sank to a low, vibrant tone. "Careful now, Joe Macaroni. These sharks here ain't so bad—but look out for those on deck. They're swoopin', belly up."

Tod nodded, strangely moved to a recurring sense of disillusionment. He understood. Oh, those "noble, brave men of the sea"! They had faded as a vision of the night.

IV : MOCK WOO OF PANAMA

Tod dipped his hands into the greasy, tepid water in the trough and ran a brush furiously round the sides of a frying pan. "By golly," he complained, "here we are at Panama—our first landfall—and I have to wash these blasted pans!" He wiped the sweat from his forehead, stopped a second, and gazed out the open port to the long line of breakwater that quivered in the morning sunlight on the placid surface of the bay.

Tom Jarvis laughed. "It's a great life, ain't it, Joe Macaroni?"

Tod slammed the brush into the water; and the hot greasy stuff splashed over his shirt. "Yes," he grunted; "now if we were only on the bridge——" He paused; he knew from past remarks that Jarvis recoiled from any mention of the navigation bridge.

"Oh, don't worry," Jarvis rejoined. "You'll see enough of the Big Ditch. It'll take us six hours to get through. Put on full speed ahead and you'll be finished by the time we tie up at the entrance."

By ten o'clock the *Araby* was moored to the concrete docks at Balboa and the inspecting doctor had departed. Tod was peeling potatoes when he was interrupted by Toppy's voice behind him.

"The mate wants ter see you, kid," he announced from the alleyway. "He's in the blarsted officers' saloon."

Without informing the cook, who had gone to the refrigerator room for beef, Tod crossed to the cabin aft. Mr. Hawkes awaited him there, seated on a swivel chair at the table. He pointed to an envelope on the green baize.

"The Old Man wants ye to take a message for him to Panama City. It'll be a good chance t' see the town."

"Yes, sir," Tod said, surprised at the sudden luck. For the last two days, the forecastle gossip with its pungent yarns of the old Spanish city had kindled his desire to go ashore at the Pacific terminal. Here, like a gift from Heaven, was his opportunity.

The mate dug his huge paw into his pocket and brought forth some coins. "Enough for your fare," he said. "You can take a jitney over the hill to this address. Give the letter to the Chink in the store, and he'll give ye some junk to bring back. The skipper wants t' take his old lady a souvenir from the Zone."

Elated, Tod took the sealed envelope and glanced at the address. The money was sufficient to hire a Ford, always cheap in Panama, and no doubt the driver would know the street well. He hurried forward to the starboard washroom, took a quick shower in the sticky salt water, and changed his clothes in the forecastle. The galley was empty when he put in his head at the door.

He turned and accosted the donkey man, who stood beneath the derrick booms of the foremast. "Seen the cook?"

"Gone down to the market," the old man informed him.

Tod shrugged. Oh, well, he'd be back in an hour or so. Since the officers would be apt to eat on shore for a change, the cook could get along without him. He went down the gangway to the wharf. He glanced upstream to his left, but save for two West Coast steamers churning north for the Atlantic side, there were no signs of canal or lock. It looked like an ordinary river.

He crossed to the street near the official buildings with their red-tiled roofs. Men in white passed him; Zone police swung by in military stride; he overtook shuffling Negroes. The glare of the sun on the concrete buildings and pavements almost blinded him. A line of carriages and Fords stood waiting for chance travellers from the ships in dock. He showed the address to a sleepy Panamanian, who glanced at the envelope with soft brown eyes.

"What's it say, mister?"

"I want to get to this address," Tod answered. "Mock Woo, No. 224 Parita Street, Panama."

"Sure, mister, I know it. Jump in." He motioned toward his dilapidated touring car.

Tod had heard stories. "How much?" he asked, warily.

"Five dollars, mister; and we'll be back——"

"Too much! I'll get another."

"Oh, señor, four dollars then—gold. Three. Wait! One dollar fifty."

"All right." Tod gave in. "Make it snappy; but let me see something of the place too."

"*Sí, señor.*"

The little car rattled down the clean paved street and turned to the right. Tod let his gaze pass swiftly over the new American buildings so like those of any town in the States. Soon they were climbing Balboa Heights, where he glimpsed Ancon Hill with its reservoir and official residences asleep in the midst of palms. Presently, the appearance of the houses began imperceptibly to change; they merged into an old-world city of mellow streets overhung with flowered balconies.

With mounting interest, Tod watched the passing faces. Though they ranged from white to deepest ebony, no two seemed of the same tint. He tried to pick out their countries: Americans and visiting Europeans; Panamanian gentlemen in fine white linen, and peons in overalls; Ecuadorians, Chileans, and Colombians; Japanese and Chinese merchants in the deep shade of open doorways. The car went down the crowded Central Avenue with its rows of modern shops, passed Independence Plaza and its Cathedral, and soon turned to the right toward the Panama water front.

Here the streets were narrow; the sidewalks were only two feet wide and sometimes three feet above street level. The balconies overhead seemed to whisper together in the shadows. The shop to which Captain Ramsey had sent him was probably a place of rare curios. At a curving point the Ford drew up and the driver waved him within.

"Him in there no good," he said in derision. "A Chino shop, a Jamaican nigger, and the boy, a San Blas Indian. Shall I wait, señor?"

"Yes, I'll be right out," the boy replied, somewhat perplexed at the cosmopolitan atmosphere about him.

In two strides he crossed the pavement and entered the Oriental shop of Mock Woo, Curios—Very Rare. It was cool and quiet within, where jalousied windows excluded the noonday light. Tod perceived large brass Hong Kong lanterns suspended from the ceiling, and beyond, dark walls lined with silks and embroideries. On the still air floated the faint, mysterious perfume of burning punks.

An old Chinese merchant in blue and gold suit and slippers rose to greet him. "Yes?" he questioned in a sibilant whisper.

"You read Melican?" Tod asked in his best pidgin English. "I gottee letter from cap'n on ship at Balboa. You sabbee?"

Not a flicker was visible on the narrow yellow eyelids. "You come, perhaps, from Captain Ramsey of the *Araby?*" rejoined the Chinese, in perfect English, with only a slight accent noticeable. "I was expecting you." He took the letter and, while he glanced down the page, spoke in a strange melodious tongue.

The tall ebony figure of a Negro rose from the shadows. He slouched across the little shop and jerked up a small Indian boy of uncertain age. "Yo-all sleep too much," he grunted. His teeth flashed in a wide grin, but his eyes, Tod noted, did not join in the merriment.

"Yo git, yuh Indian José," he drawled. He thrust the boy toward the rear door with such force that the little Indian crashed headlong into it.

The dark-skinned boy picked himself up in an instant and vanished noiselessly into a room at the rear.

This was a strange place, thought Tod. He gazed into a glass show case where curios were displayed.

"Perhaps you would like to buy," said the merchant. He opened a cabinet and brought forth long strings of jade beads, curious Chinese trinkets, carved elephants, monkeys sitting three in a row. The carved animals caught the boy's interest. He'd like to take some home. He picked up a Chinese Buddha who, fat and contented, sat cross-legged on a lacquer stand. There was something fascinating about the little fellow. Tod became oblivious of his dark, quiet surroundings.

As his glance flitted to a small cloisonné jar near his hand, he suddenly found that the room had turned black. Suffocated, choked, he stepped backward. He knew on the instant that a soft black scarf had dropped over his head.

Even as his arms instinctively flew upward, two great hands pinned them to his sides. The soft wool fabric drew tight about his face. It cut off his cries. A low chuckle came to his muffled ears. He kicked his feet; he struggled frantically; his teeth bit into the smothering cloth.

"Shut up, you!" a hoarse voice hissed in his ear.

He felt himself lifted and carried through a narrow doorway. That voice! It was vaguely familiar. Hawkes? Impossible; he was on the *Araby*. Red Mitchell's? He squirmed in impotent rage.

He fell, struggling and trussed as he was, on to a sofa.

"Yas, sah; he's a reg'lar little fightin' cock, he is!"

The words of the Negro made Tod's anger rise. His moving legs were grasped, and he felt a stout cord drawn about them. He was helpless, a prisoner.

He heard a low conversation in the room. What were they saying? What did they mean to do to him? Hawkes, of course, was back of this. What did he fear from the mess boy? Did he know that Tod was close to the secrets of the European-Pacific Company? Was the trail of Neil Moran closing in?

Tod's heart was beating in his ears like the thud of a

ship's engine. He opened his lips to speak and found that his mouth was dry and parched. "What are you doing to me?" he managed to whisper.

A sibilant murmur came back in the smooth tongue of the merchant. "You stay here, two hours, three hours —that is all."

Tod squirmed. "I'll inform the police!"

A low laugh greeted his words. "This is not Balboa; this city is under Panamanian jurisdiction. I tell them you came after dope. Oh, they know you sailors well. They will not believe you. You lose your ship—that's all."

"By golly, you got your nerve!"

"Yes? You can get another ship back to Frisco. You should not interfere with the doings of men, my boy. You are an unsuspecting fool."

Tod trembled. What a blunderer he was! So interested had he been in his opportunity to get ashore that he had played into the stacked hand of the mate. Doubtless, Red Mitchell, if it were he, was now hurrying back to Balboa in Tod's Ford. His thoughts rose in a bitter wave and engulfed him.

Silence in the room now. Someone was there, however; he could hear the faint sound of breathing.

"Let me out," he whispered. "Let me out!"

He thought he detected a movement in the room. Footfalls approached him. "What you do, señor?" whispered the voice of the San Blas Indian boy. "Why they kick you—like they kick me?"

Tod's heart leaped. Here was sympathy; here was a friend. He whispered through the enveloping cloth: "They hate me. They want me to starve here in Panama. I must get back to my ship. Let me out."

He heard the boy shudder. "They keel me if I do, señor. You 'Merican boy. They treat 'Merican boys like that, too?"

"No, not all. Let me out, José," he entreated. "I'll pay you well."

"No—no! They keel me; they keel me!" He relapsed into silence.

Tod heard a fly buzzing in the room. He lay exhausted, thinking, pondering. Jarvis would never know what had happened to him. He had vanished from the ship without a word of explanation; the *Araby* would steam on through the Canal and hit the Atlantic swells with Marseilles weeks ahead. And somewhere in the French seaport he might have found trace of Neil!

He turned over on his side. His arms ached; his head throbbed; he was almost suffocated by the cloth. How long had he been there? It seemed an hour; but it could not have been more than twenty minutes. A soft sound stiffened him into attention. The door to the shop closed.

A hand touched his arm. "Listen, señor," said the Indian boy in his ear. "I one big fool to stay in Panama. My father live in Yaviso on the Chucunaque River; he bring cocoanuts to Panama sometimes. I run away—stay here. *Nombre de Dios*, what a fool a boy can be, señor!"

"It's true," grunted Tod.

"Listen, señor. I let you go—you gimme money to get home?"

"By golly, yes! All I got. Four dollars, I think."

"It is enough. I make it on that. Quiet!"

Tod heard him go to the door again. He returned. "Woo is busy with English gentleman. The big Black gone. Quick, I let you loose."

His hands dug into the rope. Tod felt his legs loosened. His stifling cloth was released, and he glanced about the dim room while the broad-faced Indian boy unbound his arms. He stood up, swayed for a second, and grasped a table for support.

"Quick, señor. We go this way."

He led the way out a small door to the rear. Tod found himself in a narrow alley that allowed room for only one to pass at a time. The Indian showed his straight black hair as he turned down a crooked lane and, in a steady trot, made for a street far ahead. They came out panting into a market-place at the water's edge. Cries of fish venders surrounded them; people jostled them; the air was warm but delicious; the sea shone blue in the sunlight.

"We'll get a jitney," Tod jerked out. "We'll both go to Balboa. I can make the boat and you can go on to San Blas."

They discovered a driver calling for passengers for his little car. "To Balboa," Tod cried. "Quick."

They jumped within. The motor chugged, the gears ground, and they swung through the traffic to the right.

The ride seemed endless to the boy as he sat peering ahead for sight of the Balboa docks. Would the *Araby* be there? Was he a fool to try to board her? Wouldn't Mr. Hawkes try worse methods next time? Yes; but he would be on the lookout now. He must get aboard.

They drew up at the docks. Tod tossed the fare to the man, who immediately asked for more. The boy paid no attention.

"Here, José, this is all I've got. Almost three dollars."

"Thanks, señor. This a lucky day for me. *Adiós.*"

Tod raced round the buildings, where the glare of the

sun was almost blinding. As his glance swept across the dockside, his heart sank.

The berth was empty. The *Araby* had gone.

V : TO COLON! TO COLON!

LEFT behind! Penniless—and more than three thousand miles from home. Stunned by the thought, Tod gazed blankly across the dockside. Where was the *Araby?* Was she even now nosing her way into the Caribbean? He pressed his fingers into his palms and looked round. A figure caught his eye. Crossing toward the office buildings was a young man in blue trousers and shirt and wearing an engineer's cap on the back of his head.

Tod hurried toward him. "Did you see a tramp steamer leave this dock?" he queried.

"That rusty tub? Sure—she pulled out less than an hour ago."

The expression of anguish that swept across the boy's face seemed to rivet the man's attention. "What's wrong?" he said cheerily. "Left behind?"

Speechless, Tod nodded.

"That's rotten luck. You can probably catch her, though, by taking the train to Colon." He passed on into the office.

The railroad! Yes; he might make it yet. But he had no money. He went forward to the edge of the wharf where the blinding sunlight dazzled his sight. He must get aboard the *Araby*. Could he appeal to the port authorities to advance him enough to get to the Atlantic side? Must he beg?

Presently, he noticed the engineer walking toward the wharf again. Tod saw that he was heading for a long oil tanker moored some distance down the docks. On a run Tod started after him.

"Are you going through to Cristobal?" The question came, smothered, from his lips.

The man turned and surveyed him. "Sure. But aren't you going by train?"

"I'm broke."

"The deuce you are!" He meditated a moment. "Well, if you think there's a chance of overtaking your ship, you can go through with us. I'm the third. Come on."

Tod followed. They crossed to the dock where the tanker was making ready for her departure. He made out her name on the stern: the *West Corinto* of San Francisco. The engineer said over his shoulder: "Keep close to me and walk along as if you belonged—see?"

Up the gangway they went to the superstructure amidships. Here Tod glimpsed the officers' quarters. They turned aft and went across a spidery bridge that hung over the steel deck with its innumerable hatchways. The black funnel climbing up so close to the stern seemed strange and out of place.

"Better stay aft, kid," the third said genially. "The officers for'ard won't notice you here. When we tie up at Cristobal you can slip ashore. See you later."

Tod passed the firemen's quarters and climbed to the deck above, where, abaft the funnel, he was partially screened by the lifeboats. Everything was painted and polished with meticulous care, certainly in every respect unlike the woebegone aspect of his own tramp freighter.

Presently the tremor of the ship's propeller informed him that they were getting under way. Slowly the *West Corinto* drew out into the stream and headed north. Docks and warehouses and huge machine shops slipped by. Tod peered ahead. There was no sign of the *Araby*. By this time, doubtless, she had passed through the locks that lifted her to the bridge of water high above, and was slowly churning through the Canal toward Gatun.

The tanker must have gone nearly six miles before the river-like shores swung to the left and gave him a glimpse of the first set of locks, their white concrete sides shining in the sunlight.

The third engineer joined him at the deck's edge. "Miraflores," he explained. "Been through before?"

"No; and it doesn't look as I expected. Where's the Canal?"

The man grinned. "Old Culebra Cut is the only real canal part; the rest is either river or lake or bay." He pointed ahead to small electric locomotives that stood waiting on the concrete docksides. "See those four little goats? They pull us through the locks." He grunted sarcastically. "The powers that be don't trust a ship's engines here."

Ahead lay two long slips of water shining between gigantic parallel walls of concrete. As the tanker drew into the one on the right, a lumber schooner came slowly from the other slip. Tod perceived that a double system of titanic stairs allowed one ship to rise without interference while another ship dropped down to sea level. The beetle-like locomotives, two on each side, now put forth long lines fore and aft. Deliberately they advanced, swung up the inclines to the level above, and drew the tanker through the open gateway into the first lock.

Above the puny ship towered colossal concrete walls. Gradually, the steel gates of stupendous size closed behind them. The ship seemed to lie at the bottom of an immense oblong well. The soft wash of water against the plates of the tanker made Tod glance downward. He started. Great gushers of bubbling water stirred the surface into little rippling waves. Quietly, almost imperceptibly, the ship began to rise.

"The first step," chuckled the young engineer. "Some stairs, eh?" There was an air of proud satisfaction about him as he pointed out the giant mechanism of the lock. "We did it, kid—after the French had failed. Every time I go through this Canal, I forget all my doubts about old Uncle Sammy. If he can do this, he can do anything—if he'll only get down to brass tacks and throw his everlasting red tape overboard."

The water now had risen so that the tanker was thrusting her funnel above the sides of the lock. Graceful concrete light poles came into view; next, the red-tiled tops of the watch towers; and last, the small electric mules. Then they were once more above the glittering pavement, and the immense steel gates before them were swinging open.

"The next step. We might see your ship above."

Again the locomotives dragged the tanker into the level water of the next lock; the gates closed behind; and again the ship climbed slowly up the massive walls. The gates ahead now opened into a wide stretch of water.

"These two steps lead to the Miraflores Lake. A mile and a half ahead we hit old Peter McGill."

The locomotives were soon left behind and the tanker carefully shoved her way through the placid waters of the lake. Tod strained his eyes toward the opposite shore line. No tramp steamer was visible, however. Only a white motor ship passed them, making for the Pacific side.

"Diesels," the third said laconically. "That's what they're all coming to some of these days. The Swedes and the Danes clung to their sailing ships so long that they found the steamers of other nations carrying their cargoes. They learned their lesson; now they lead the world in the use of motor ships. God, they're beautiful things! I wish I were engineer on one."

Fifty minutes later, the tanker had passed through the Pedro Miguel Lock and was steaming quietly between the palisades of twisting Gaillard Cut, that immense slice through the hills which had threatened by its slides to make the Panama Canal only a vision.

"Do you think the *Araby* is far ahead?" Tod asked.

The third puffed lazily on his pipe. "It takes an hour and a half to get from Gatun Lake down the locks to sea level. She's not there yet. We may overtake her in the locks."

How the minutes dragged their weary way down the afternoon! If the tanker could only put on full speed ahead, instead of this snail-like progress bound by rules of the Zone. Tod stretched himself in the shade of a lifeboat, watching the tropical shore slip past.

The Rio Chagres widened to a lake; the encroaching jungle crept down to the very water's edge; clusters of vivid orchids shone against the green. Between enchanted islands of waving fronds, the tanker steadily steamed on the route marked out by the buoys and lighthouses.

Tod, peering eagerly ahead, saw only a white heron flying gracefully toward the distant shore line.

Turning northwest, the route spread out across Gatun Lake, surrounded by gently sloping hills of green. Innumerable islands were passed; here and there a tree stuck its wintry branches out of the water. The great dam at Gatun, in flooding the jungle valley, had drowned the vegetation; only remnants of the forest were left to thrust their stricken tops above the surface, dying thus that man might carry his ships across the mountains.

Tod ate supper with the third in the engineers' mess room. The food, he noticed, was infinitely better than any furnished by the larder of the European-Pacific Company. When they came out into the short twilight, the tanker was entering the first of the three mammoth locks which were to drop them down to sea level again. Going forward to the forecastle deck they saw far below them the silver ribbon of the Canal running out to meet the sea. Tod caught his breath sharply. It was strange thus to be standing aboard a ship looking down upon the ocean as though they were resting on a mountain-top. A ship was rising in the middle lock on the left. Another was just leaving the lower lock on the right and starting for Cristobal.

About him the tropic night was closing down, but even in the distant twilight Tod made out the familiar outlines. His heart leaped toward the dawning stars. The *Araby!*

"There she is!" he cried. "My ship."

"You may make her, then," the third conceded.

The tanker was drawn into the first lock, the gate closed behind her, and the water receded into secret tunnels below. The buildings, the electric mules vanished above. The ship lay quietly at the bottom of the well. Then the great steel gates in front swung open; lights flashed along the water's edge; the tanker was drawn forward into the middle lock.

On the instant, Tod turned his searching gaze seaward. The *Araby* had vanished in the night.

A sudden tropical shower, so common in Panama, deepened the darkness. "And they call this the dry season," commented the third. "Yeah—nine months rainy and three months wet."

They hurried under cover amidships. One bell sounded behind them, and the third went aft to prepare for his watch below. Tod followed as far as the firemen's quarters, where he walked nervously to the rail.

Two hours later, when the *West Corinto* had tied up at the Cristobal docks, the sky was once more clear. The arch of the Milky Way gleamed silver. Ships rode at anchor in the harbour; round lights flashed from open ports; moored to the bunkers for coal, other steamers lay, silent and dark save for their regulation lights fore and aft. Tod looked across the dark town, across the railroad tracks to Colon. Front Street quivered with lights; doubtless, her night life, famed in deck-house yarns, was now beginning.

Where was the *Araby?*

Tod slipped down to the wharf. At a run, he went to the left, searching the steamers in port for a sight of the rusty tramp. In half an hour, he found her. She was moored to the docks below the bunkers. He rushed up the gangway, breathless with eagerness. How the familiar deck echoed with his footsteps! It was like coming home again.

Abruptly he hesitated. A heavy-set figure loomed up in the alleyway ahead. His heart missed a beat. The first mate blocked his path.

VI   TOD SHOWS HIS FISTS

"WHADDA ye mean?" growled Mr. Hawkes in his beard. "Tryin' to jump ship at Balboa, was ye?" He came forward, grasped Tod's arm, and pressed it cruelly.

"I wasn't," the boy murmured. "You know I got left."

"Yeah, I know it!" He pushed him toward the galley entrance. "Better take care of this infant, Jarvis," he called.

Tod leaned against the bulkhead and turned his eyes on the retreating form of the mate. He was joined at the gangway by the captain, and the two talked for a moment in low tones.

"Mr. Burton," came Captain Ramsey's voice.

"Yes, sir," answered the young third mate from the deck above.

"We're going ashore, Burton; and it's up to you to see that none of the crew leaves. No liquor smuggled aboard, either—see?"

"Very good, sir."

The two men descended the gangway to the dock. Tod turned to the galley. The cook was filling two pans with new-made bread dough and setting it on the shelf until morning.

"Hello, Tom."

"Sufferin' mackerel!" Jarvis surveyed him with delighted eyes. "Where you been, Joe Macaroni?"

Tod sighed. "I thought I'd lost the ship for good," he admitted. "How'd she happen to stop here?"

The cook grinned broadly. "Oh, I told the Old Man that there'd be no meals if I didn't have a mess boy for help; and I wouldn't take a nigger, either. So we tied up to wait for you."

"By golly, I'm glad to be here."

The cook's smile vanished as he scrutinized the boy closely. "You're a little fool, Joe Macaroni, to come back to this tramp. Don't you see that the mate's got about as much use for you as he has for a broken tail-shaft?"

"I know—but I've got to get to Marseilles."

"Why Marseilles?"

"I'll tell you some time, but not now. I want to see Red Mitchell."

The cook crossed his tattooed arms and, leaning back against the table, nodded slowly. "Oh-ho! So you think you want to fight, eh?"

"I do. The mate sends me on a wild-goose chase to a Chinese shop where Red Mitchell slugs me on the head. Thought he'd fixed me. Wait till I see him."

"Better slug the mate too, hadn't you?"

Tod's mouth and eyes wrinkled into a smile. "I'll do that later."

"Listen here, Joe Macaroni, you go slow. That little coal-passer is strong as a whale."

"Yes, but he doesn't know how to fight. And I do. Why do you suppose I've been practicing boxing these last three years in the gym? Well, for just such a chance as this."

Jarvis threw back his head; his deep laugh boomed forth. "A regular stormy petrel. That's what you are, Joe Macaroni."

Tod, not a bit amused, turned and left him. He crossed the deck, where the open doors of the two forecastles gleamed pale yellow. At the top of the stairs, with his foot on the iron sill, he paused. The forecastle was dark with men. Voices rose with the cloud of smoke from pipes and cigarettes.

"Yeh, beat it, he did," came a voice. "A-scared he was. Ain't I right, now?"

"Blimey, you're off yer nut, Red. The kid ain't scared o' the likes o' you."

"Oh, he ain't! Then why did he jump ship?"

"Yah, Red—you yoost wait. He'll come. Yoost wait."

"Stow the gaff, you fellers," said the boatswain. "You darn stokers always think you can run this here ship. Always blamin' the deck hands fer somethin'. Better go back to your own fo'c's'le, Red. The air's better for you there."

Red Mitchell snarled angrily. "Yeah, just like what Blackie Judson says—you fellers in here are all afeardt to fight. Ain't I right, now?"

In the little roar of rage that ensued, Tod went down the ladder. He met the men in the act of heaving Red Mitchell up the companionway.

"Blimey, it's the kid!"

"Yah—yah. Didn't I say yoost wait?"

The men fell back and unceremoniously dropped the little coal-passer. Tod saw surprise light the countenance of the rat-like face.

"Where was you, kid?" asked the boatswain.

Tod felt his anger rising. "Ask Red Mitchell. He knows where I was. He knows why I lost the ship at Balboa."

Toppy flung out a shrill cackle. "Blast yer hide, Red, if yer knew and didn't tell yer messmates."

Red Mitchell's mouth drew down at the corners in a snarl. "Naw. Don't ask me. Whadda y' mean, kid? Is you insinuatin'?"

Tod surveyed him coolly. "I suppose, Red, you never heard of the oriental shop of Mock Woo—Curios, Very Rare."

"You're talkin' through yer hat!" scowled the other.

Tod stepped forward. Throwing his cap on a bunk, he slipped out of his coat. "This isn't the first bit of dirty work you've tried, Red Mitchell. But it's the last. Get ready."

"Blimey, he's peelin' his sweater. Strike me bline."

The boatswain put up a restraining hand. "You fellows wait."

"Wait, nothin'!" Red spat upon the floor. "He can't bamboozle me—the toff! I'll stow his gaff!"

"Yeh, bose, it's time," said Toppy, stepping between them. "But wait a minute. We ain't got things ready. Look—the cap'n and the mate is gone to Colon on business." He laughed shrilly. "Treats us like little boys ten years old. We cawn't go ashore, oh, no. But we can stage a fight. In half an hour. We'll git the men together. It ain't fair to let them miss this here show."

A chorus of approval came from the bunks. "A fight.
. . . Five rounds. . . . A regular bout. . . . Toppy, you be
referee. . . . Where's yer fightin' kit, Toppy, what yer
talked about?"

Red Mitchell fell back, and Tod crossed to his bunk.
The little Londoner was down on his knees, wrenching
open his dunnage bag beneath a lower bunk. He came
out with two pairs of short drawers and canvas shoes.

"Stole the bloomin' things," he grinned. "They came
straight from the ringside at the Liverpool docks."

"Py yiminy! A real fight."

"Here, Red, take yer things and dress. We'll call yer
in twenty minutes." He turned to Tod and thrust into his
hands the fighting kit. "Here's yours, kid. Make ready."

"All right." Tod nodded. He waited until Red Mitchell
had climbed above and gone to the firemen's forecastle,
then he followed. He determined to take a shower first.
Already Toppy was clearing the benches from the floor,
and fixing a shade over the electric bulb in the deckhead.

"Blast yer hide, if this ain't the real show," he murmured. Tod heard the rising voices behind him. The men
were eagerly making ready for the fight.

He crossed the dark deck to the washroom with its
smell of lye and damp wood. The cool salt water seemed
to clear his mind. He rubbed himself briskly and slipped
into the short tight pair of gray trunks. He put on the
canvas shoes, and rose, finding himself fit and eager. With
his coat on and his clothes in his hand, he went down the
starboard alleyway. A light burned in the cook's cabin.

Stepping within, he dropped his garments on the chair
and looked at the Tattooed Man, who lay in his bunk,
reading. Tod's eyes met his surprised, incredulous stare.

"Sufferin' whale oil, what you doin'?" The cook rose to a sitting position and ran a hand through his short hair. His huge body seemed to quiver in amazement; but his eyes flashed darkly. "Joe Macaroni, you goin' to fight?"

Tod nodded, and Jarvis rose and motioned him to the berth. "Lie down—rest. When is it coming off?"

"In twenty minutes. Toppy is fixing up the fo'c's'le. Both gangs will be there."

"I don't like it, Joe Macaroni," the cook went on as Tod stretched himself on the bunk. "Are you tired out?"

"I oughtn't to be. Did nothing all afternoon."

"Excited? No, you're not. Here, let me have your arm. Cool, now. Remember what I told you about the fight on the Bund at Shanghai. You must play the same game. Red can last all evening, but you can't stand the strain. Get him before you tire."

Jarvis was talking serenely now. "I've seen this coming, kid; and I hoped it wouldn't. This flotsam on the *Araby* isn't for the likes o' you, Joe Macaroni. Why did you ever sign on?"

"I had to."

Jarvis sighed. "Well, you're here now; and you've got to fight. The men have driven you both to it. I've seen 'em talking, whispering when the officers wasn't near. Down in the engine room, too, it's been the same."

Tod closed his eyes. Yes, he knew that this was more than a personal quarrel between him and Red Mitchell. The smouldering jealousy between the engine room and the deck, between men who slaved in the inferno below and those who worked in the cool air above, had kindled into hate at the death of the stoker. Alive, he had been growled at by his messmates; dead he had become a friend to be avenged. Hatred flamed forth in all its fury. Red would avenge the wrongs of the engine room; the kid would uphold the rights of the deck.

"Five rounds, you say," Jarvis went on. "That's too long for you, Joe Macaroni. Red's muscles are made of iron. Behind each blow will be months of trimming in the bunkers, throwing coal down the chutes to the stokers at the furnace. Older he is, too; but he has no science. You think you know how to box. Then use it, every bit. Take it easy at first. He is cowardly. Find his weak point, then press—press and give no quarter. He means to fight to a finish. This is no child's play."

"I know. I've found none on this ship."

"Aye, growing up you are, Joe Macaroni. Almost a man. Rest, now—close your eyes. My heart is in this fight."

Footfalls sounded in the alleyway. "Ready, kid?" whispered Toppy. "The gang's waiting. Fight 'im—fight 'im. We 'spect you t' hold up the honour o' our bloomin' fo'c's'le."

Quietly the three went out. At the main deck they hesitated. The last members of the firemen's forecastle were streaming down the companionway. Suddenly, there arose a shout of mingled voices.

"Red's come," whispered Toppy. "Hush! Wait!"

On the boat deck above them had sounded the steps of an officer walking forward. Evidently the noise had caught his attention. He waited for a moment at the rail, then went back to his room beneath the chart house.

"That's Burton," Jarvis commented. "Listen, there's the fourth engineer playing his darned ukulele."

Tod heard the sounds of soft-stringed notes drift down and a voice singing in a high falsetto:

> "All de world am sad and lonely,
>   Ebery where I roam . . ."

That song wasn't true, the boy thought swiftly as they crossed the deck. The world was neither sad nor lonely; it was exciting and filled with people. At the seamen's forecastle he stopped, while Toppy led the way below.

"Cool—cool, Joe Macaroni. Make him angry, tire him, then light in."

Grudgingly, the stokers sitting on the companion steps moved aside to let the three descend. Between Toppy and Jarvis, Tod let his glance sweep over the place. The light above the entrance had been turned out and a shade flung around the single globe between the bunks, so that a blue cone of light cut down through the smoky atmosphere. Red Mitchell's gang lined the stairs and the after bulkhead; Tod's crowd rose tier on tier in the bunks forward. The forecastle was hot and stale; it was damp with sweating bodies. The ventilators, trimmed to the wind above,

and the open ports on the right side let in only a feeble
flow of air. Voices rose, murmurous with eager lust for
blood. Pipe and cigarette smoke sent a continual haze up
to the deckhead where it hung like a cloud, black and
stagnant, threatening as a coming storm.

As Tod and Jarvis crossed beneath the glow of the
light, a roar of welcome came from the throats of the
seamen.

"Yer blarsted fools!" shouted Toppy in rage. "D'ye
want ter 'ave the horficers down on us? Pipe down!"

In the apex of the forecastle, where its narrowness allowed only one tier of bunks, Tod took a chair arranged
for him. Over it were flung several towels; a water bucket
stood on the floor.

From the cleared space in the centre, Toppy gave his
orders in a shrill high voice. "Close the door, Judson.
Blimey, I know it's bloomin' 'ot; but youse guys make
too much noise. Johnson, keep yer glims peeled on the
arfter deck. And don't yer fergit to sing out if any bloomin' horficer pipes up. I'm runnin' this fight 'cause I'm the
only one as knows the old Mark o' Queenberry's rules—
see? And I'm the friend of them both. We'll 'ave five
rounds—more if necessary."

"We won't need 'em," broke in Red Mitchell from his
bench at the foot of the stairs. His partner and helpmate,
Black Judson, laughed deeply.

"He's too sure, Joe Macaroni," whispered Jarvis as he
rubbed the boy's arms. "Let him go the first round; then
surprise him."

"No blarsted dirty work allowed," pursued Toppy
from the ring. He motioned to Mitchell, who rose.

"Red Mitchell, of the Black Gang."

A low burst of applause went up from the throats of the engine-room gang. Clearly, they were certain of victory. Tod turned his gaze on his opponent who stepped into the full glare of the light. Red Mitchell smiled with the easy assurance of a champion. His pasty skin was blotched and none too clean. He drew in a long breath and expanded his chest; the muscles of his upraised arms swelled and rippled under their covering. Raising one foot quickly, he sidestepped; and his limbs, their length accentuated by the short black trunks, showed the easy play of practised muscles.

Tod watched him closely, as this play to the spectators brought a rising roar from the fireroom men. Red was five foot eight; just the boy's height; but the coal-passer was built more compactly, more solidly. He weighed perhaps one hundred fifty, against the boy's one hundred thirty-five.

"Remember my words, Joe Macaroni. Take the first round easy. Now, go."

Toppy flung out his arm. "The kid, representing the deck."

A burst of applause went up from the seamen. Tod, stepping forward beneath the light, felt the vibration of their cries as it swelled to a mighty thunder.

"The kid. He's got guts!"

"Yah—yah. Yoost wait. He wins!"

"Pipe down!" squealed Toppy. "Any more noise like that an' th' blarsted fight is off. Blimey, ain't yer got no sense?"

His warning struck the spectators into silence. A profound hush came over the little forecastle. Tense, breathless, they waited. Tod was dimly aware of a circle of gleaming eyes rising to the deckhead. It all seemed unreal, as though he were no longer Tod Moran, but a wooden puppet decked out in fighting tights and canvas shoes, and now shoved before an audience to make his bow. Mechanically, he put forth a hand to shake with his opponent.

Red Mitchell showed his teeth in a snarl. "I don't have t' shake with this whelp. Ain't I right, now?"

A low murmur of approval rose behind Red. How the Black Gang hated him! Why? What had he done to them?

"There ain't no gloves," went on Toppy mildly. "It's goin' ter be the naked fists—the raw 'uns."

A welling roar rose to the cloud of smoke above. It was like the cry of a pack at sight of the hunted, more animal than human. Tod and Red Mitchell stepped back.

Toppy raised his voice. "Remember—three-minute rounds." He paused. "Seconds out!"

In the silence the gentle slap of water against the hull was heard. All eyes were focussed upon those waiting figures beneath the light. Toppy's throat moved convulsively.

"Time!"

VII : BLACK GANG VS. DECK CREW

THE two white figures sprang into instant action. Red came at Tod with his face down, his red hair flaming, his lips drawn back over his teeth. Tod circled. Keeneyed, cool, with his chin in and his arms close to his body, he moved his legs with the litheness of a practised boxer. No movement of his antagonist did he miss. A great driving blow flashed toward him. He avoided this, and his left shot out and just touched the other's chest.

"Attaboy! . . . Ye got him, kid! Knock him cold!"

"Oh, my! Our little red rooster got hit."

"Blimey! First touch! Cocka-doodle-do-o-o-o!"

Tod saw the crimson leap into Red Mitchell's face. His mouth contorted in a snarl; his red-lidded eyes gleamed with malice. That was good. Red was getting peeved.

The coal-passer, slower than the boy, more solid on his feet, now attacked furiously, trying to batter down the boy's defence. Tod stepped aside, waiting. Red came at him, his head still down, his back bent almost double. The terrible onslaught of those flashing arms forced the boy to retreat. He dodged, ducked, and found himself pushed back in the narrow apex.

Laudatory cries rolled from the firemen. "Hit him, Red. . . . Ye got him now."

"Wow! Wot a knockout."

A crashing fist had caught Tod straight on the ribs. As he staggered back against a bunk, he saw Red's eyes alight with joy.

"At him, Joe Macaroni! Send him back!"

Tod flung himself forward at his antagonist. They fell into a clinch. Red's hot breath was on his left shoulder; blows rained upon the small of his back.

"I'll kill you, you little pup!" Red hissed.

"Lookit the butcher!"

"At it again. He likes liver, he does!"

Toppy sprang between them. "Break, you fellers! D'you think this is a dance?"

They separated and stepped back. Tod went at him; his fists moved like the piston rods of an engine. Thud—

thud! Thud—thud! Red was defending. Tod pressed him closely. The boy took a glancing blow just over his heart, then swung up his left and sent it crashing against his opponent's jaw. The dull thud echoed in the stillness.

"Time!"

Red swore softly as he wiped his chin. "Just when I got goin'. Ain't I right, now?"

Black Judson chuckled grimly as he drew Red into his seat, and Tony the Wop let out a deep laugh. Immediately, the forecastle resounded with raised voices. Bets flew back and forth. Cries for their champion cut across the room.

As Tod lay back in his chair, Jarvis wiped a towel quickly over his sweating body. "Great stuff," he whispered. "You got him goin', Joe Macaroni. He's gettin' mad—fightin' mad!" He pressed a wet sponge into the boy's mouth and wiped his heaving chest. "Watch him. Play him up. Let him get wild—then slug. Watch your chance—this round!"

Tod nodded. With head thrown back, arms and legs outstretched, he lay in his chair, breathing deeply. Vaguely he was aware of the boatswain's commending voice, of Swede Jorgenson delightedly cheering him on.

"Time!"

Again the sudden silence, broken only by the heavy breathing of excited men. Again the rush of Red Mitchell's compact form. Tod waited his chance, saw an opening, and with all the force of his arms and legs let drive a blow straight for the other's tight-drawn face. It caught the man directly upon the nose. A burst of blood went streaming down his jaw, dripping to his glistening chest in great wine-red splotches.

"Lookit his bloody beak!"

"Yah—yah—yah!"

Bedlam broke loose. The noise was like the roar of animals at the first smell of blood. The boy felt suddenly sick. He and Red were fools thus to be entertaining these beasts. He hesitated. Even the furious expression of startled hate on his antagonist's face had no power to move him. And in that instant Red Mitchell drove a swinging crash upward. Behind it was all the strength of those daily five hundred shovelfuls of coal. With a resounding thud, it smacked against the boy's jaw and struck him to the deck.

Full length he lay, with his head almost at Jarvis's feet. *One . . . two . . . three. . . .* The bulb of the light was an immense moon swinging giddily through the sky. The rising clamour of the men was the thundering roar of a distant surf. He listened, eyes closed.

Four . . . five. . . . They were counting him out. The second round! Well, he didn't care; it was heaven here on the floor. What did he care for those bellowing men with their gloating eyes! *Six. . . .* He stirred, his eyes opened.

"Up, Joe Macaroni! Up!"

Seven. . . . By golly, this would never do. He struggled to an elbow. Drawing an arm across his mouth he knew that his lips were cut and the blood trickling down his jaw. *Eight. . . .* He was on all fours now. He braced himself, swayed an instant, then rose to his feet.

"Attaboy!"

"Well, I'm hanged if he ain't got grit!"

"Guts, I call it!"

Yes, that was the word. Not to fail now. Not in the second round. He swung into position; he staggered slightly. Red came at him.

"Time!"

Heavenly relief. Lurching, swaying, he backed to his chair. Dimly he felt the sponge at his lips, his face wiped clean, his body rubbed. Just to rest—never move. His head sank back.

What was that? Who was talking close at hand? Jarvis, of course. He opened his eyes. The cook bent over him. His mouth was a straight line in his square jaws; his eyes, set in the broad cheeks, glittered in the shadow.

"Take it easy," he counselled; "you ain't whipped yet—not by a long shot. You stopped short, Joe Macaroni. What got into you?"

"I dunno. I was thinking."

"Sufferin' tripe! This ain't no time to think. Wade in. You can lick him. He's yellow."

Jarvis turned as the bellowing roar behind him increased. Men jumped from the bunks; the Black Gang surged forward to meet them. Angry murmurs rose.

"Back! Back, you fools!" Jarvis strode to the centre of the ring. "This fight ain't over yet. No sirree! The kid ain't licked—not yet. He's got a come-back, he has. Just wait—and watch."

"Yah—wait!"

Muttering, cursing in their throats, the two factions separated. They climbed back to their seats; their eyes stared hungrily down at the open ring.

"Rested?" Jarvis was back at Tod's side. "Watch your chance. Red thinks he's already won. Fool him! Press—press. Remember—my heart is in this fight. You'll win!"

Toppy was talking again with upraised arm. What was he saying? The voices of the men drowned his words.

Jarvis leaned closer. "It's all right, Joe Macaroni. Red don't want any more rounds. He wants to fight to a finish this time. I said yes."

Tod nodded and rose, even as the spectators hungrily took up the cry: "No more rounds. A fight to a finish!"

"Time!" Toppy whirled to the ringside.

Red Mitchell came to meet Tod with a smile playing about his lips. Tod knew from his expression that the little coal-passer thought the fight was already as good as over, that one blow would finish the kid. By golly—by golly, Red was going to get a surprise! He'd make him go down too; he'd make him feel the deck beneath his outstretched body.

"Think yuh can stand up again, do yuh?" taunted Red. "Yuh ain't got it in yuh. No—not in your family." He drove forward, head down. "Ain't I right, now?"

Tod pressed his lips tightly. He felt sharp anger surge up within him. Cool—cool, Joe Macaroni! A hard smile drew down the corners of his mouth.

His mind was on his work now. He avoided a blow, dodged, struck his opponent on the ribs, and dove in. Thud—thud! He battered down the weak defence. Thud—thud! The blows hit, but it was like hitting a rock. His knuckles were bruised and cut. But they were hard too. Oblivious of the mounting tumult in his ears, the shouts, the cries, the curses, he pressed, pressed, continuing his battering punishment.

A look of pained surprise came over the rat-like countenance of the coal-passer. In that stirring instant Tod knew that fear had flashed for the first time through the man.

Above the clamour he heard a voice: "Joe Macaroni—now!"

An unfathomed strength flowed through him. He shot forward. Twinkling feet, flashing legs, swinging arms with their lashing impact drove Red Mitchell backward.

"Wallop him, kid!"

"Red, you fool, fight! Fight!"

The coal-passer seemed appalled at the jolting, mauling fists. Recoiling, swerving, he was yet unable to sidestep those punishing blows. With his face a sallow gray, he parried awkwardly, and drove his right into the boy's ribs. Tod in that unguarded second, let fly his left with all his strength, all his weight behind it. Straight toward the rat-like jaw it leaped. The dull thud of it resounded through the forecastle. Breathless, the crowd waited.

Red Mitchell staggered, flung out his arms, and pitched backward. He dropped in a huddled heap.

"Blimey, wot a knock-out!"

One . . . two . . . three. . . . Tod stepped back. His eyes were fixed on that motionless form. *Four . . . five. . . .* Red stirred; he moaned slightly.

"At him, Red!"

"Don't let that lubber win!"

"Get up, you blasted fool! Shake a leg!"

The firemen swarmed from their seats and crowded about the prostrate figure. "Up, you fool!" The voices were heartless, brusque with anger.

Seven . . . eight. . . . Tod glimpsed round him the burning eyes, the leering mouths, malignant, crying for blood. *Nine. . . .* Red slowly rose on one elbow. His face was screwed into lines of bitter hatred. Then he collapsed again in sobbing breaths.

Ten.

Shouts swelled to a thunderous roar that detonated through the forecastle—a bellow of victory from the deck hands, a rising scream of disappointed fury from the Black Gang. At the sound, deep antagonisms were loosed at their moorings. The floor beneath the cone of light was abruptly filled with moving men.

With outstretched hands Tod stumbled through the frenzied turmoil. The sweltering forecastle, the stench of dirty bodies, the bestial howls, and the driving, thudding blows on the instant stifled him. He wanted air—air.

He felt himself lifted; he knew that Jarvis had picked him up as he would a child and was wading through the sweep and surge of that flooding tide of battle.

"Out of the way! Back—back!"

The companion steps were reached. He felt himself borne up, up—and the next moment the fresh cool air of the night caressed his moist and weary body.

VIII : CAPTAIN TOM JARVIS

"Never such a fight, Joe Macaroni. Never such a knockout."

Tod leaned against the bulwarks; his moist hands gripped the curving edge of the steel plates. Wiping the sweat and blood from his face, he looked out across the harbour. The dark hulls of steamers loomed up in the roadstead, their sides relieved by the glow of open portholes. The sound of muffled oars drifted across the water and brought to Tod's mind the thought of other ships' officers who now perhaps were returning to their boat.

"Has the third mate heard?" he whispered huskily.

Jarvis gazed aft toward the shadowy superstructure. "Burton is deaf if he hasn't," he rejoined in his deep tone. "Listen to th' animals. How they roar!"

Tod turned and faced the forecastle bulkhead. The dark figure of Tony the Wop emerged from the open companionway and proceeded with low intermittent moans to the firemen's quarters. Behind him came the reverberating echo of the fight: shuffling feet, stifled oaths, the muffled clamour of the uproar. The injured man stumbled across the iron sill of the second forecastle and vanished down the ladder.

"Is he hurt bad, Tom?"

"Draggin' his arm. Serves him right."

"Look—there's Red."

Accompanied by the stoker, Black Judson, Red Mitchell stepped to the main deck. He flung off the arm of his companion and turned to stare back at the commotion below.

"The blasted beasts," Red shrilled. "Did ye hear 'em yell? 'At 'em, Red,' they says. 'Kill him. Fight! Fight!' Yeh—I hopes they gets some of it themselves, the beasts. Yeh, I hopes they kill each other." He stumbled toward the open door of the firemen's forecastle. Evidently, he became aware of Tod and the cook standing at the bulwarks, for he paused and eyed them intently.

"Yeh, I hopes they get killed. Ain't I right, now, kid?"

Tod's hand slipped along the rail. In surprise he heard himself answer: "By golly—I hope so too."

A moment later Red had disappeared with Judson down the companionway. Jarvis made a sound like a chuckle in his throat. The boy looked up; but when he dimly saw the big man gazing aft he followed his glance.

Mr. Burton came hurrying forward.

"What's the racket, Tom?" the young third mate inquired, hesitating near them. "They've had booze?"

Jarvis nodded. "But mostly a friendly fight."

"It sounds like it." Burton crossed to the open door. His voice shouted down the stairway; then his figure blocked the entrance for a second as he descended.

In silence, the two at the bulwarks waited. If any difference below was noticeable, it was merely an increase in the hubbub. Mr. Burton soon returned.

"They've gone crazy," he ejaculated in an angry voice. "They refuse to obey." He started aft. "I'll get my automatic."

"I wouldn't if I were you, Mr. Burton," Jarvis said serenely. "Here, I'll give you a hand.—Wait a minute, Joe Macaroni."

He turned with his swinging, powerful stride. His huge form blocked the dim light of the forecastle entrance. Tod heard his voice boom out as he went down the steps. "All hands on deck! Muster aft! Cut the fight, you fellows!"

Presently the pandemonium below decreased to a low murmur. At that commanding presence, the boy thought, the men had jerked themselves back into order. Commanding! That was Tom Jarvis. He knew how to handle men.

Tod watched them come up on deck. In little disgruntled groups they went their way, some down to the firemen's forecastle, others toward their quarters amidships. Even Chips and the donkeyman and the boatswain seemed to have lost their heads. Jarvis, reappearing, dispersed them in sharp ringing notes like the crack of a whip. A moment later the deck was deserted and silence once more enfolded the ship.

"Get a shower and a rub-down, Joe Macaroni, and come to my room."

Tod went. He felt like his old self again when he stood under the twisted tin shower and rubbed himself into a glow. Surveying himself in the cracked mirror

fastened to the wall, he sighed. The wide gray eyes that stared back at him beneath the tousled crown of sandy hair were bright and clear; the uptilted nose had escaped all injury, but the mouth—— If that blow had hit his eye, he would be needing a raw beefsteak plastered on it. He chuckled.

Toppy's cockney voice greeted him over his shoulder. "Fixin' up, kid? Gawd blimey! but you walloped him. Wot a knock-out. Oh, that mouth ain't bad. Red'll be needing a whole cow tied around 'is bloomin' body." He laughed in his high falsetto. "He don't fight none too fair, does he, kid?"

"Aw, fair enough."

"No, he don't. He ain't square. But there ain't anythin' that fights square on this blarsted tub. Even the cooties got the 'abit. They bites where you cawn't 'it back." He went out, grinning.

Tod found the cook in his cabin reclining on the settee. The boy slipped into singlet and dungarees and then lay down on the bunk.

"I've got somethin' to ease up those bruised knuckl[e] of yours." The man busied himself with salve and ban[d]ages. "I'm proud o' you, Joe Macaroni. And as for [?] seamen's fo'c's'le—well, I suppose you'll be a little god there now."

He smiled as he took his place again on the s[?] "Some fight! I only hope that when I get my han[?] a certain young man that I give him as good a b[?] as you gave Red."

Tod opened his eyes and observed Jarvis. Th[?] a grim twist about the firm mouth, a distant lo[?] Tartar eyes. "You've got an enemy then, Tom?"

"Yes—but he's a coward. He'll never fight back."

Tod sighed. "Well, I pity the poor fellow when you get your hands on him." He gazed at the swelling muscles that bulged from the thin white singlet. Such a man as this was not made for a ship's galley. The length of limb, the lithe movements of the powerful body, the poise of the head, all told of a commanding presence. Tod looked at the man narrowly. "You've been commander of a ship, Tom Jarvis. I know it. To-night I could tell."

Jarvis answered in a low, measured tone. "Yes; now I'm cook on an ocean tramp—but once I was captain of a cargo carrier. . . . But I want to forget that." He drew his hand across his brow as though he would wipe away a picture he dared not face. "Yes, I've had my command —and lost it."

"Lost it!" The words were like an echo.

"Oh, I'm not crying over it." The man lifted his head and looked earnestly at the boy. "Five years ago, I was like that young third mate, always studying, always learning navigation at school and on ships. Then I got my first command—at twenty-five. Can you realize what that means—master of a ship at twenty-five years old? Oh, how young I was! And I thought I knew so much. I was proud of that freighter. She was such a beauty. Then—then I lost her. Yes, lost her—and the Board of Inquiry fixed the blame on me."

He paused. His hands clenched his knees in an iron grip. "Oh, I know that every master who ever loses a ship says he isn't to blame; but I was made the goat, I tell you. . . . We were making the Columbia River one night in a fog. It had shut us in ever since we had passed

Cape Mendocino lighthouse on the starboard beam; the foghorn had been wailing across the waters every minute; and the thing had got on everybody's nerves. I had signalled to the engine room for half speed ahead; for hours we crept along.

"Then we passed the Blunt's Reef light vessel, and I breathed easier. My calculations in the chart room had been correct. Just ahead lay Point Adams. It was at that moment when I stood on the bridge thinking we had made it safely that the thing happened. I don't know exactly what it was—only a little sound, a slight concussion below and aft. Almost at once the second officer brought word that number four hold was filling rapidly, that we'd have to take to the boats.

"I remember distinctly the surprise I felt. This wasn't fair—my first command! The second took my place and I hurried aft. Looking over the casing of number four hatch, I was certain it wasn't that bad. There was a hole in her side above the Plimsoll mark; it was only the heavy seas that filled her when she rolled. Once across the Columbia bar and in the river, she wouldn't take more than a drop. It was to be a race, then; and I felt sure that we could win.

"I had the pumps manned and the watertight doors in the bulkheads closed. We crept across the bar, but she settled almost before we reached the channel. The engine room had filled and the steam pipes burst. The sliding door leading aft from there to the shaft tunnel was open. Someone had opened it again; I hadn't known until too late. Half an hour after we had left in the boats she went down. . . . My ship."

The voice stopped. Tod raised himself on his elbow.

The man's head was bowed in his hands; the closely cropped hair was ruffled between his spread fingers.

"They blamed you?" Tod said gently.

"Yes; the captain. Then I realized why the company had given me, young as I was, the command. Because in my crazy pride I didn't suspect them; I was putty in their hands. They were crooks; they collected the insurance, and I lost my master's papers for a year. A year! . . . It might just as well have been for life. Every place I went the story followed. 'Oh, didn't you know? He lost his first command. Yes, his certificate for a year, too. . . .' Always the same story. I couldn't get a berth. The company knew I suspected the truth; so they hounded me from port to port. I mustn't be allowed to get a good name again. I might talk, you see. . . . But I was in no hurry; I was after the man who knew the truth. The first mate and the chief engineer got money out of it, I know; but the purser, somehow, seemed different. He had gone below, he told me that night in the open boat, and seen the chief slide open that watertight door. He promised to testify, if the inquiry came off. But he didn't—he disappeared. I couldn't find him. . . . I'll get him yet. I'll let the world know that Captain Tom Jarvis is equal to any master on the Pacific. And look—here I am, a cook on this rusty tramp." He spoke the last words bitterly. His eyes, the boy perceived, were gray and dull like burnt-out coals.

"But you're a blamed good cook, Tom," the boy insisted.

The big man laughed softly. "Sure I'm a good cook— and I'm not ashamed of it. Cooking can be an art; but hardly on the *Araby*. Learned it on the China Sea. That's where I got these pretty pictures." He pointed ironically to his chest. "I was on the beach in Shanghai for two months, and when I got a berth on a barkentine for the States I had these. . . . That fixed me. I decided that I'd gone down far enough. I had my mate's papers, but I wanted my master's; so I jumped ship at Seattle and studied and worked and fought for them. And I don't intend to lose it all without a fight, either." He sighed as he drew his hands across his moist brow. "Only sometimes I get mighty tired out, discouraged."

"If I were ever a mate on a ship," Tod put in eagerly, "I'd like to sail under you, Captain Tom Jarvis."

"You mean it?" The burnt-out coals of his eyes glowed with sudden feeling.

Tod nodded. "You'll win out too. I know it. You'll get that rotten company yet."

"It isn't much of a shipping firm," the other replied slowly. "It's mostly one man—a smooth devil. He organized a new steamship line a year ago."

Tod's mind flashed back to San Francisco, to certain words that Sheila Murray had said about the European-Pacific Steamship Company. Loose strands were gathering and weaving themselves into a pattern. "Is it Swickard?" he hazarded.

Captain Tom Jarvis looked up with a start. "Jasper Swickard. You know him?"

"Aye, the manager of this line." Tod paused as full understanding swept over him. "Now I know why you're here."

"Careful, Joe Macaroni," retorted Jarvis with a smile. "I ain't no ship's officer now."

"Yes; but you will be when you find your man."
Tod's cheeks were flushed; he felt his pulse quicken.
Now he understood the man, understood his strange si-
lences, the look of deep absorption in his eyes. He was
a person who knew life, too. He'd tell him of Neil.
Surely he would help. And whom would he rather con-
fide in than Tom Jarvis? Weren't he and Neil akin?
Hadn't they both been judged guilty by Jasper Swickard,
at one time a director of the Jamison Line, now manager
of the European-Pacific Steamship Company?

"Yes, now I understand," Tod repeated; "Swickard
would never suspect that the cook on the *Araby* might
be the former captain of—of—what was her name?"

Jarvis pronounced the name softly, with a caress in
his deep voice. "The *Annie Jamison.*"

Tod grew rigid. The *Annie Jamison.* On the instant, he remembered the time when Neil had come home with the news of the wreck in the Columbia River. No one had been hurt, though; Neil had gone off almost at once on his trip to the Amazon, where he had contracted a tropical fever. Forgotten incidents welled up within him. His mouth felt abruptly dry.

"Who—who was this man who ran away? Why didn't he give evidence?"

Tom Jarvis laughed thickly. "Money, I guess. And yet I felt certain that he was the one person who would back me up. I depended upon him." He leaned back against the bulkhead; his eyes half closed. "He was the purser."

"The purser." The words barely escaped the boy's lips. There was a feeling at his throat as though something clutched his windpipe.

Tom Jarvis rose. His huge bulk loomed up almost to the deckhead. His hands clenched, his muscles grew taut; the dragons writhed on his chest and about the cords of his neck. He flung out the words with an oath, words that in an instant built up again that impenetrable wall between them.

"Yes, the purser—damn him! ... . Neil Moran."

THE STONES SANG WITH THEIR EAGER STEPS.

PART THREE

ON THE TRAIL OF NEIL MORAN

MARSEILLES HARBOUR
FOREIGN AND OFFSHORE VESSELS
IN PORT
Arrived 3 April am. Stmr. *Araby*,
Ramsey 37 days from San Fran-
cisco. Mdse to Granet et Cie.

Journal Maritime

I : A SECRET MEETING IN MARSEILLES

RISE and shine! Up, you lubbers! Marseilles—on the starboard bow!"

Tod Moran turned out with a yawn, climbed the ladder to the forecastle head, and watched Marseilles rise out of the classic waters of the Mediterranean. Over the network of masts and funnels in the harbour, a soft mist wavered; then the first rays of the sun dispersed the haze and brought into view the church of Notre Dame de la Garde, which, from its height behind the city, gazed serenely down upon the turbulent water front.

Port formalities are ceremonial functions in France; it was afternoon before the quarantine officers departed and the *Araby* moored to her dock in the New Harbour. Tom Jarvis and Tod rushed through the evening mess with a gaiety which they had forgotten had ever existed. The cook became a boy again. Two years had elapsed, he told Tod, since he had stepped foot in the great cosmopolitan city; and his memory went back to those days when his ship had made regular passages from New York to Mediterranean ports. Land! Marseilles! The laughter of throngs in the cafés in the Rue de la Cannebière. Heigho! for France.

Night enveloped the city when Tod went with him down the gangway to the quay. The stones sang with their eager steps. Gas lamps burned along the water front; above shone the deep blue of the southern sky.

"By golly, isn't the air wonderful?" Tod exclaimed. "It's land air!"

Jarvis threw back his head and laughed. "Joe Macaroni, you talk just the same as when you came aboard at Frisco. 'Isn't the sea wonderful, Mr. Jarvis?' Sufferin' sea gulls! You smell the water-front alley."

"You mean they're dirty?"

"I do."

"Oh, well, it's land air, anyway—and everything seems different. Even you, Tom."

"Me?"

"Yes; officer's blue serge makes you look nifty—like a captain, for sure. Where do we go?"

"Everywhere. To the theatre, to the opera, to the movies. We're going to saturate ourselves with song and dance. Ah, here's the old can o' beer."

He spoke with a delighted catch of his breath as they turned from the Quai du Port into Marseilles' greatest thoroughfare. "It's French from now on, *mon ami*. Can you parley?"

Tod sighed. "A little. I wish I'd studied more at school. A restaurant menu is about my limit. What theatre, do you think——"

He paused; his hand went out to clutch Jarvis's arm. "Look! There's the Skipper and Hawkes ahead of us!"

Tom Jarvis came to a sudden stop. He pulled Tod away from a gleaming street lamp into the shadow of a doorway. At this point the Rue Cannebière was thronged with promenaders. Café doors blazed with light; merry chatter struck Tod's ears in a tongue strange yet pleasing.

Silently they waited with eyes fastened upon the movements of the two familiar figures a few yards ahead. Arm in arm, the commander of the *Araby* and his mate were swinging up the pavement. Before a brilliantly illumined entrance, flanked by two small trees in tubs, they paused while a group of people came out. Then they lurched within.

"Yeh, I thought so." Jarvis nodded slowly. "Hawkes is gettin' the cap'n liquored up, as usual. I wonder why?"

"You mean there might be a reason?" Tod queried, looking up at him.

"With Hawkes there is always a reason—and one of the worst, generally. If he is trying to get rid of the Old Man, he'll bear watching."

Tod followed his companion's glance across the street where a café displayed its tables on the pavement. "The very place," Jarvis went on. "We can watch from there without Hawkes ever being the wiser."

A moment later found the two Americans seated at a small round table before the Café du Soleil where a potted palm half hid them from passers-by. Here, beneath the awning, Tod sipped his grenadine and surveyed with mounting interest the life of this strange seaport. There was a gay, carefree atmosphere about the place that made one think of carnival time. Figures brushed slowly past by ones and twos, laughing, throwing nimble jests in foreign tongues: soldiers clad in sky-blue with women on their arms, sailors from an English man-of-war in the harbour, dark-skinned Moors from Algeria, shifty-eyed Levantines, Italian merchants with flashing glances. He seemed to be sitting by the wayside, watching the world go by.

So immersed in the scene was he that Jarvis's voice, abrupt, incisive, broke in like a thunderclap. "Hawkes! And alone!"

Tod's glance flashed through the fronds of the palm to the café opposite. The first mate stood in the doorway, looking up and down the pavement. At length he advanced to the curb and hailed a waiting taxi.

"Quick," cried Jarvis as he rose and flung a ten-franc note on their little pile of saucers; "we must keep him in view."

"Can we follow him?"

"We must. He may have an appointment somewhere. It's about the *Araby*, I know. I'm certain they never mean her to reach San Francisco again. But what do they intend? . . . Our ship!"

Already Mr. Hawkes was entering his cab. Jarvis pushed his great bulk through the throng to the curb. "Here's a taxi."

Tod brushed past two Zouaves in red and blue, and followed him to the edge of the pavement where, behind the taxicab, they were securely hidden from any one opposite. Jarvis spoke to the driver, who sorrowfully shook his head.

"No, no, monsieur," answered the man. "Did I not just tell an Englishman that I have a fare inside the café? *Pas possible,* monsieur."

Jarvis smiled, put his hand into his pocket, and unrolled several French notes. "Now, monsieur taxi driver," he said, "we want your car bad—right now, *pronto, vite! C'est compris?*"

The driver's small black eyes glowed; his teeth flashed white in a grin of understanding. He was down on the pavement in a second; the door swung open. "Jump in, messieurs! *Merci bien.* In Marseilles, nothing is impossible."

Tod jumped in. Jarvis hesitated. "See that blue taxi just starting across the street? Follow it, driver. Keep it in sight and there's a fifty-franc note extra for you."

The taxi throbbed. They were off. Tod, from his deep seat in the cab, kept his eyes on the blue car ahead. Jarvis leaned forward in anxiety. The driver was manifestly one who knew this business well; he threaded his way through the traffic with a practised hand. The other car turned into a side street to the left. Their car gave chase.

"Not too fast, driver," warned Jarvis. "Don't let them suspect we're after them."

The blue taxi now speeded up; apparently Mr. Hawkes was in urgent haste.

"Where are we?" Tod asked in a low tone.

"I think this is the Avenue de la République. Hawkes seems to be shaping a course for the docks."

As they followed at a safe distance Tod perceived that they were once more in the mean gloomy streets near the harbour. The dark stone houses seemed to press together above them, to blot out sky and air. Noisome odours struck his nostrils. Occasional sailors passed on the narrow sidewalks where gas lamps gleamed dully in the night.

With a soft grinding of brakes, their taxi pulled up sharply. "They've stopped, monsieur," called the driver in a hushed voice.

"Wait," Jarvis cautioned.

The man descended and, opening the long hood of the car, pretended to tinker with the engine. Secure in the darkness of the interior, Tod and his companion watched Mr. Hawkes step from his cab, pay his driver, and with a quick glance to left and right, enter a dimly lighted doorway.

"Some little wine shop," Jarvis affirmed. "Who can he be meeting there!"

A moment later the blue taxi disappeared round a corner; the dark street was empty. Only a few wanderers strolled up from the quays toward the Rue Cannebière. Jarvis and Tod descended, dismissed the cab, and quietly crossed to the other side of the street. Here the shadows protected them from any prying eyes which might peer from the wine shop. Opposite the doorway through which they had observed the mate vanish, they slipped into the darkened recess of a grimy entrance.

"He's talkin' to someone in there," Jarvis ventured.

Tod saw that the wine shop opposite was a poor little

place, probably frequented by the riff-raff from ships in port. It was a silent place, too, this April night. Within, a gas light burned dimly; behind a high counter, a large fat woman poured out drinks undoubtedly for the two men who were vaguely visible through the dirty casement windows.

"Listen, Joe Macaroni," Jarvis whispered. "I'm going closer. You stay here and watch. I've got to see who that other fellow is."

Tod waited in the darkness of the doorway, while Jarvis noiselessly crossed to the edge of the café window where he might glimpse the interior. Two seamen went by, singing. A late produce wagon passed noisily on the cobbled way. With shortened breath, Tod saw that his friend was slowly edging toward the dark, cobwebby windows. At the same moment, a lounger rose from a hidden table near the counter. His figure was instantly outlined in the doorway.

Tod's heart leaped, seemed to drop. It was Red Mitchell.

Too late Jarvis observed him. He began to move

swiftly away, but the little coal-passer was already on the pavement, grasping his arm.

Tod heard a rasping voice cut the stillness of the air. "Whatcher doin' here, cooky?"

At the sound of the shrill voice, Hawkes left his companion at the table and came up quickly to the doorway. "What the devil's the matter, Mitch?"

"Here's the big cook sneaking round. Is that right, now?"

In a flash of despair Tod realized that the game was up. Fools! Why hadn't they known that the wily first mate would have one of his henchmen on guard! He pressed his slim body back into the kindly darkness.

"The tattooed cook!" Mr. Hawkes swore volubly. "What in thunder are ye followin' me for, Jarvis?"

Amazement overwhelmed Tod as he saw the huge form of his friend lurch toward the curb. Then a drunken voice spoke in deep, raucous tones. "Me? I'm just goin' back t' the blasted ship. I'm broke already, Mr. Hawkes. Say, now—can't yer let me have a little on the side?"

"Oh, he's drunk, is he?" The mate stepped forward. "Yeh, the whole blamed crew'll be drunker'n a bell buoy by mornin'. Sure I can let yer have a little." Tod thought he detected relief in the tone. "But I wants' yer on board to-morrer mornin', see? You go with him, Mitch. See that he gets back O.K."

"All right; but the blasted savage ain't the kind of company I'd choose, Mr. Hawkes. Is yuh through with me to-night?"

The mate's glance swept up and down the cobbled way. "Yes—keep yer eyes on the cook. Here, take this."

"Aye, that's a good feller," said Jarvis with an assumed swagger. "We'll git aboard some time, won't we, Mitch?"

Red Mitchell put his arm through the Tattooed Man's, and the two figures, one towering above the other, went swaying down the pavement. Mr. Hawkes stood in the doorway, watching. A moment later, he turned back to the table where his unknown companion waited.

Tod clung to the darkness of the recess. What should he do? Yes, he must follow Mr. Hawkes.

The street became quiet again. A chill wind began to blow up a cobbled alley from the sea. The gas lamps flared. Once, far down the street, he glimpsed a *gendarme* making his nightly rounds; and soon after a blurred figure went by on the opposite pavement singing *"Toute la longe de la Tamise"* in the bawdy voice of a cuirassier. In the wine shop Tod saw the massive *patronne* counting her money, preparing to close for the night. Presently, the two belated customers rose; their figures showed mistily through the windows. He heard their murmuring voices as they paid and crossed to the door. Beneath the lamp, they paused to survey the deserted street.

Tod felt his heart suddenly jump. His mind flashed back to a fog-enveloped wharf office in San Francisco, to a sardonic face with sleek dark hair over eyes narrow and crafty. His throat tightened; his hands clenched. Mr. Hawkes's companion stood revealed.

It was the manager of the European-Pacific Steamship Company—Jasper Swickard.

THE THIRD-CLASS COMPARTMENT

THE instant realization that all of Jarvis's surmises had been correct, that the mate was in league with the manager of the European-Pacific Steamship Company, sent Tod's thoughts whirling. He was on the right trail, then. Could he find the secret? Could he get news of Neil? Tod's hands itched at his sides. By golly, he'd show them! These two men had swept Jarvis from their path to-night mainly because his great height and bulk could be seen; but a youth of seventeen, slim and quick, could more easily follow, unsuspected.

He waited in his secure retreat until the Americans were half a block ahead; then, from his own side of the street, he started in pursuit. Evidently they were no longer in fear of detection. They were in earnest conversation; not once did they glance round. At a lighted corner, they stopped, and Tod perceived that they were waiting for an electric tramcar, looking toward the harbour.

They were going east then, toward the other side of the city. He must get on that trolley too. In the shadow of a doorway he halted. Presently a tram came thumping along the Boulevard des Dames; it paused and he saw Mr. Hawkes and Swickard take a seat on the front platform and face the other way. On the side he saw the sign: Gare St. Charles. The station! Were they leaving town, going to Paris, perhaps?

He darted forward and, as the car started, slipped aboard the rear platform.

"Where to, monsieur?"

"The station."

"Four sous."

Tod pulled his cap low over his eyes, turned his coat collar up, and slouched into a seat as though he were cold. For the present at least he was safe.

As the little street car passed the Arc de Triomphe and turned into the Boulevard de la Paix, he was arguing to himself. What should he do? Suppose Mr. Swickard and Hawkes were going north to Paris. Should he follow? He had a handful of francs in his pocket, but that would not take him far. If he could only get hold of Jarvis, talk to him. But that was an impossibility; he must decide for himself. He must watch his step, too. While Mr. Swickard probably would not recognize him, Hawkes most certainly would.

Abruptly the tram swung round a corner and the conductor shouted: "*La gare!*" Tod waited. Would the two men descend? He peered through the glass toward the front.

Jasper Swickard and the mate stepped to the ground. They paused for a second, talking, then Hawkes shook hands and swung himself aboard another tramcar going back toward the city. Mr. Swickard went swiftly forward to the large station which blazed with light.

Tod's fingers curled inside his pockets. Should he follow Hawkes? No; Swickard was bigger game. Realizing that he was now safe from detection, he jumped to the ground and hurried after the manager. Through the bustling throng at the great entrance they went. Jasper

Swickard stopped at a window, passed a handbag to a porter, and went to the right toward the gate of the departure platform.

With eager eyes Tod looked through the iron grilling. Where was the man going? If he had stopped at the ticket window, the name of his station might easily have been overheard; but there he was with the porter leading him to a long train standing waiting, its engine ready for its journey. Despair clutched his heart. Must he stand there and watch the man vanish to the north in the night? Perhaps he knew where Neil was; perhaps he was even going there. Neil might easily be a prisoner in some remote hamlet in the mountains. Jasper Swickard must be followed—he must!

Already the porter was returning through the gate. Tod stopped him. "Oh, monsieur," he asked in bad French, "where is that train going?"

"You are English?" smiled the porter. "That is the express, bound for the Riviera and Italy."

Italy! Of course. To Genoa, where the *Araby* was bound.

"And the American?" Tod hurried on. "Does he go on to Genoa?"

"Name of a name of a name! Am I to keep track of every traveller in the station? That man? Bah, he gives no gratuity like other Americans! His ticket says Cannes."

"Cannes. Where is that?"

Mon Dieu! Do you not know the great winter resort on the coast? It is halfway to the border—three hours distance. The express leaves at once."

With a muttered word of thanks, Tod rushed back

to the ticket window. "One to Cannes," he gasped.

"Second class, monsieur?" asked the man in excellent English.

"Is there a third?"

"Yes, monsieur."

A moment later Tod was darting through the iron gate to the departure platform. He heard the guard slamming the compartment doors. The rear cars were marked third class, and to these the boy ran.

"Vite! Vite!" the guard motioned him in.

He dropped on to a wooden seat. The slamming of doors went down the line of coaches. A trumpet shrilled. The train started.

Wild-eyed, Tod watched from the narrow window as the express swung round the lights of the city and headed down the Mediterranean shore for Italy. What lay ahead of him? Was he a fool to be leaving on this wild-goose chase? What did he know of France? Very little indeed. But for Neil, for Jarvis, he must go on. In Mr. Swickard, he divined, lay the key to the enigma.

He settled himself in the seat, surveying for the first time his strange surroundings. He was in an oblong compartment running across the train, a meagre box with two wooden benches facing each other. Although there were seats for eight, only three other people occupied the compartment. One was a petty naval officer who, he soon learned, was returning to his ship at Toulon; the other two were an old peasant couple bound home to Ville-franche. Tod, striking up a conversation with the sailor, could not repress a smile at the broken English the man spoke; then, as it occurred to him that the French which he himself spoke was little better, he sobered. From this curious conversation he soon learned much about the district that runs along the matchless shore of the Mediterranean from Marseilles to Genoa, the French Côte d'Azur and the Italian Riviera. It was the playground of the world, the home of retired princes and money kings, a leisured class that spent much of its time in the gambling halls of Monte Carlo.

At Toulon the sailor left. As the express once more swung along into the open country, Tod could see the lights of his ship winking in the harbour. The old couple opposite now brought forth diminutive pillows from their bag and, turning down the electric bulb until it was a sombre glow, proceeded to go comfortably to sleep. Tod nodded also.

He awoke with a start to find the train drawing into the bright light of a large station. He put his head out the window and read the name—Cannes. Seizing his cap, he opened the door and stepped to the platform. Slowly he strolled forward, his eyes upon the first-class coaches. In vain he waited for the familiar figure of Jasper Swickard to descend. As the moments passed, as the new travellers took their places and still no American did he see, his fears began to mount. Had he allowed his quarry to escape while he slept?

If he could only get inside a first-class coach! Unlike the cheaper coaches, however, only one door was visible at each end, and these were guarded by men in uniform. Tod, feeling that, at least, he had little to lose, approached the conductor nearest him.

"Monsieur," he said, "I thought I saw a friend of mine buy a ticket in Marseilles for Cannes. He is an American, smooth-shaven, dark, in your coach."

"Oh, that American. No; he is within. He decided to go on to Monte Carlo. He likes a game, he says, now and then." The man smiled.

With relief, Tod turned away. The game that Jasper Swickard was playing was a bigger game than any played at Monte Carlo that night. He hurried back to the rear of the train and regained his seat in the third-class compartment.

Once more the express sped on through the night. This time, however, there was one person who did not nod in his seat; this time, Tod told himself, he would be ready. Mr. Swickard's change of plan might signify that he would again alter his course.

Half an hour later, the train slowed down as it approached what in the darkness appeared an unimportant fishing village along the shore. A small wayside station, open to the night, stood by the tracks. Across a clump of roofs Tod saw dim moonlight playing on the sea. Unexpectedly, he started. A lone figure with a black bag had descended from the first-class coaches and was walking quickly toward the station.

As the train began to move, the boy jumped for the other side of the compartment. Stumbling over the outstretched feet of the peasants, he threw open the door and flung himself into the darkness. Headlong, he plunged down into soft earth. He picked himself up and watched the lights of the express disappear in the night toward the Italian border. Somewhere in the village a clock struck one.

Across the tracks Mr. Swickard was entering the station. Tod waited until he had passed beyond, then cautiously followed in the moonlit gloom. A single electric globe above the little entrance illumined a sign which read: Antibes. A strange village. A strange country. A wave of intense loneliness swept over him. He was far from friends and home, in a lonely hamlet of which he had never heard, and following his enemy. Yes; Jasper Swickard would bear watching. A ticket for Cannes, then another for Monte Carlo, only to descend at this deserted spot where doubtless only fishermen dwelt!

Of a sudden, he heard the wheels of a carriage grate on the gravel beyond the station. Step by step, he went quietly forward till he stood within the shadow of the little building. There, at a corner, he pressed his slim straight body against the wall, listening.

"You are here, Jules?" It was Mr. Swickard speaking in French.

"Yes, Monsieur Leighton."

"Is everything quiet at the Villa Paradis?"

"Quiet, yes—but I do not think he is so well."

Tod heard the manager climb into the carriage. The driver whipped up his horse as they clattered off noisily down a dark road to the left. Tod stumbled on after them in the shadow of the trees. Mr. Leighton! So the manager of the steamship company had assumed another name while in Antibes. And the man at the Villa Paradis? Who was he? Could it be Neil—Neil, a prisoner?

He increased his pace. Ahead, the carriage turned east along a white sea road that seemed to run straight along the coast to Italy. Jules was probably urging his horse faster; steadily the carriage gained upon the boy. His run became uneven. By golly, in a moment he'd get his second wind! Life on shipboard, however, had not prepared him for this form of marathon. The carriage became a dark blur on the road; the patter of hoofs grew fainter.

He must have run nearly a mile when he slowed down to a walk. His breath came in gasps; his knees trembled. He lurched to the roadside where he dropped exhausted to the ground. Far ahead came the distant sound of hoof-beats; then that was lost in the night and he was alone. He gazed around, strangely incurious. To his right gleamed the rippling surface of the Mediterranean; to his left rose hills covered with orchards. Above, the sky was a luminous blue with a full moon riding low in the heavens; toward the north and east loomed snow-covered peaks from which a sharp wind blew.

His overheated body felt suddenly chill. He rose and, crossing the road, discerned the tracks of a trolley run-ning parallel with the highway. Slowly he advanced, his breath coming steadier every moment. Once the lights of a motor flashed down the road and whizzed by with a quiet, purring sound. Then silence again enveloped him.

At length he plodded into the shadow of a small tramway shelter. His hands touched a cold wooden bench, protected somewhat from the wind; and here he crouched, chilled and depressed, his arms about his knees. Silently gazing at the unbroken line of sea, he understood how it felt to be alone and friendless in a foreign country. Between him and his home, a sea and a continent encircled half the globe. There were even a hundred miles of coast line between him and that bit of American soil he had trod in the shape of the hard-wood decks of the *Araby*.

The *Araby*. . . . He remembered, with a little catch

in his throat, how snug his quarters appeared in the forecastle. He could see the men lurching down the three steps to their bunks from their first night ashore. He could see the cozy cabin opposite the galley with the cook reading late into the night, and the cat scratching at the door for food. Was Jarvis on board now? Was he wondering what had become of him? Did he intuitively know that Tod Moran would go on and on, searching, searching? For him? Yes—and, although Jarvis didn't know it, for Neil too.

He shivered; but whether from sheer weariness of spirit or from the frosty air, he did not know. He couldn't sleep. Not here, anyway. He rose and struck off toward the east again, trudging slowly on through the moonlit night.

An hour before dawn a peasant in a creaking cart picked him up. Tod lounged gratefully against a sack of onions. The old man, bound for the municipality of Nice with vegetables, flicked the reins of his decrepit horse and chattered amiably in a patois that his passenger could just make out.

"You come from America? I have a cousin there—in Montreal. Perhaps you know him, *hein?* No? Well, I'd like to go there too; but it is across the water, is it not? God put me here on this bit of land, and here I shall remain. But what a wonderful people—you Americans! A nation of millionaires! Is it not true?"

He turned and surveyed the boy with a puzzled frown. The impression had no doubt entered his simple mind that his passenger was not in the least like an American millionaire. "How happens it, *mon enfant*," he added, "that you walk the coast this early morning?"

"My train was late," the boy carefully explained. "I missed the home of my friends."

"What! You have not slept this night? Ah, always have I said you were a strange people, you Americans."

"Do you know any hereabouts, monsieur? A Mr. Leighton?"

The old man shook his head. "There are many foreigners on the Riviera during the season. Do you know the name of his villa? All houses have names, you know."

Tod's sleep-burdened thoughts drifted back to the station at Antibes. "Yes—he told me. Villa Paradis."

"The Villa Paradis! *Certainement.* Many times have I left potatoes and artichokes there. Yes, I know Jules and Madame Thérèse." He laughed shrilly. "It is two kilometres ahead. Go to sleep, *mon petit ami.* I will let you know."

Dawn came. Light spread over the mountains; the wind whipped the surface of the sea into little whitecaps. Tod dozed, while the cart crept drowsily along the road. Gradually, the almost-forgotten odour of orange trees invaded his sleeping senses. Why, he was home—home! Neil was there, gaily coming up the path to the porch, his handsome face jubilant at his arrival. He waved; he shouted. Gay, careless Neil.

Tod stirred. Opening his eyes he saw that they were passing between long rows of villas set in the midst of parks and hedges. Before them crawled other wagons loaded with produce for Nice. The peasant, drawing up the weary sorrel, pointed to a lane on the right which wound away toward the sea.

"That, monsieur, leads to the Villa Paradis," he said.

III : AT THE VILLA PARADIS

TOD walked on, more asleep than awake. The villas ended, the road dwindled to a cart path, a farm was passed on his right hand, and then, before him, lay a rutted cart track leading across a small neck of lowland jutting out into the sea. At the far end, the leaden roof of a house was dimly visible, shrouded in the deep green of trees and garden.

"A lonely place, this Villa Paradis," he thought. As he went impetuously forward his feet sank into the soft warm earth. On each side, a salt marsh crept to the very edge of the roadway; sparse grass waved in tufts here and there; a noisome smell hovered above stagnant pools. Beyond this the ground rose slightly, and here he grew more cautious. Presently, he came to a high iron gate. It stood like a row of spears in his path, flanked by walls, old and gray, that led down to the water on each side. Cut off thus from the mainland by marsh and wall, the villa might have been an island set in the azure Bay of Nice.

With his face pressed furtively to the iron grilling of the gate, Tod saw that the house was almost hidden by tangled growths of trees and underbrush; evidently, the place had long before surrendered to the encroaching marsh. The sun had not yet tipped the mountains; the garden lay in shadow, wet with dripping dew. Two long rows of plane trees lined the grassy drive which curved to the rear; rose bushes grew rank in the garden; weeds lifted exultant heads above the flowers; birds fluttered in the thickets. Over all hung a silence profound and disturbing.

A fishing smack went by toward Italy, its lateen sail bellied in the breeze. Two men sat in the cockpit eating great hunks of bread. Tod promptly remembered that he was ravenously hungry—and sleepy too. His hand closed on the little roll of paper francs in his pocket. He didn't have much money. Before he spent any for breakfast he'd better get some sleep. It was early, surely not more than five-thirty; and in all probability no one would be stirring in the Villa Paradis for several hours yet.

He stepped to one side and dragged his tired legs through the long damp grass by the wall. At a point where the weeds grew thick, he pressed them down into the semblance of a nest and flung his weary body upon them full length. It was peaceful here; the only sound was a slight rustling in the grass as though snakes were gliding away in the shadows. Even that thought had no power to disturb him now; he went instantly to sleep.

The sound of approaching cart wheels wakened him. He sat up. The sun was already halfway to the zenith; it must be ten o'clock. He beheld a decrepit sorrel horse pulling a cart along the roadway, with a peasant in a smock slumbering on the seat. Realizing at once that here was his opportunity to get within the wall, he hurried to meet the old man.

His benefactor of the early morning gazed at him in astonishment. "What, *mon enfant!* You again!" he exclaimed. "Did you not rouse your friends in the villa?" His brows knitted in a frown as he pulled up his horse.

In a flash Tod determined to be frank. "Monsieur, let me ride into the grounds of the villa with you. I will pay you three francs, five francs. But not a word to them within. *Compris?*"

The peasant nodded sagely. "Well, I like not the Villa Paradis myself. What can one expect when the owner brings a dirty pair from Marseilles to care for the place! Look at it. In another year, the weeds will be growing from the chimney. Ah, those Marseillaises! Ugh! they are cutthroats." He drew his hand expressively across his throat.

Tod climbed over the large cumbrous wheel and crouched on some sacks behind the plank which, when the cart was empty, served as a seat. The sorrel gazed round curiously; then, with a look of dumb resignation, he began once more his even, funereal pace. At the villa gate, they stopped; the old man descended and jerked on a handle at one side. Immediately, the shrill jangle of a bell broke the morning stillness.

"That'll bring Jules," he said, nodding complacently as he climbed to his seat.

A man came hastening down the path from the villa. Tod watched him closely as he turned a huge key in the lock and swung back the gate. Jules was a small thickset man dressed in corduroy trousers and blue shirt; he had the grim countenance of one who is bred in dirty seaport alleys and has never looked upward at the sun. His glance swept them narrowly. Motioning them within, he flung out a greeting in a voice harsh and guttural. "And whom do you bring with you in the cart?" he added.

"Only a little friend from Cagnes," replied the old man as he picked up the reins. "He rides with me—now and then."

The cart creaked; they passed the gate and jolted up the sombre avenue toward the Villa Paradis. The plane trees sighed overhead; the weeds brushed the wheels; a rabbit bounded away into a thicket. A moment later, the house rose before them, a straight, high dwelling with dark windows which stared sightlessly out at the day.

They rounded a corner to a kitchen door, from which issued the rattle of dishes. A cry from the old peasant brought a woman to the doorway. She was tall and erect as a youth, though the hair that fell in wisps about her face was gray. On her upper lip a black moustache was visible. As she crossed to them, her eyes, black and beady, favoured Tod with a brief scrutiny. He was glad when the onions and lettuce drew her attention. Jules now joined his wife at the cart, and immediately they began haggling over prices.

Tod let his keen glance run over the square stone house, once a proud villa set in luxuriant grounds, now a mockery of its former self, in decay, in disfavour, rotting away beneath the onslaught of the damp seas about it. Was Jasper Swickard sleeping somewhere in those rooms above? And Neil—was he a prisoner beneath the eaves in the attic where the sun rarely penetrated? Tod shivered. The unkempt garden, the mildewed house, the ruffian and his evil-looking wife with their churlish voices, all made him abruptly sicken. He trembled at the thought of Neil confined in the darkness of such a lair.

"To-morrow, Madame Thérèse?" The old peasant was pocketing his money.

"No—Saturday, you fool!"

Jules, with a gruff laugh, put out his hand. "And the other—you have brought it?" he asked in a lowered tone. "Our English vagabond could not live without it."

The peasant smiled grimly. Reaching into a pocket beneath his smock, he brought forth a tiny package. Jules's large hand closed upon it.

"He is better, perhaps?" inquired the old man.

Jules gave Tod a quick glance. "Better? No—worse!" His mouth broke into a snarl as he glanced over his shoulder. "Here Moran is now—the worthless dog!"

Moran! In the stillness of the morning the word rang loud and clear. Tod heard his pulse beating in his ears. His fascinated gaze was directed upon the tall figure of a young man in soiled overalls who came round the house. In one hand he carried a rake, in the other a shovel. Neil! Neil! But as Tod stared, his heart sank.

Instead of the Neil of laughing mouth and glowing eyes, the Neil of gay gestures and engaging manners, this was a Neil who was a stranger to him. The handsome face was pallid and drawn, the mouth drooping, the eyes life-

less as burnt-out coals. He walked with slow leaden feet that might have echoed down the corridor of a tomb.

Madame Thérèse uttered an evil chuckle. "Do you think he improves, monsieur?"

At his brother's approach, Tod clung to the wooden sides of the cart; his knees of a sudden had turned to water.

"I'm going to clean up the grape arbour, Jules. Is that right?"

The voice was Neil's, but the accent another's. Tod had heard him speak French many times after his return from his passages to Europe; he had insisted that his younger brother learn it too; never, though, had the soft French words sounded so dulled, so remote from reality. Over the boy ran a terrified quiver of apprehension. Neil was seemingly not a prisoner; rather did he have the appearance of a person in hiding. What did it signify? . . . Bit by bit, there crept back into his mind all those accusations that had been like sword thrusts to him—the words of Jasper Swickard in the wharf office in San Francisco, the deprecating tone of Hawkes when he told of Neil's disappearance, the thrusting keenness of Red Mitchell's attack in the forecastle, the bitter accusation of Tom Jarvis in his cabin. Was Neil immersed in the schemes of the European-Pacific Company, regretting his part perhaps too late, half-heartedly hanging on to the shreds? . . . Why did he not look his way? Didn't he intend to recognize his brother?

"Vegetables, Madame Thérèse?" Neil murmured, with all the old ringing notes gone. He came close to the cart; his hand, white beneath the soil that clung to it, strayed along the wheel. Glancing forlornly upward he met the widened gaze of his brother.

Something deep within the boy stirred at sight of those upturned eyes, dulled yet tortured, beseeching. They pulled at his heart like the wistful eyes of a caged beastie of the woods. It came over Tod that there were bars more subtle and strong than any forged by the hand of man, that there were darker chambers in a tortured mind than any prison cell. And Neil—Neil was in such a room now, with the darkness about him, peering out between bars in helpless misery.

The old peasant took up the reins. "*Bonjour*, Madame Thérèse. *Bonjour*, monsieur." The cart swung round and started down the grassy drive.

Tod still clung to the side of the cart. All the flood of words that surged within him refused to rise through his tightened throat. He wanted to shout, to cry out: "Neil, I'm here! Here to help. I don't understand—but you're caught as Tom Jarvis was caught. Wait—I'll get you out! . . . Some way——"

Out of the flood, however, no tide arose. He heard the

slam of the great iron gate, the turn of the key in the rusty lock. The Villa Paradis lay behind them.

"Well, *mon petit ami*," said the peasant softly. "You saw them, *hein?*"

Tod did not answer. His head had dropped on his motionless hands.

The cart jerked and tossed in the ruts; the driver grumbled to himself as he urged his horse forward. "Ah, those Marseillaises! I like them not. And that man. English? Bah, he is American. Can I not tell from his talk? But he is ill—very ill. May *le bon Dieu* help him in such hands!"

Tod looked up. "What's wrong with him? You know?"

"*Mon enfant*, there you see a man who has dulled his brain with beguiling drugs. He is not long for this earth of ours. Jules says he will not live through the summer."

A stab—a wrench! Not live through the summer!

"What! *Mon Dieu*, where are you going?"

Tod was already clambering over the wheel to the ground.

IV : THE PRISONER

SUMMER—summer! The word was singing through the air. Summer! . . . Even now it was stealing up from the South, up from African deserts and across the sea to this dreaming shore. It was about him too—in the soft warm caress of the sunlight, in the pigeons wheeling against the sky, in the lateen sails like blots of red and brown on the deep blue of the water. And Neil would not live through the summer.

As he raced toward the Villa, his thoughts reverted to the events of the last few weeks. Yes, Neil and Tom Jarvis had been caught and wounded in the machinations of the European-Pacific Company; they had both been cast adrift as worthless; but while Jarvis was doggedly fighting his way to safety, Neil had given up and was going under. Was it already too late to help him? It couldn't be—not yet.

Once more at the wrought-iron gate Tod peered into the deep shade of the garden. He could see no one. Neil must be working in the grape arbour. Where was it? His gaze swept across the weeds and flowers. There it rose, a long dark tunnel of green, to the right near a little cliff where the wall ended. He left the gate and with quickened step went along the wall for a hundred yards. He must be almost opposite that wild growth of covered arbour. He listened. In his ears sounded the dull thud of an ax on wood, followed by the prolonged rustle of severed vines.

"Neil," he whispered. "Neil!"

No answer came. The sharp rending of vines continued. There were no voices—surely Jules was not at work also.

He called louder this time. "Neil! Neil!"

The noise ceased. The clear notes of a bird came to him, then the murmur of wind in the olive trees which topped the wall.

Tod put his hands to his mouth. "Neil, say something. It's Tod—Tod!"

Silence. He leaned against the wall, his eyes strained upward. If he could only get to the top and look over. He glanced about him. Near by, in the grass, were stray bits of driftwood. Not big enough. He searched down toward the swamp ground until he found a timber four feet long; this he carried, water-soaked and heavy, back to the wall. Planting it against the stones, he scrambled up, his hands pressed into the damp niches where moss grew. He stood up, balancing himself, and found that his fingers curved over the top of the stones.

A sharp pain in one hand informed him that glass lay there, broken in small pieces and strewn along the flat surface to keep invaders out. He scraped it carefully away. With a little leap, he dragged himself up until one knee was atop; his hands touched the other side, a foot across. Flat on his belly, he looked down through the gray olive branches into the garden.

Standing there watching him was Neil. His pallid countenance was suffused with a look of expectant hope; his fingers moved nervously on the ax he carried. For a moment, they stared at each other.

Neil broke the silence. "Is it really you, Tod?"

"Of course it is." Tod's voice was slightly angry. "What's got into you, anyway? Can't you talk?"

Neil came closer; a trembling hand touched the wall. "I don't know. . . . Everything is like a dream. I thought you were only—another vision." His vague glance drifted across the garden. "I haven't spoken English for months —years, it seems. And now to see you——" He dropped the ax and leaned against the stones. "For God's sake, Tod, get me out of here. They're killing me." The last words rose to a hysterical note. "They're killing me, I tell you!"

Tod surveyed him steadily. "Aw, cut it out. Why don't you climb over the wall and get away?"

"Away? Where to?" He paused and raised a pair of gray, listless eyes. "I haven't got the strength yet," he sighed. "They dope me, I think. Every night I sleep as if they'd drugged the food—or the wine. And last night —Swickard arrived."

"Yes?" Tod said. "And then?"

"I saw him this morning. He says that I'd better stay here, that he's keeping me out of prison. It's a lie, Tod. I didn't take any of their money. Someone else messed up the books, and it looked bad for me—that's all. He didn't give me a chance to straighten things out. Oh, I know why he keeps me locked up here. I know too much! Too much about the doings of the European-Pacific Steamship Company."

"Well, get a ladder and climb up here." Tod's tone was full of easy assurance. "We'll beat it. Now!"

Neil smiled wanly. "Do you think it's that easy to get out of this hole? I haven't the strength. They'd have us, anyway, before we got halfway down the road. Oh, I've tried! He nearly killed me the last time—Jules, the blackguard!"

"Then when it's dark. Tonight."

"There's only one way. I've thought it out. A boat."

"A boat?"

"Yes—there's a little beach behind the house. If you could land there—— Hush! Listen."

A voice, deep and strident, was calling across the garden.

"That's Jules!" Neil's face was suddenly distraught with terror. He stooped with surprising quickness and picked up the ax.

Tod contemplated him in amazement. It soon turned

to pity, however, as he surmised the life that Neil must have led under the vigilant eyes of Jules and Madame Thérèse.

"Wait—wait!" Tod's voice was low and eager. "I'll get a boat, Neil. Tonight—at nine. Can you get to the beach?"

"They lock me in," he whispered dully.

"Where's your room? Can't you climb out?"

"It's the window above the kitchen. I'd never make it without a ladder."

"I'll get one, then."

Neil flung him a look of gratitude. "Nine is too early. Swickard's here, and they'll be up. Later."

"At midnight, then. Hush."

Neil was gone through the weeds and rose bushes. His voice drifted back from the grape arbour. Jules evidently was near.

Tod dropped quietly to the timber and jumped to the ground. At midnight! Good heavens, what a changed Neil! How dull his eyes were; how childlike he seemed. At times, he had always been somewhat of a fool, Tod told himself. Leave it to a brother to know the crazy things a fellow did. It was only when Neil was viewed across a sea, wrapped in the glamour of a ship, that he attained heroic proportions.

Tod trudged wearily toward the roadway. Neil wasn't more of a fool than he himself was. Why did he always envision marvellous heroes who never breathed outside the pages of a story book! Why did he always dream of things, not as they were, but as he would like them to be! Gentlemen adventurers never at a loss for high-flown words and deeds. Ships that sailed into the sunset. They

were all right till you touched them—then they vanished.
And yet . . . There was left—just Neil.

Was he himself made of the same stuff? Would Tod
Moran fail at the crisis, when the supreme moment came?
Would he dissolve like a mist, too? Well, he didn't know.
He'd be prepared, at least; with him there would be no
wavering doubt.

He sighed as he turned into the road and faced the
hills far ahead. Over the pools of the marsh, the air quivered with insects. The mosquitoes would be out in swarms
that night. Well, let them bite. He and Neil would soon
be off for Marseilles. Yes, he'd get Neil out, even though
Swickard was there, and Jules, and that vixen Thérèse.
They were doping his brother, doping him as he had
heard the boarding-house masters did when they started
a man on the shanghai passage. Let them watch out! Tod
Moran was on to their tricks. He'd show them. That very
night. . . . At midnight!

V : ESCAPE

ADRIFT off a strange coast in a rented skiff, Tod shipped
his oars and let his gaze run over the water to the
illumined windows of the Villa Paradis. It was after
eleven. He hoped he and Neil would be out of the grounds
before the moon rose; for even now it was not too dark.
Stars danced on the surface of the sea, and when he
jabbed them with his hand they rippled away in fragments. The great lighthouse on the Cap d'Antibes shim-

mered faintly on the water. On the other oar, the myriad
lights of Nice curved round the shore against the deep
gloom of the Maritime Alps.

Presently, one by one the lamps in the lower floor of
the villa were extinguished; a moment later two appeared
on the second floor. These soon went out, and the house
was wrapped in profound darkness. Still he waited; he
wanted to be certain that Swickard and the caretakers
were sound asleep. A moist coolness touched his neck,
and looking round, he saw that a long low sheet of fog
was creeping in from sea. It would soon be about him,
blotting out all sense of direction. As in haste he put the
oars into the rowlocks, determining to land at the slip of
beach and wait there, he beheld a lamp shine suddenly
from a window facing him. He gave a little start. It was
the window above the kitchen door. Neil was ready then,
waiting. Tonight, Tod told himself, his brother had no
doubt refused the food. He turned the boat and saw over
his shoulder that the house was again in darkness. At the
same moment, there reached his ears, clear yet distant,
the sound of a clock striking the hours. He counted the
strokes. Midnight.

The fog began to close about him as the stem of the
skiff whispered on the sand. He beached the boat and
reached for the ladder which lay lengthwise in it. He had
rented them both at a fishing village two miles down the
shore. It had taken all his francs, for the shrewd fisherman had insisted upon security until the boat was returned. He'd have to return both safely or he and Neil
would never reach Marseilles.

He lifted the ladder and carried it to the cliff which
soared upward to the grounds of the villa. A narrow path

could be distinguished up the side, and with the ladder dragging on one end, he slowly ascended. At the top he hesitated. Already the mist had obscured the house.

Determined to reconnoiter before he brought the ladder to the kitchen door, he went forward step by step. The smell of damp earth filled his nostrils. The weeds, heavy with moisture, brushed his legs. He felt the dampness through his thin shoes. Olive trees hung down above him; branches scraped his face. He brushed them aside and finally came to a clearing between a latticed summer-house and the villa. He listened intently. Over the grounds brooded the profound silence of sleeping things. A dripping from the trees told him that the mist was thickening.

He suddenly remembered stories of men who had been shot as they climbed into houses at night. He remembered a case of a man sentenced to years in prison though he had only been in search of food. It was funny how you thought of these things just at the time you shouldn't! Strange, too, how your courage vanished with the sun. With his heartbeats loud in his ears, he gazed up at the dim outline of the dwelling. After midnight. Surely the inmates were lost in their first sound slumber.

He spun about and returned with the ladder. With infinite caution he carried it, heavy and awkward, toward the rear of the house. A little esplanade was passed at one side; then the kitchen door detached itself from the gloom. To get the ladder up to the stones of the window ledge without any noise—that was his problem. He rested the ladder on the step, wiped his sleeve across his brow, and pushed back his cap. He lifted the ladder carefully and walked his hands down the rungs. The end swayed precariously in the air.

With his arms outstretched, he stepped backward. He stumbled. In a terrified instant he knew that he had lost his hold.

The ladder crashed down the uneven stones, thudded to the ground. The stillness was shattered by the noise.

Had Jules heard? Or Mr. Swickard—or Madame Thérèse? He mustn't let himself get nervous. It hadn't been such a loud sound. He'd better be quick, though. He lifted the ladder again. This time it grated softly on the window ledge directly over the door. He looked up. Neil should be ready now. Why didn't he come down?

No movement from above, however. What was the matter with Neil? He surely must be waiting at the window. He ought to be left behind; it would serve him right. Tod started up the rungs.

Near the top he paused. His head was almost even with the sill. The window was closed. He tapped softly on the pane. With his heart jumping he saw the sash slowly rise.

Neil leaned out. "Careful," he warned in a whisper. "Someone just went past my door—and down the stairs." His hand moved convulsively on the sill. "You made an awful noise. I think Jules heard. He sleeps next door. One second!"

Tod muttered to himself. Leave it to Neil to make a fuss. Just like him. He was frightened, that was the reason. The place had got on his nerves. Thank heavens, he himself hadn't——

An abrupt click from below sent him flat against the rungs. He stared downward. With panic-stricken eyes he discerned the screen door opening inch by inch. He felt himself go pale. The sweat started out on the palms of his hands. Jules!

At the same instant a window to his left slid noisily up. A head emerged. A woman's voice let loose a stream of invective into the night.

"Thérèse!" Neil was at the window again.

"Quick!" cried Tod. "Come out."

He was already sliding down the ladder. A low laugh of satisfaction brought him to a halt. The figure of Jules stood waiting below. Tod saw a knife glistening in his hand. Without thinking, he ran up the rungs once more. Even as Neil grasped his arms, Jules had kicked the ladder from under him. He struggled over the sill. He was in Neil's room, locked in, and below, Jules, no doubt, was snarling gleefully in approval.

"The door!" his brother whispered. "The lock isn't strong."

As Tod rose, he heard Neil drive a chair against the knob. Once—twice—the blows echoed through the house. The knob rattled to the floor. The door stuck. Neil beat on it madly, kicked it with his foot. The lock gave way. The door swung back and the hall lay dark before them.

"This way." Neil tossed the words over his shoulder. Grasping Tod's hands he started through the encompassing blackness. A door to one side opened and a lamp gleamed in the hand of Madame Thérèse. Tod glimpsed her angry lips shadowed with their line of moustache. He heard her cry out. As she raised a hand, a revolver flashed.

Neil, swooping, flung her arm upward. A shot cracked out, detonated through the hallway. The woman pitched backward; she screamed. The pistol rattled to the floor, and the light flashed out.

Tod darted after his brother. He heard another door

open and Jasper Swickard's voice calling: "Jules—Jules!"

"The stairs," Neil blurted over his shoulder.

Tod plunged downward, his hand sliding on the banisters. "Which way?" he gasped as he touched the newel post.

"Here." Neil's hand guided him through a door to a room where low French windows were visible. Tod heard a handle turned deftly. The windows swung open. They were outside now on the esplanade.

"This way," Neil whispered. "They'll think we're running for the gate."

He plunged ahead into the dripping darkness with Tod at his heels. It came over the boy in a flash that he was glad to let Neil take the lead. This was worse than he had expected. He had been a silly fool; he had thought it would be simply play. Instead, it was deadly earnest.

Behind them, shouts resounded from the house. Another voice took up the cry, this time in the garden to-

ward the front gate. Jules was hoping to head them off.
They raced through the shrubs and weeds, through their
clinging tendrils to the cliff's edge. Here they paused.

"The path!" Tod gulped. "Sufferin' sea gulls!"

They had reached it now, were running, sliding, falling down the incline to the beach. Above them came the
cries of their pursuers. Their means of exit had been discovered.

A shot echoed in the night. It whizzed harmlessly overhead. Then they had come to the soft wet sand and were
searching for the skiff.

"Where is it?" Neil's voice was eager, ringing with
exultation.

"Here." Tod touched the stem.

"Get in," his brother commanded. "Take the oars. I'll
shove off."

Even as Tod took his seat on the thwart, the stern
swayed upward and water murmured round the sides.
Behind him Neil stumbled into a seat and reached for
the extra oars on the bottom. The boat turned. Breathlessly they pulled out toward the open sea.

Cries came from the gray line of beach. A shot hissed
by in the fog. The muffled sound of the oars no doubt was
plainly audible on the sand. An instant later, a second
shot snapped out. It thudded on the bottom.

"By golly, he's hit us," cried Tod.

The cries grew more distant. A light flashed up on the
beach and through the haze they saw Swickard holding
aloft a flaring torch.

"Stop rowing," ordered Neil. "If they can't hear us,
they won't know where we are."

Tod perceived that they were drifting toward the Cap

d'Antibes. The flare went out; the fog closed in. Vainly they tried to pierce that gray-black wall of gloom.

"Can we make the shore?" Tod whispered.

"Sure. I know the outline of the coast. This mist will help us hide. There isn't a boat at the villa. They can't follow." His voice was almost gay. The cowed, listless Neil had been left behind.

With firm yet quiet strokes they resumed their rowing. It was like trying to pierce a wall that moved with them. The mist beaded their brows and lashes with moisture; it coiled about their necks with caressing dampness. Tod on a sudden felt his feet cold as ice. He moved a foot. Water swished about it. He put down a hand.

"By golly, Neil, the boat's leaking."

"They all do," came the even reply. "It won't matter."

Tod rested on his oars. "Do you hear a gurgling sound? I think that last shot put a hole on the stern."

Neil swore softly. "I'll find it and stuff a handkerchief in it. Have you got one? I haven't."

He was down in the slushing bottom, feeling in the darkness of the sternsheets for the leak. "Keep rowing, Tod," he urged; "it's filling swiftly."

Tod knew by the drag on his oars that the skiff was beginning to wallow. The water crept over his ankles and rose higher about the calves of his legs.

"Quick. Here it is. Throw me your handkerchief.— That's the stuff."

Tod jerked his cap from his head and began to bail. The movement took him back to another night so like this, yet so different. There were no seamen to help him now, no commander in the stern to cheer them on. There were just Neil and himself.

"I'll row," his brother announced; "you keep on bailing out."

Cautiously they advanced. Tod lost all sense of direction. He was not gaining on the water, either; the boat was wallowing more heavily. Neil's breaths came in gasps as his shoulders strained to the oars.

"We've got to land, Tod," he said in a grim tone. "And we can't be very far from the villa. Have you any idea which way we're headed?"

"Not the slightest," Tod confessed.

Neil laughed shortly. "Neither have I. We're in a fix all right; but thank heavens, we're out of that hole."

Above the low bank of fog the moon must have risen, for a strange ghostly pallor hung over the sea. From the direction of the dim gray light, they judged the shore to be almost directly opposite. Turning the boat, Neil swung his oars furiously through the dragging water, and presently the stem touched sand.

"We must have hit the lowland, Tod. God knows how we'll ever make it across the marsh."

Tod sprang out. They pulled the boat as near to shore as possible. Walking to the left, they found their feet sinking into the ooze of the mud. To their right, a small beach circled back toward the Villa Paradis.

"Any way but that," Neil remonstrated. "We've got to cross the marsh."

"Can we do it?"

His brother considered a moment. "We might, but I doubt it."

"Can't we fix the boat?" Tod suggested.

They set about it at once. They dragged the boat up and tipped out the water. Tod searched for a stick that might be whittled down into the hole. A moment later, Neil raised a warning hand.

"Listen. Do you hear anything?"

Tod put his ear to the sand. "Someone's coming. From the Villa Paradis!"

"They've heard us land," Neil whispered.

"Can't we hide?"

They looked along the beach toward the sound of the approaching footfalls. A small ray of light was dimly visible.

"They've got an electric torch! Tod, what'll we do?"

"We'll hide in the marsh. Maybe they'll pass us."

Shouts sounded down the beach. The next moment the two fugitives had entered the marsh. The earth gave way beneath them, sucked at their shoes; the long grass sank into the mud with a gurgling whisper. Above them the pallor of the mist had lightened; the moon threatened to pierce that low blanket which hung over the bog. The rains of the last few months must have settled in the lowland in little pools; an odour of decaying vegetation drifted upward; it was corrupt with rotting things.

Neil stumbled once into a pool from which a swarm of insects rose. He threw himself violently backward. "Watch out, Tod," he whispered. "It's like quicksand. We'll wait here."

In breathless silence, they crouched on their haunches. Their burning gaze was fixed on that moving point of light which pierced the gloom. As the torch flashed on the stem of the skiff they saw two shadows gesticulate. A low murmur of voices came to them. The round gleam of light turned and flashed their way. Jules and Jasper Swickard were following their footsteps.

"Come," whispered Neil. "Follow me. It's the only way—now."

He rose stealthily. With a sucking sound, the marsh dragged at his heels. Tod rose to follow; and in that instant a pistol shot exploded like the crack of a whip. The bullet tore through the air above them with a hissing breath.

Neil broke into a run. Tod, following in his brother's footsteps, cast a terrified glance over his shoulder. Once more the mist had closed in; the flare of the torch had vanished.

"Not so fast," Tod whispered. "They can't see us now—and they don't seem to be following."

Neil slowed down, laughing shortly. "I guess they think—we'll never make it through this bog." He meditated a second, then looked about him. "But we can—we must."

Slowly, cautiously, they made their way forward. Tod wondered if they were going round in a circle. The bog seemed endless. The drone of mosquitoes sounded in their ears as the insects were stirred from their hiding places. Neil stopped. Ahead, a wide pool shone dimly. "We've got to go round," he said.

He turned and vanished suddenly into the gloom. Tod heard the moist crunch of his footfalls in the ooze. Starting to follow, he felt the ground tremble beneath him. The earth gave way; mud and slime bubbled up about his knees. It sucked at his legs, dragged him down. He flung himself backward, but his feet did not yield. He lost his balance and went headlong into the slime. The dark warm slush closed over his head. He came up gasping, his eyes blinded. The stench in his nostrils almost overpowered him. He seemed to have stumbled into the heart of corruption. He kicked and knew that he was swimming. Well, he'd make the other bank; it might be more solid there. He touched bottom. The mud rose about his ankles, lapped at his legs; long growing tendrils entwined themselves about his body, pulling him gently under. He kicked madly, threw himself at the earth. His hand touched coarse grass. He pulled, and it gave way. A mass of flying dirt filled his eyes. A thousand insects swarmed about his face, piercing his skin, droning like the faint hiss of escaping steam. The surface of the pool was alive with little scuttling spots. Bubbles, black and oily, floated up to the air.

"Neil!" he called. "Neil!"

The mist wavered about his head; it seemed to rise and let down the wan glow of the moon. In the light he saw small black heads with piercing eyes coming along the surface toward him. Water rats! Didn't they mean to wait even till he died before gnawing his bones? He splashed at them. They swung about and disappeared. He put out an arm to grasp the tussock near him, and instantly his hand was covered with a mass of stinging needles.

"Neil—Neil!"

A strange muffled sound to his right made him cast a quick look that way. He started. A few feet away a ghostly head was swaying in the water. It was so ghastly, so over-laden with slime, he thought at first that he had come upon the body of a dead man whom the swamp had buried weeks before and was now disgorging. Then a pale hand rose wraithlike out of the slime, and in a tortured instant he knew that it was his brother.

Tod beat his way toward him. His tightened throat refused to yield word or cry.

"I'm all right," Neil quavered, spitting the ooze from his mouth. "I heard you fall—started after you and tumbled in. God! I thought I was never coming up. Here—get hold of this log."

Tod put up his hand and grasped a branch. It came away in his grip with a mass of scurrying beetles. He dropped it and dug his fingers this time into the rotten pulp of the trunk.

"I think I can get out, Neil," he said hoarsely. "Give me a lift—then I'll pull you out."

Resting his knee on his brother's shoulder, he gripped the log and flung himself upward. A second later he was prone on the grass. He filled his lungs with air. It was fetid; but he was out—out. Insects buzzed around him. He reached down and grasped his brother's hand, pulled, dug his feet into the mud, threw himself backward.

Neil crawled to the bank like a Mesozoic creature out of the slime. It was almost solid here. Their feet sank a few inches into the mud; but they could see. They jumped from tussock to tussock, balancing themselves danger-ously near the pools. God! would they never get out of this quagmire? Jasper-Swickard, Madame Thérèse and Jules seemed infinitely easier to cope with than this corruption.

To Tod, hours elapsed before they came to solid ground and saw in the moonlight the line of the roadway before them. Peace hung over the bog; not a sound came to their ears. Who could surmise that so near lay a pitiless death waiting to entrap its unwary victims?

Tod drew his hand across his face and looked at Neil. Heavens, what a sight! He himself must be a mess too. His cap was gone; his clothes hung wet and cold on his body; his toes curled in the slush of his shoes. He breathed deeply; they were free—free. Yet no sense of victory, of elation, came over him; rather did he feel weary, forlorn, depressed.

"Tod, do you think—they'll follow us?" The tone was listless, dead.

Tod turned. Neil was shivering, his teeth chattered loudly in the silence.

"We'd better run," Tod advised. "Maybe we'll warm up."

They started in a slow, loping trot up the roadway. Neil hung back, and Tod let his own pace slacken. They passed a farm on their left; villas took form and lined the road.

Neil drew to a stop. "Tod, I'm all in," he murmured. "I can't go on."

It was the Neil of the Villa Paradis who spoke, the Neil whose body and brain had been beguiled by soothing drugs. Tod, putting his hand on the other's shoulder, felt the spasm of pain that shot through the tall form.

"Neil, you mean," he stammered, "that after all this

time you can't do without it? Perhaps—if we could get some——"

Neil jerked away. "No! . . . I'm through with it—through for good."

Tod saw him tremble, saw him drop to his knees and sway with his fingers writhing at his lips. "I won't—I won't!"

That aching need, his brother knew, was torturing him now; it was crushing him down again, striking him to the ground.

"He needs a bed," Tod thought, "and sleep. We're broke—dead broke. And Marseilles is a hundred miles away."

VI : THE STORY OF THE "ANNIE JAMISON"

THE hours that followed were like a horrible dream to Tod, a terrible vision of the night which he could not shake off.

He led his brother down to the shore. They stumbled upon a fishing smack turned keel up on the sand; and here the boy took the dripping clothes off his brother and wrapped him as best he could in an old tarpaulin that he found near by. Neil dropped into an uneasy sleep. When the sky lightened at the false dawn, Tod waded into the surf and scrubbed their clothes, hung them out to dry when the sun should rise, and crawled, shivering, beneath the boat with a spidery net drawn about him in misty folds.

When he awoke, the sun was beating in on them. Neil, yawning, flung him a weary smile. "I feel better," he observed. "Only hungry—and tired."

"How are we going to get to Marseilles?" Tod asked, as he brought their clothes and they dressed. "We haven't a penny."

"I'll get some grub. You wait." Neil turned toward a fisherman's hut that rose from the shore toward Nice.

Tod sat with his arms about his knees, thinking. Neil was willing to beg in his hunger, beg like the outcasts he had seen in Panama, like the riff-raff along the Marseilles water front. They had come to that, then—they were beggars.

Neil returned with an immense hunk of peasant's bread and a slice of home-made cheese. "Eat it, Tod," he said. "I paid for it—with your watch." He laughed shortly. "You dropped the thing on the ground, so I picked it up. I got two francs extra—enough to take us to the American Consul at Nice."

"Well, my Ingersoll wasn't worth much more," the boy admitted. "By golly, this bread tastes good."

With the food warming them and the walk toward the tramway loosening their chilled muscles, they waxed almost gay. Spring had caught them on the Azure Coast and their hearts refused to be sad, refused even though Neil lacked cap and coat and their clothes had a scarecrow appearance.

"So you've been helping the cook on a freighter," Neil pursued, as they sat on the forward end of the Cagnes trolley bound for Nice.

"Yes, the *Araby* of the European-Pacific Steamship Company."

"Good heavens, Tod, that's Swickard's outfit."

"I know it. Sheila Murray got me the job."

"Sheila! How is she? You saw her?"

"Of course. She thinks you're a piker." As he saw the expression of pain that swept like a tide across Neil's face, he hurried on. "Aw, don't let me kid you. She was the one who said you were being made a goat by Swickard. I—I like her."

Neil smiled gaily. "Thank heavens, we can go home now. But how can I get myself right, how can I prove all this crooked work of the company?"

Tod gave him a searching look as he said: "We're not the only one who wants to do that. The cook does too."

"Why the cook?"

"Because he happens to be Captain Tom Jarvis of the *Annie Jamison.*"

Neil's slender hands gripped the knees of his old trousers, then nervously went up to the buttons of his worn blue shirt. "Captain Tom Jarvis!" he breathed. "I suppose he thinks I ran away from the inquiry."

Tod looked out toward the passing row of villas. "He told me he counted on you—you of all men on his ship. And you failed him, Neil. Failed him. Why?"

"Because I didn't think the Board of Inquiry would fix the blame on him. Swickard said it was only a formality, that the blame rested on no one. I went to Brazil on the *Panama* for coffee and didn't learn about it until months later. It took me weeks to figure out just what had happened." He paused and ran his hand through his uncovered hair.

"Just what did happen, Neil?"

"You remember it was my first trip as purser. It was

our third night out from San Francisco, bound north for Seattle. I remember that I came on deck during the second dog watch, perhaps seven o'clock in the evening. We had run into a fog bank two days before, and the whistle was shrieking every minute or so. I could just see the Point Adams lighthouse winking on the starboard beam. The Columbia River bar wasn't many hours ahead.

"I had been sitting in the chief engineer's cabin amidships, and some sudden noise, I don't know what it was, made me get up and go on deck. I think now that it must have been an explosion in number four hold. Captain Jarvis was laying out the course in the chart room, and what with fooling with the ruler and compass, he must not have heard. It was the second mate who hurried for'ard with the news that number four hatch had blown loose, that the hold beneath was filling with water.

"Captain Jarvis hurried aft as cool as you make them. He didn't know then that it was not only the sea he had to contend with. I heard him order the pumps manned and the watertight bulkheads closed. The crew were a weak bunch, and the chief engineer one of Swickard's friends that I didn't like. I don't know what it was that made me go down to the engine room a half hour later. Perhaps I sensed that something was wrong there. Well, there was! The chief had reported to the skipper that all was O.K. below. O.K.! Good heavens, the engine room was filling with water and the steam pipes liable to burst at any moment. I didn't realize until later that they dared lie to the skipper, that they had not closed the bulkheads. They opened them."

Tod listened breathlessly. "Yes—and then?"

"After that, the pumps were useless. A column of water

half the size of a man's body was being projected verti-
cally up into the hold; it seemed to come through the
manhole of the ballast tank on the port side of the tunnel.
The captain realized then that he couldn't save the ship.
He gave the order to clear away the boats and signalled
to the engine room to stop the engines. By that time, there
was such a list to port that the starboard boats couldn't
be lowered. Provisions were got out and all hands took to
the boats. A half hour later, we were drawn up a half mile
or so from the ship, when we heard another explosion
—the pressure in the forehold, probably.

"We had left the fog bank behind, and the captain had
turned the *Annie Jamison* as near to land as he could.
We watched her sink, stern first. It was awful—the crew
shivering and the captain not saying a word.

"Next morning, at dawn, we were picked up. A coaster
took us in to Portland."

"That was all?"

"Yes. I went back to San Francisco, thinking that if
the steamer might perhaps have been saved, it was because of the crazy crew and the chief engineer not trying
very hard. I didn't think that they had meant to sink her.
I didn't know then that such things happened in everyday
life. Well, I know better now. She was overinsured; and
the cargo, for all I know, may have been faked crates of
tinned goods, with water in them instead of fruit."

Tod turned earnestly to his brother. "Could you and
Tom Jarvis prove it now—if you got together?"

Neil shook his head. "I don't know how. We suspect,
but that's all. Only——" He stopped and his eyes
widened. "Tod, only if they are trying to pull the same
stunt on this *Araby!*"

Tod trembled in his eagerness. "They are, Neil. Jarvis thinks so, too. Swickard's got a captain on her that's drunk half the time, and a first mate that runs things to suit himself. Jarvis says that the Company doesn't mean to let the ship reach San Francisco again."

"They'll have to be mighty careful. The underwriters aren't asleep, you know."

"What are we going to do, then?"

"The American Consul ought to advance us enough to get to Marseilles. We'll see Jarvis, and together go to the insurance office. If the *Araby* is loading a fake cargo in Marseilles for San Francisco, we'll have them just where we want them."

"The Company has a general cargo waiting at Genoa. We load there for home."

"Then we'll have to go slow. We've got to get them, this time. I can't prove a thing against Swickard yet. I suspect; I know; but there is no direct evidence that would convict him in any court. He's slick, he's smooth. But how can we get him?"

"Tom Jarvis knows. I'm sure he knows more than he says. He's waiting—waiting to spring a trap on them. That'll prove he wasn't to blame. And we'll help him, Neil; we'll let him know that he was mistaken when he said Neil Moran ran away."

Neil turned and gripped his brother's hand. "Put it there, kid," he said. "We'll show him—yes."

Ten minutes later, they descended in the Rue de France, where a *gendarme* pointed out their way. Before the American Consulate in the Boulevard Victor Hugo, a flag was flying, a flag that made Tod's heart give a little leap. Home! Home!

The American Consul himself was not visible; but his secretary proved to be a middle-aged man of kindly countenance and with a humorous twist about his mouth. He listened to their story as told by Neil, and smiled.

"H—m. Sailors away from your ship, eh? Want to get back to Marseilles. Where's your papers?"

"I haven't mine," Neil acknowledged; "but my brother has his all right."

The secretary looked them over. "Steamer *Araby*. One moment." He turned to his desk, brought forth a shipping guide, and ran his finger down a list. "Here we are. Marseilles Harbour, offshore vessels in port: *Achilles, Algonquin, Antonio Giomi, Anyo Maru, Apremont, Araby*— here it is. Captain Ramsey, merchandise to Granet and Company. H—m! How long did you say you had been ashore?"

"Three days," Tod replied.

The secretary gave them a quizzical glance. "The *Araby* cleared for Genoa last night."

For an instant Tod thought the room was whirling. He steadied himself.

"For Genoa!" Neil's voice was hoarse with disappointment.

"The mate probably filled your places when you didn't turn up. Too bad. I'd better give you a letter to the office in Marseilles; they will see that you get a berth for home. New York, probably, though. Do you mind that?"

"But we've got to get back on the *Araby*." Tod's voice trembled with emotion.

"Of course you have; but you're too late. She's gone."

Neil put his hand on the desk. "Couldn't you advance

us enough to get to Genoa? Our ship will be there a week or ten days. We could send you the money soon."

The secretary sat down and fingered a paper knife. "Same old story with you sailormen," he said shortly. "Always want to go where we can't send you. Sometimes it's Barcelona; then it's Havre or London. One young fellow said his ship was tied up at Paris." He smiled at the memory. "If you want a coat and cap, I'll give you both."

"But it's very important that we make her," Neil entreated. "I'm purser. It isn't as if I could get another job to-morrow."

"You should have thought of that before you skipped ship for Monte Carlo."

"But we haven't seen Monte Carlo——"

The secretary cut in sharply. "Look here, now; I want to be reasonable. It's the border formalities I'm thinking of. One of you hasn't his seaman's papers and both of you are broke. There is a visé fee when you cross into Italy. All that means unnecessary work." He paused and looked at them earnestly. "Come back in an hour and I'll have your tickets for Marseilles ready. If you can't take them, we'll see what the Consul can do. He's busy just now."

He nodded; and they found themselves going out the door. In the Boulevard beneath the shade of the plane trees they talked it over as they turned east.

"Shall we go to Marseilles, Tod?" Neil's voice was languid.

"No—no. How can we? We must get hold of Jarvis. That is our one chance, Neil, to square things. We've got to get to Genoa. Can we walk?"

"We might; but we won't. That secretary was just trying us out. His office gets taken in so often by seaport bums that he's getting careful. But we're Americans, aren't we? And so is he. We'll go back and see the Consul himself. Bet you a dollar to a doughnut that we'll be on our way to Genoa by morning."

"I wish I had the doughnut," said Tod hungrily. "I'm as famished as a porpoise."

After all, Neil was right. The American Consul was American. That afternoon, with tickets to Genoa and ten francs in their pockets, they boarded the train at the P. L. M. station.

In a third-class compartment Neil sank down happily, humming a little tune. He counted one by one the buttons on his frayed and ill-fitting coat. "Richmen, poormen, beggarmen"—he grinned wanly—"that's us, Tod."

The train plunged on through the afternoon. Ahead in the dusk lay Italy.

VII   SHANGHAI PASSAGE

THE Mediterranean Express slid into the great Genoa station at nine that night. Among the stream of travellers it debouched were two scarecrow figures in seamen's clothes. The brothers found themselves in the midst of the seething crowd outside the platform, with a long line of drivers shouting, calling, gesticulating.

"*Hôtel de Milan—Helvetia—Hotel Liguria—Savoie!*"

It was all strangely different, strangely exciting. Neil pushed his way ahead to the street. "We'll walk, Tod," he remarked; "we've just enough money for some bread and sausage and a flop somewhere in a sailors' lodging house. I know one—cheap—down by the water front."

They descended a narrow street, dark and silent, to the curving Via Carlo Alberto. Here little waterfront cafés shone in the night; opposite them the harbour spread out with its crowded shipping at anchor within the breakwater. Far out, a huge light was winking amid the stars. At a busy corner they went down a flight of stone steps to the *Trattoria del Porto*. A restaurant by day, a café by night, it catered to the foreign ships in the harbour and was now aflare with life.

Beneath the pavement, they crossed between crowded tables where seamen of all nationalities sprawled on the marble surfaces. A steady drone of voices filled the smoky air; behind swinging doors to the rear a wheezy accordion belched forth a Venetian waltz accompanied by the continuous hiss of sliding feet. At a secluded table against the wall, the two Americans seated themselves.

"*Pane—salame—cioccolata*," Neil ordered. He darted cautiously over to the high counter where a miniature ship reposed in a glass case, and returned with an evening paper. Quickly his eyes ran down the shipping news. "She's here, Tod," he said. "The steamer *Araby* arrived this morning. Loading near the Ponte Calvi Docks."

Tod munched the butterless bread and the thin slice of sausage with its tang of garlic. "Should I go aboard to-night and find Jarvis?"

"He'll probably be ashore with the rest of the crew. Better wait till morning."

Tod relapsed into silence again, watching swaying sailors descend the steps to the café and with a crooked walk navigate the narrow aisle toward the music. With a start, he recognized one as Blackie Judson, fireman on the *Araby*. "Is he looking?" Tod asked, turning so he would not be observed.

"No; he'll be drunk for a week," Neil replied. "I know their kind; they take enough booze to burn out their 'tween decks."

Once the swinging doors crashed outward and two Portuguese sailors with earrings danced in drunken mirth out into the aisle. To the delighted cries of the onlookers, they swung in an unsteady circle until the *proprietario* laughingly drove them back as he might two clumsy cows.

Neil and Tod sat long over their frugal meal. It was after eleven when they climbed to the pavement above. There, for a second, they halted. Arc lamps flared along the harbour front; French and Portuguese seamen swung past; two policemen in dark clothes stood on the corner.

Tod's attention was focussed on two approaching figures, both vaguely familiar—one a tall blur, the other short and square. His pulse quickened. It was Jarvis and Mr. Hawkes.

The boy pulled his brother unceremoniously against the iron railing about the stairway, as the two men halted before the café. Neither immediately glanced their way. Tod perceived that the first mate was making a night of it; he talked boisterously; he gripped the handrail to steady himself going down. Tom Jarvis, starting below, let his long Tartar eyes sweep toward them; but no sign of recognition gleamed in them. Had he seen? Tod breathed quickly.

"Did you see him, Neil? Jarvis."

"Captain Tom Jarvis! Good heavens, I didn't notice. Let's get him." Neil started toward the stairs.

"No. No." Tod hung back. "We can't talk to him now. He's with Hawkes, Swickard's man I told you about."

Neil nodded. "Very well. Let's turn in, then; I'm sleepy as a turtle."

"Where do we go?"

"Along this *vicolo*," Neil said as they turned into a narrow winding street that climbed toward the town. "Ever been to a sailors' flophouse, Tod? No? Well, I hope that you're not too particular."

Tod laughed. "If I were to tell you all the little unmentionable things about the *Araby*——"

"Save yourself the trouble. This place is bad enough. And it calls itself a hotel!"

The Albergo Morosini flaunted a huge sign above a small dark entrance. A narrow stone staircase led up to an office in which several seamen lounged, swapping yarns, no doubt, of passages good and bad.

"Yes, meester, I spik English," the man behind the counter informed them. "Beds feefteen and seexteen."

Again they climbed a narrow stone stairway, shadowy and cool. At the top, in the yellow glow of an oil lamp, they hesitated before the open door to a room containing two tiers of long wooden structures like immense bunks, one upon the other. This was the flophouse, Neil explained, where sailors for five centesimi obtained the privilege of rolling themselves in a blanket and throwing themselves in huddled heaps on the flat boards, their heads on the raised side against the wall, their feet planted against the footboard running along the aisle.

"We belong to the aristocracy," Neil went on; "we have beds."

They turned toward the front and entered a high-ceilinged dormitory with an aisle visible between two long rows of cots. Though a lamp burned in a bracket at one side, the twilight of the room was like thick smoke. Counting the beds, they proceeded down the aisle. Beneath light gray blankets, a seaman snored querulously; another tossed near by with bestial mutterings.

"By golly, I'm glad we're near the window," Tod remarked as they found their cots at the end of the row.

"Yes, and closed, of course," Neil returned softly. He stepped to the nearest casement and flung it open. Little squeaks from the hinges echoed through the room.

At once an Italian voice broke in with a curse.

"Sure, I'll close it," Neil replied as he opened the other. "Go to sleep, *caro mio.*"

Tod slipped from his outer clothes and dropped into his cot. "By golly, this is a queer place, Neil."

"Is it? Well, wake me in the morning or I'll sleep the week out. This is heaven."

Tod pulled his blanket round his neck. The doorway, far down the aisle, was a yellow square in the shadowed wall. From the windows a chill wind blew; somewhere out beyond the breakwater a steamer was whistling; from a café round the corner came the muted notes of an accordion playing a gay little air, soft and languorous as the Italian sunlight. It kept running through the boy's mind. He couldn't sleep, though he heard Neil's even breathing near him.

His mind was occupied with thoughts of Jarvis. Had the big man actually seen them and yet showed no sign of recognition because of some new aspect of the situation? Did he, perhaps, really believe that he, Tod Moran, had jumped ship in Marseilles? Had he known Neil, the man for whom he had been searching this last year or two? Or was Jarvis in reality mixed up with Hawkes in some double dealings, tired of his effort toward clearing his name that led nowhere, willing in his bitterness of spirit to wrench what he yet could from life? Let Jarvis just wait till morning and he heard this news of Neil, this corroboration of the danger impending the *Araby*. His eyes would shine then with renewed hope.

Steps sounded on the stone stairway. Two seamen lurched down the aisle, hunting their numbered cots. Tod recognized their talk as bastard French. One of the newcomers kicked off his shoes and flung himself down on his blankets; the other hiccoughed, spat on the floor, and with his cap still on, pulled the covers over his head. Except for the sound of breathing and the snoring of a drunken sailor near the doorway, silence enveloped the long room.

Tod slept only fitfully. Through the minutes, other seamen wandered in and, groping in the dark, found an

empty bed. Strange tongues spoke in whispers across the room; strange words drifted into the boy's consciousness.

Presently he started into sudden wakefulness at the touch of hands on his blanket. "I want a bunk!" a voice, gruff and deep, broke in. Tod perceived a dark face bending over him, a face with only two eyes visible beneath the mass of black hair. "Take yer blanket," the man said thickly, "and go back to the blamed chicken coop."

"Get away!" Tod retorted. "There's an empty bed across the aisle."

The man merely nodded. Now thoroughly awake, the boy looked up intently. He knew the fellow. It was the burly stoker, Black Judson, of the *Araby*. Tod felt the man take hold of the long iron side and lift. A second later he found himself on the floor with his two blankets writhing about him.

"I want a bunk!" grumbled Black Judson. "Git out, you cockroach!"

Neil stirred in his bed. "What the deuce is wrong?" he asked sleepily.

"Some drunken fool tipped me out on the floor."

"The devil he did!" Neil, so slow in avenging his own insults, was up in a flash at this ignominy thrust upon his brother. He darted across Tod's reclining form and jerked the man by the arm. "Get outa here, you dago, or I'll scuttle you! Get me?"

"Me? By thunder, I'll toss yuh in th' furnace." Black Judson sprang, hurling his great body on the tall American.

Tod kicked the blankets from his feet. Jumping up he saw that the two men were locked in a fierce, warlike embrace. Swaying, struggling, they pitched into the aisle full length. Neil rose first and stepped back. His assailant swayed drunkenly for a moment like a beast on all fours; then, in a horrified instant, Tod saw that, as the stoker rose, his right hand fingered a sailor's sheath knife. It glimmered in the lamplight like an evil thing.

Black Judson staggered forward. Even as he lunged for Neil, the knife gleaming dully in his hand, Tod sprang between them. His arm flew upward to ward off the blow.

"Tod, get out!" Neil blurted.

Already the big fireman had closed with the boy. Of a sudden, Tod felt a swift stab of pain in his left side. He staggered. Men tumbled out of their cots; cries, curses, broke the stillness. Hands grasped the two writhing figures. Tod glimpsed the burly form of the fireman disappear in the midst of the crowding seamen. Neil's voice sounded in his ears as if it were miles distant.

"Hurt, Tod?"

Tod stumbled backward. "No—only a scratch. He got my side."

Dark forms appeared silhouetted in the square light of the doorway. Footsteps came crowding down the aisle. A volley of oaths ripped open the air. "What! Theese American! Why you fight? Thees is good house—never fighting here."

"Nom d'un chien, il est mort!"

"Dio cane!"

"Aw, hell, stow the gab!"

Cries, echoing like distant shots about him. A swaying jumble of people, and Neil striding forward. "Yes, where's that devil with the knife? It's prison for him."

"Poleece!"

"*Guardie!*"

"The cops—the bulls!"

Strangely unmoved, Tod watched the aisle clear as if by magic. Facing him and Neil were the dark-clad forms of two policemen. Over the shoulders of these, two other faces, familiar, appearing like figures in a dream, stared at him, their eyes alight with hatred. They were Mr. Hawkes and Tom Jarvis.

The gruff voice of the first mate boomed across the room. "That's them, officer. Those two there. Tried to jump ship, they did. Running away."

"It's a lie!" Neil sputtered.

Tod stepped backward as the two policemen swooped like birds of prey and pinioned their arms to their sides.

"What's this mean?" Neil gasped.

Mr. Hawkes smiled grimly. "Now, don't try to lie outa this, young man," he interposed. "We got yuh this time, and we got the Genoa law behind us. It's the ship's brig for yuh both."

Neil struggled uselessly in the iron grip of his captor. "Cut it out," he remonstrated. "Don't try any shanghai passage stuff on us."

Tod turned his bewildered eyes upon the cook. "Tom," he whispered. "Tom."

The face of the Tattooed Man wore an impassive mask. Not the slightest emotion stirred his features; only his eyes, as he glanced at Mr. Hawkes, gleamed narrowly.

The first mate laughed in his beard. "Ain't these the flyaways, Mr. Jarvis? Ain't they?"

Tom Jarvis let his gaze settle upon Tod's face with a gleam of understanding. Although his lips did not move, the boy read his message. *Play the game, Joe Macaroni. Play the game.* Tod unconsciously nodded as the cook's quick glance passed across to the former purser of the *Annie Jamison.* The impassive mask of the moment before slowly vanished as he stared, transfixed, at Neil Moran. Hatred, intense and overwhelming, swept across his bronzed features. The pupils of his eyes dilated; his mouth slid into a straight hard line.

"Yeh, that's the men," Jarvis jerked out in a tone full of menace. "We'll take 'em back, officer. Get 'em dressed."

At the words, Tod felt his heart go cold; a clammy perspiration broke out on his body. An abrupt trickle at his side, warm, slow, caught his attention. He screwed up his right arm where a stabbing pain gnawed his ribs. Looking down he saw that his hand dripped with blood.

His throat grew tight. "Neil——" The murmur of voices receded; the room tossed about like a skiff in a storm. He swayed.

On a blinding instant, the square yellow light in the doorway flashed into a thousand fragments; the floor rushed up and caught him.

"GET BUSY! PRESSURE'S DOWN TEN POUNDS!"

PART FOUR

THE DOOMED SHIP

REPORTED LOST
American stmr. *Araby*—2952 tons
European-Pacific S. S. Co.
Cleared Genoa for San Francisco April 16.

La Gazzetta d'Italia

I : HIGH ADVENTURE

IN THE recess of his forecastle bunk, gray with shadows, Tod Moran lay with his flushed face turned toward the quivering plates of the hull, his eyes staring sightlessly through the porthole at a starlit sea which flooded past. It was only his fever-racked body, however, that lay there; his mind had cleared for ports afar.

He was back in the sailors' flophouse at Genoa where the twilight was like thick smoke. Someone had drawn a keen knife across his ribs, and it hurt. It hurt so intensely that, although he tried to stifle the sound on his lips, he cried out in agony. Neil was there and Tom

Jarvis; yet neither stepped forward to give him a hand. It wasn't quite fair, was it? when they knew he had asked for aid? Well, he wouldn't beg.—What was that? . . . *Richman—poorman—beggarman.* . . . It was a lilting, slightly wistful song that someone trilled above the wheezy notes of an accordion. Beggarman! . . . Yes, almost he had come to that.

Now he was on a train thumping around a shore toward Marseilles. It made a noise like drumming in his ears. A peasant in a smock pointed to a road out the window, and said: "That, monsieur, leads to the Villa Paradis."

In a street of crowded villas, a garden was hidden by gate and wall. The gate was securely locked, so he climbed over the wall. Neil awaited him there near a skiff on a sandy beach, and at once they put to sea. Then the fog closed in. It pressed about them, moist and chill; no matter how they rowed they failed to pierce that encircling gloom. They heard the beat of drums from the shore. It was to warn ships off the rocks. The fog, thickening, wrapped itself about them as though it meant to choke out all life with its wintry blanket. It numbed him, so that he lay quiet, not caring to move. From the mist emerged the face of Red Mitchell, cruel, sardonic, beneath its film of coal dust.

"It's Neil, Tod—Neil."

"Naw—get away. It's Red. I know you. You slugged me in the side."

But it wasn't Red, either; it was a San Blas Indian boy and he was telling Tod how to escape. Escape? . . . Escape from what? By golly, kids were foolish; they ought not try to get away. Look at Neil, now. He made no effort; he stood locked in the ship's brig, peering out between iron bars. Then someone opened the door—he couldn't see just who it was—and Neil, the fool, at once jumped overside. The boatswain threw over two life belts, but Neil had vanished in the darkness of the wake.

It was dangerous to put out in a boat, because you could hear the muffled beat of drums from the coast, and that meant shoals. But the captain let him man the little skiff *Annie Jamison*, and he went after Neil. Straight toward that drumming he steered. Every moment the rhythmic tattoo grew more intense, more menacing. He stood in the sternsheets, singing, for that drowned the unceasing roll of the drums.

In a trough of the sea was a life ring, and clinging to it, a man.

When they had lifted him, dripping, inboard, they found that a shark had gashed his side. The wound lay open, raw and bleeding. They brought him back to the seamen's forecastle and stretched him in a bunk. He must be very ill, because everyone came and went softly; everyone spoke in whispers. Then, in some strange, unaccountable way, he himself merged into the sick man; it was he, Tod Moran, who now lay stretched in the bunk, and it was Neil who came at times and looked at him.

Neil was always telling him to lie down and be quiet so the men could sleep. They were tired; they had worked; they didn't like anyone to cry out at night. But because Neil now looked surprisingly like a nigger, he wouldn't obey his brother. He wanted to watch the doorway for someone who never came. Who was it? He listened intently as the footfalls descended the three iron steps; each one kept time to that distant drumming—one, two, three!

His heart leaped when he heard a familiar step, but the tobacco smoke marred his vision.

"The kid—he sleeps yoost now."

"I'm not seasick, Swede."

"Now yoost lay down, matey." A hand wiped his brow and smoothed his crumpled hair. "Yah, you got fever. You'll be up in couple o' days."

"Couple of days? Say, I'll be serving breakfast in the cabin tomorrow morning."

"Yoost lay down."

"You tell the blooming cook I'm not sick. And tell him I think the sea is wonderful! By golly, this is the best little freighter that ever hit the Pacific."

He heard above him the deep-toned sound of the bell on the forecastle head. He heard the watch below turn out with surly grunts. Tin cups rattled; the aroma of coffee penetrated his nostrils; innumerable feet climbed the companion steps to relieve the men on deck. All through the middle watch, he heard the bell strike off the half hours. Presently, as eight bells crept round again, he dozed.

Voices brought him back to consciousness. The men must have been washing down the decks, for he heard them take off their heavy sea boots and fling them under bunks. Low murmurs drifted up to him; someone told a yarn of windjammer days at sea.

"Yeah, we lay becalmed for weeks waiting for the Trades, and the grub gettin' more rotten and the lazarette more empty every day. Then I goes to the cap'n and says: 'Cap'n, let me have yer gig and I'll get a mess o' fish, I will.' He nodded, so I took my bunkmate and put out in the gig that night with two lanterns and a net. We stretched the net between the oars lashed to stem and stern. Then, with lanterns lighted, we waited. Our fishing soon began. The silly flyin' fish would leap at the light, and we'd hear them plop against the net. We'd grab 'em then and knock their heads in. It wasn't more than an hour before we had a mess for the whole ship's company. Made me bos'n for that, the cap'n did. Yes, sirree. 'Johnson,' he says, 'yuh got brains.' And bos'n I've been ever since."

Loud guffaws greeted the end of the yarn. A derisive voice cried: "Brains! It's a lyin' tongue yuh got, if yuh asks me."

The boatswain answered in a tone of hurt reproach; the conversation waxed stronger, higher. "Key down," said a voice. "You'll wake the kid."

The weather-beaten face of Nelson the Dane leaned over Tod. "Feelin' better this morning, ain't you? Want anything?"

"Yes, please—a drink of water."

The tin dipper clinked in a bucket and the man returned. As Tod gulped down the cooling liquid, he heard shoes scuff on the steps. Neil stood beside the bunk.

There was a quiver at his lips when he spoke. "Thank heavens, Tod, you've been better this last week. You're almost yourself again!"

Tod Moran forced his weary eyes over his brother's tall figure. Neil wore an old blue shirt and dungarees, both black with coal and grime. A powder of sombre hue covered his face; little beads of perspiration made trickles of white down his jaws. All that remained of that appealing presence was a steady gaze from gray eyes that yet had the power to charm.

They charmed Tod now in a manner that lifted his

mouth in a smile. "In the stokehole?" he queried faintly.

Neil nodded with a rueful glance. "Stoking." He took the sweat rag from his belt and wiped his neck. "Locked in the brig below for six days while we loaded in Genoa; then they put me in the stokehole. Hot work."

"Where are we?"

"Passed Gibraltar three days ago. In the Canaries Current now." He took the dipper from Tod's feeble grasp. "Hungry?"

"A little. How's the cook?"

Neil turned away. "The cook? . . . Oh, he's all right. He's sent you soup and canned milk from the galley; he came for'ard once or twice. Oh, he's all right.—Well, I'll go and wash up and then come back."

Tod Moran lay quiet. The morning sunlight pierced the after bulkhead with two golden spears which quivered on the littered floor. Through the open door and the ventilators turned to windward, the sound of the chipping of paint came to him on the drowsy air. The swish of the water along the plates of the hull was like the scarcely audible music of a dream. Coats and shirts flapped lazily on their pegs; the soiled light-curtains swayed in the somnolent breeze. It was good to be here, lying in a bunk and listening to the sound of the morning's work on deck. He kicked off his blanket, and in a surprised moment realized that his limbs were so tired and weak that they trembled at the unwonted exertion.

Presently the inspecting officers appeared in the doorway on their morning round. The faces of the captain, the first mate, and the chief engineer peered within; but only the commander of the *Araby*, acting as the ship's doctor, descended the steps.

"Well, Moran, I'm glad to see you better," he remarked in his treble voice. "I've doctored many a man on the sea these last twenty years; and I generally pull them through. Yes; I don't want to appear boastful, but I generally pull them through. I sometimes think I missed my calling. I should have been an M.D." His lean face broke into a smile; little wrinkles formed at the corners of his red-rimmed eyes. "Mighty lucky that your brother could come along and nurse you. Have him give you a kerosene bath and then get some broth from the galley."

He left with almost a swagger in the swerve of his thin shoulder blades.

Later in the morning, refreshed by the bath to which he had submitted like a child, and the few spoonfuls of beef broth, Tod Moran surveyed his brother with brighter eyes. "What are we going to do, Neil?"

"Heaven knows, Tod. All I care about is getting home. We're bound west for Panama."

"Will we reach there?"

"Hush!" Neil glanced furtively round. "Be careful what you say. I was scared stiff when you were delirious, for fear you'd talk too much. I don't know what to think. Maybe we will—though Toppy has told the men that in Genoa he saw the rats trying to climb over the tins on the hawsers. Funny thing. I don't know—and I care less."

"You take things so easy. Everything's an adventure to you. You seem to eat it up."

"Do I?" Neil grinned. His handsome face was once more visible, his dark hair brushed back from his high forehead. "Well, it's all experience, isn't it? I want to try everything once before I croak."

"Even firing in a stokehole?"

"Sure thing. It's rather awful down there—and mighty hard work. The temperature is working up to a hundred twenty degrees; soon it'll be climbing toward thirty. But I'm learning things down there, Tod."

"Learning things? You never do, Neil."

"Well, I get a different viewpoint, anyway." He paused and ruminated for a moment. "If anything is going to happen to this old tub, it'll happen before we hit the Canal. There's plenty of islands in the Caribbean; we could land on one easily."

He crossed to a bench before the table and sat down. "I'm off till four. Want me to read you something?"

"What?"

"Here's a book the fellows have been devouring in the firemen's fo'c's'le. It's called 'The Lookout: A Romance of the Sea.' It's pretty good."

Tod Moran smiled listlessly. "I thought I tossed that overboard. It's rotten, that book. I know; it's the one I read on the train going to San Francisco. I thought it was the real stuff then; but now I know it's all lies."

"Oh, it isn't so bad. Listen to this:

"'Cursed luck,' said Captain Titherington, 'with this barometer falling and the pirate devil chasing us!'
"'No sloop can overtake us, Captain,' said his mate. 'Pago Pago isn't far ahead. The guns are out and the decks cleared for action. Let us turn and fight!'
"'Mr. Fallon, you are ever avid for a fight,' said the captain. 'I cannot risk the lives of my noble, brave men of the sea, so loyal——' "

"That's enough," Tod cut in sharply. "I can't stand

any more. The fool that wrote that stuff hasn't even been to sea."

"Maybe he has," Neil said with a smile. "Perhaps on a passenger liner—or a private yacht."

Tod sighed. "Yes; he might even be a ship's officer. But he better not try to pull any stuff about the men in the fo'c's'le."

"Well, listen to this, then:

"Climbing aloft the lookout was almost choked by the smoke and din of the fighting. At the crow's nest he swore a mighty oath. The man whom he had been sent to relieve lay wounded nigh unto death! . . ."

"Now that's better," Tod murmured as he settled himself into his mattress. "Read some more."

Neil's voice droned on. Tod forgot the little world of the ship in which he lay. He forgot the men who commanded her and the doom which lay ahead. He was aloft with the lookout man, leaping through deeds of high adventure. By golly, this was good. It was like a shot of dope; it made you forget. He thrilled to the story of this gentleman adventurer who had smuggled himself on to the ship; he smelt the smoke and the burning powder; he heard the sharp rattle of musketry. This was a hero for you; he never failed. Tod sank into restful, satisfied slumber.

Drums again, drawing closer—a sharp tattoo like pagan armies gathering for an attack; so close they came that he felt their soft vibration in the air. He opened his drowsy eyes. On the crossbeam above him, a cockroach crawled swiftly out of sight. In his ears sounded the musical slap of water along the starboard strake.

His eyes caught sight of a rose-tinted book lying on his
blanket. He reached for it, clenched it in his hand. By
golly, he'd had enough of such opium. He stretched his
arm across to the slanting plates. "The Lookout" vanished
through the porthole.

He lay back with a sigh, listening. There it was again—
drumming. The tremor of the steel plates at his side drew
his attention. He caught his breath sharply, for a thought,
which seemed to steal into the very recesses of his heart,
swept him up. That was it—that was the drumming: the
steady soft pulsation of the steamer's engines driving the
Araby homeward.

## II	MR. HAWKES SHOWS HIS HAND

THE rusty tramp had shoved her nose southwest across
the twentieth parallel before Tod Moran was once
more able to take his place on deck. He did not return
to the galley, however; the boatswain brought word that
the second mate had ordered him to chip paint in the
alleyways. It was not difficult to sit on his haunches and
chip the dirty white scale from the steel plates with a
small, edged hammer; but whenever he raised his arms
to reach overhead he felt his wound gnaw quietly but
surely at his side. Bits of paint flew like sand in his eyes;
the grit dug into his skin, and itched. He kept at it steadily, grinding out the long daylight hours on deck.

From the open door of the galley came the sound of
the cook at work: the hiss of the meat saw, the clang of

the range door, the rattle of dishes. Tom Jarvis now went
about his duties alone, relieved only slightly by the former
coal-passer, Red Mitchell, who had taken over the care
of the cabin aft together with the officers' mess.

On the second morning of his new drudgery, Tod heard
a sudden uproar in the galley. It was after eleven and Red
Mitchell had just come forward from setting the officers'
table. His voice came to Tod, raised high in expostulation.

"Cut it out, cooky! You can't treat a friend of Mr.
Hawkes like that. Ain't I right, now?"

"Get out before I heave yuh overside. The sight o' your
face makes me sick."

"I'll complain to the captain, I will!"

"Get your tray and beat it. Gut me if I can stand you!"

Red emerged from the doorway, a tray in his hands.
He hesitated and glanced in Tod's direction. His mouth
curved in a derisive smile. "How d'ye like yer new job?"
he essayed in a low tone.

The youth did not pause in the short swings of his
hammer. "Pretty good," he said shortly. "How do you
like being mess boy?"

"Mess boy, me eye! I'm the officers' steward, I am."
He licked his chops. "And I don't have ter eat the gar-
bage they gives the fo'c's'le now." With a triumphant
grin he departed for the cabin aft.

At eleven-thirty Tod dropped his tools near the winch
and procured his mess gear from the forecastle. The food
was handed out the galley door and brought by Swede
Jorgenson to number one hatch where the men crowded
round it like wolves about a carcass.

"Now the kid ain't in the galley no more, the grub's
rotten," commented Chips.

"It fair sickens me. Blimey, if it don't. Swill, I calls it. Swill."

"Yah, the cook—he don't like it neither."

"Aw, he don't, huh? Well, why does he serve it, then?"

"Blimey, he's got to—that's why. Got the blarsted stuff cheap, they did, in Genoa. The spuds, now, they all run to sprouts; and the meat—it fair stinks." Toppy dipped his thin nose into his pannikin and wrinkled his face in a frown. "Phew! I wouldn't give this to pigs, I wouldn't."

Tod Moran crossed to the shadow of the forecastle and dropped to the deck near his brother, who was conversing with another fireman, Tony the Wop.

"This stuff is awful," Neil commented. "Can you go it, Tod?"

"A little. I'm not very hungry."

"You be seeck again, you eat these." Tony waved a spoonful of stew in a precarious gesture of disdain. "It maka me seeck, too."

Neil stretched out his long legs in their dungarees and set his tin upon the deck. Breaking a piece of bread, he revealed innumerable weevils baked in the dough. With a frown of disgust, he tossed it overboard. "The men won't stand this much longer," he remarked. "The first place that hits them is their stomachs. They're almost ready to mutiny."

"Thees boat rotten." Tony wiped up the gravy with a slice of bread and gulped it down. "Why I ever leave San Francisco! I dunno. I stay there next time." He broke a long black cigar in the middle and passed half to Neil. "Theese Tuscano—heaven." His brown eyes, shadowed by dark lashes, smouldered with unquenched fire. "Those officers—*Dio!*"

Tod drank the lukewarm beverage of chicory and let his eyes sweep out across the sea. Sunlight shivered along the waves; here and there leaped bits of spray. "That looks like an island off the port beam, Neil. Is it?"

Neil nodded gravely. "We're near the Caribbean at last." He rose and scraped his tin plate overside.

A moment later, Tod followed him down the slimy steps to the washroom where the stench almost overpowered him. "We're drawing close to the time," Neil whispered as he hurriedly washed his mess tins. "I know it. Watch out."

"Oh, I'm all right. I'm on deck," Tod returned; "but, Neil, you might get caught down there in the stokehole. It's like a rat trap; you'd never get out."

"Hush!" Neil flashed him a warning glance as the grumbling seamen appeared above in the doorway.

In the forecastle, Tod dried his cup and plate and put them away in the cupboard beneath the steps. He turned in surprise to find the forecastle crowding with firemen as well as deck hands. What did it mean?

"Draw lots," rumbled the deep voice of Black Judson, "and see who goes aft with the complaint."

"Yeh, think they can feed us swill, they do. Blimey, we'll tell 'em! Got to get better grub at Cristobal or we'll complain to the port authorities."

"Yah, roll the bones."

"Takes too long. Say, there's the kid." Black Judson surveyed Tod with narrowed eyes. He spoke to the men now lining the bunks. "Say, what's the kid been doing lately? Nothin'. Let him go aft. Huh?"

Several men nodded in approval. "Sure thing. Let the kid be th' goat."

Tod Moran, crossing to his bunk, suddenly swung about. "No, you don't. I'll take my chances with the rest, but that's all."

"Blimey, now, don't get sore," Toppy soothed from his seat atop the littered table. "If yer talks nice, maybe the skipper'll put yer back in the galley."

"No, thanks, I've had enough of the galley. But why don't you ask me like a man?"

Toppy's lips curled in a wide grin over his yellow teeth. "Gawd strike me pink! The kid thinks 'e's growed up."

Tod glanced round at the circle of faces, eight or nine seamen and ten or twelve firemen; he perceived that they were immersed in a heated discussion. Beneath the surface of their caustic criticism lay unplumbed depths of bitterness. Driven like cattle, fed like swine, they had little recourse to the tyranny of their officers. It was not strange, he thought, that their bovine eyes appeared so stupid and their revels at times so sharkish.

A feeling of pity rushed through him. "All right," he conceded; "what shall I tell the captain?"

"Tell 'im we cawn't eat their bloomin' grub, that's wot. Tell 'im we wants better eats or we complain at Cristobal."

Tod listened to the flood of suggestions from the men. "Sure, I understand. I'll put it strong."

"Yeah, hurry up. Go now." They sat still to await his return.

With quickened heartbeats, Tod Moran departed. In the starboard alleyway he halted at the open door of the galley. The cook's powerful body was bent above the stove. At length he turned, long of limb and splendidly erect, and regarded Tod with an impassive gaze.

"Hello, Joe Macaroni. How are you?"

The youth thrust his hands deep in his pockets. "Oh, pretty good," he replied in a low tone. "The men are sending me aft to complain about the grub."

"Gut me, if I blame them! I hope they get filled with such officers." His curious eyes gleamed with unexpected fire. An iron fist thumped the table. "Don't they know I've raved till I'm black in the face? If the Old Man don't get better grub at the first port, I'll walk out." He stopped suddenly; a ruminating look came into his eyes. "Only— only——"

"Yes?"

Tod saw the singlet grow taut across the mighty chest. He waved a deprecatory hand. "Go on! Tell the cap'n— with my compliments."

Tod left with his thoughts absorbed by a question. Where did Tom Jarvis, so aloof, so unfathomable, now stand in the presence of the *Araby's* impending doom? Had the man done his best in the matter of the seamen's food; or was he in reality using his power as a wedge to separate still further the forecastle from the cabin aft? Tod, almost before he was aware of it, had knocked upon the cabin door.

"Come in," answered the gruff voice of Mr. Hawkes.

At the table beneath the open skylight, the first mate sat at his noon meal. Tod started as he beheld the recumbent form of Captain Ramsey lying on the red plush settee, one hand hanging limply overside.

"What d'ye want?" said the mate, pausing with knife in air.

Tod Moran wet his lips. "The men, sir, have sent me aft to speak to the captain."

"The cap'n?" Mr. Hawkes threw back his bearded face and laughed. "There he is." He pointed to the sodden figure on the settee.

Captain Ramsey, Tod saw, slept in a drunken stupor. His yellow skin hung over his bones; his weak mouth lay open with deep breaths sighing between his teeth.

"What do the men want?" pursued the mate.

"They have a complaint to make, sir."

"Oh, they have." Mr. Hawkes put down knife and fork, and chewed vigorously for a moment. "Out with it—what's the trouble?"

"It's the food, sir. It's not eatable. The bread's full of worms and weevils; the meat's tainted; the potatoes——"

"That will do." Mr. Hawkes was on his feet. He picked up a slice of bread. "Does this look like it's full of worms?"

"That isn't the kind we're served, sir. I could bring you a piece."

"Do you dispute my word? The grub on this ship is first rate! I'll have no complaining yokels coming aft."

Seating himself, he speared a slice of *salame*, thumped it down on the bread, and munched it in cheerful serenity.

"Come and see their food, sir," Tod insisted. "Then——"

He stopped as the mate rose in a flash and strode his way. He saw the man's mouth break into a leer of triumph; a hairy paw caught him by the tender flesh of his side. A cry of agony rose to his lips. The clutch was just over the wound, and the short fingers, biting to the ribs, slowly twisted.

"Make lying complaints to me, will yuh? I'll learn yuh."

Tod Moran drooped. A stabbing pain tore through him. "Don't," he whimpered. "Don't."

Mr. Hawkes's malignant face bent over him. "Yuh never been no use on this ship, yuh haven't. I'll give yuh a real job now—you can go down to the stokehole." He twisted the flesh again, chuckling. "Yeh, that'll git yuh, all right—passin' coal in the bunkers."

The youth collapsed against the wall. "Captain Ramsey," he called. "Captain Ramsey!"

Mr. Hawkes flung him away with a laugh of derision. "When yuh want the cap'n of this ship, call me."

Tod Moran picked himself up, swaying against the bulkhead. Through burning eyes he saw the mate go to the settee and shake the drunken captain into wakefulness. "Git up, you blamed fool," he scowled. "This here kid wants t' know who's master o' this ship. Is it you, or me?"

Captain Ramsey struggled to one elbow. "Gimme drink, old man," he hiccoughed. "Yesh, I'm master."

"You—master!" Mr. Hawkes chuckled scornfully.

"All right. Then cut out the drink. Get up to the bridge."

The commander of the *Araby* swayed to a sitting position. "Gimme drink, Mr. Hawkes."

"No more," the mate snarled. "You get up to the bridge."

"Gimme drink, Mr. Hawkes." The man's mouth slid open; his bleary eyes, between granulated lids, peered out vaguely at the table.

The mate swung about with a swagger and filled a glass from a decanter on the sideboard. "Who's master now, Mr. Ramsey?"

Tod saw the captain's eyes fasten greedily on the brimming glass. "Yesh, Mr. Hawkes—you in charge now."

A deep laugh greeted the words. "Here, you swine, drink this. I'm commander now."

The mate spun about toward the youth; his beard shot forward. "Go tell that to the crew. They can eat it, see? Now git!"

Blindly Tod Moran stumbled to the door. Outside, his shoulder came in contact with an empty tray; behind it he glimpsed a flaming thatch of hair above a rat-like face.

"Say, why don't yeh look where yer goin'?"

Tod gave no answer. He groped his way to the nearest hatch and dropped upon it. His hands came up to his throbbing side.

A step followed him. "Kid, you ain't got no sense. You don't know how to git along. Ain't I right, now?"

"Get away. Leave me alone."

Red Mitchell heaved a deep sigh. "What's the matter? What d' yeh want, anyway?"

The question brought a pang. What did he want? . . . He only wanted to creep home. He wanted a room of his own where in privacy he might throw himself down with his face in his arms. It wasn't merely the pain in his side; it was the pain in his heart, as well.

A shudder passed through him. He raised his eyes, looked across the sunlit deck, and rose. Slowly he went forward. In the starboard alleyway he hesitated. Grouped about the forecastle doors were the firemen and deck hands, their eyes focussed aft.

Tod Moran, dropping his hand from his side, staggered to the fore-deck.

"Gawd strike me bline!" shrilled a voice. "There comes our answer."

III : IN THE STOKEHOLE

NEXT morning, in the eight-to-twelve watch, Tod Moran went on duty in the bunkers.

As he emerged from the forecastle to the main deck, he presented a different appearance from the trim youth who had served the officers' mess in the cabin aft. Instead of a starched white coat with shining buttons, he now wore an old blue shirt and overalls. He started with a brisk step, nevertheless, toward the starboard alleyway; but paused when his eyes caught sight of a fireman climbing from the stokehole fiddley. The man, a Portuguese, lurched to the bulwarks where he rested his arms on the iron wall. His naked torso streamed with sweat; his powerful shoulders writhed in convulsed movements as his rough-hewn face contorted in jerks of agony.

"What's wrong with him?" Tod inquired of Nelson the Dane who sat against the mainmast splicing a frayed hawser.

"Ignorant cattle, that's what's the matter," commented Nelson with unwonted energy. "They're told not to drink so much water down below; but they will do it. They gulp it down by the gallon, and suffer for it. Lookit the beast! Ain't he a nice sight?"

Tod stared in silence at the anguished sufferer. The man moaned slightly now; bits of speech in a foreign tongue came, stifled, from his lips. Tod Moran dragged his eyes away. Looking up, he beheld a gull soaring against a burnished sky which dipped to a sea that was glazed.

The youth stirred, then proceeded slowly aft. He entered the engine-room entrance and was instantly struck by the terrific vibrations and the oppressive warmth of the place. A volcanic breath swept by him up toward the open skylight. He compressed his lips, swung down the iron rail of the ladder past the cylinders to the middle grating. Here the chief engineer, his Scotch face screwed into a frown, stood looking intently at the flashing rods and gleaming metal. Tod passed him and swung down the second ladder to the plates of the engine-room floor where an oiler, black and grimy, went about, oil can in hand. The cadenced throb of the engines almost deafened him; the steel plates beneath his feet vibrated as if they were alive. The hot atmosphere pressed about him even as the bunkers filled with coal pressed about the sides of the engine room. By golly, it was hot.

The second engineer, coming to relieve the third, called above the pulsing tumult: "How's the steam?"

Tod waited while the second peered at the blackboard and tried the gauges. He was a small but well-built man with a taciturn countenance that seemed overburdened with the weight of his constant watchfulness. The third engineer toiled up the ladder, and the second turned to Tod with a gruff "Come on, snipe, I'll show you your work."

He led the way past the telegraph with its indicator pointing to *Full Ahead,* around the ventilating fan to a small iron door leading forward. Tod stooped, entered a dark tunnel to one side of the boilers, and came out a moment later into the long black stokehole. The narrow compartment, its ceiling lost in the gloom above, ran directly across the ship. The boilers rose aft, an iron bulkhead forward, broken in the centre, Tod saw, by the fiddley opening with its ladders and grating.

Here, in this sombre hole, encased in steel, three men were at work. Before the port boiler near Tod, Tony the Wop looked up from his pile of coal; beyond him, Blackie Judson mopped a sweating brow before the centre; and in the murky distance a huge Finn clanged shut a furnace door of the starboard boiler. The men, stripped to their waist and wearing black dungarees, appeared in the flickering shadow like half-human figures, apparitions of a disordered brain. Sweat and grime ran down their flushed bodies; their faces were so black that Tod could barely make out their features. High on the bulkhead behind them, two electric bulbs, wire covered, tried vainly to pierce the dust-laden air.

"Get busy!" shouted the second above the steady draft of the furnaces. "Pressure's down ten pounds!"

At once the men jerked into action. Tony the Wop,

lean flanked and powerful of shoulder, closed the forced draft checks on number three furnace, swung open the door with a clang, and thrust a long slice bar into the glowing clinker. Blackie Judson opened the door of number five, which emitted a leaping tongue of flame. Instinctively, Tod stepped back against the bulkhead. His hand went to his eyes to shield them from those fiery throats which spat forth scorching heat. The draft roared. Shovels scraped the steel flooring. Coal shot quickly into the yawning mouths.

Tony the Wop swung shut his door, opened the forced draft checks, and swung about to lean exhausted on his shovel. He wiped his tortured eyes with a sweat rag, breathing deeply the faint breath of air that drifted down the ventilator openings. Tod gazed at him, fascinated. Tony's profile, as beautifully modelled as a Tuscan urn, shone clear in the firelight. Turning, he gave Tod a wry smile and an eloquent gesture that embodied centuries of vanished splendour.

"This way." The second waved his hand forward.

Tod crossed to a black doorway behind the fiddley ladder and stumbled up the dark incline of a tunnel into the bowels of the ship. He knocked against an iron wheelbarrow. Moving slowly thereafter, he cautiously circled the open mouth of a chute in the deck plates and gazed up at the dim region of the bunkers. An electric light gleamed feebly overhead; the bunkers, rising about him, faded away into deep obscurity.

"Here, Shorty," called the second, "show the kid what to do."

The second departed with a word of warning about keeping the stokers well supplied, and then Shorty the

Greek, a black statue of a man, told Tod his duties. The bunkers just forward of the stokehole were empty; the ones on the port side were now being drawn. He was to fill the barrow—long easy sweeps, not too quick—wheel the barrow back to the chute, and dump the coal down to the stokehole.

"By golly, it's hot here!"

"Hot?" Shorty the Greek snarled sharply. "You wait. It's hundred-eighteen now; at noon it be over twenty. . . . So long, kid."

Left alone, Tod Moran set to work almost with eagerness. In the dark and soot he soon lost count of the hours as he hurriedly shovelled coal into the iron barrow, wheeled it jerkily down the plates, and tipped the contents into the chute. His thighs and biceps ached; his breath choked on the dust that enveloped his little world like a fog. Remembering a bucket of water which he had seen near the stokehole tunnel, he rushed for it and plunged his caked lips into the tepid liquid. He drank it down in eager gulps. Suddenly he stopped. His mind had envisioned the pitiful figure of the Portuguese fireman on deck. After that, he dared not take more than a mouthful, even though his head swam and his lips grew dry and brittle.

"Say, keed," called Tony once from the tunnel incline, "you work too fas'. You never las' four hours. You crazy."

Tod soon learned to throw the coal in steady, even movements; but by ten o'clock his side was beginning to make itself felt. He wiped the film of dust from his face with a damp sweat cloth which came away black, set his teeth grimly, and stooped again over the coal.

All thoughts of fatigue vanished, however, when he

turned his flaming eyes into the darkness at the end of his narrow alley. Dimly he had been aware of a watertight door in the steel bulkhead aft; but immersed in the toil of the first hours, he had not given it a thought. Now, through the swimming heat, a thought had floated to the surface of his consciousness. Beyond that door lay number three hold.

In the days of his convalescence, in his days of chipping paint on deck, he had often glanced at the covered hatches and vaguely wondered what lay below in the holds of the *Araby*. Here, in the 'tween-decks, he had stumbled upon a doorway. Could he open it and peer within?

He dropped his shovel and crept aft. The door was probably three feet high and half as much across; it was set a foot or more above the plates of the 'tween-decks. An iron handle was screwed fast behind a cleat; and, tug as he would, he could not dislodge it. He was weak yet; that was the trouble. He needed a hammer.

A step sounded behind him. "Hey, you snipe," admonished the second; "the steam's going down and you ain't got no coal below." He punctuated his words with a stream of oaths.

Tod fled back to his barrow. As the man came swiftly toward him through the murky gloom, flinging out an arm in an angry gesture of command, Tod perceived that the second possessed the soul of a junior officer, bullying yet servile.

"Get busy, you scum!" he cried. "The mate'll be complainin' to the chief, and you'll have him down on our heads."

Tod picked up his shovel, slid the blade beneath the coal, and threw it into the barrow. The second vanished

toward the throbbing heart of the *Araby*. Tod lifted the
handles and pushed the load along the plates. With a rolling clatter and a rising smoke of black dust the coal disappeared down the chute.

Furnace doors clanged below. Water hissed on fiery
clinkers. Above the muffled beat of the engines, voices
raised in altercation drifted up the incline. Tod bent his
weary head, listening. Something was wrong. He dragged
his legs over to the tunnel leading to the stokehole.

Oaths ripped across the heavy air. The second was in
a tantrum. "Can't keep 'em going?" he shrieked. "I'll
make yuh!"

Wide-eyed, Tod Moran stared into the stokehole. The
second, with his back to Tod, faced the wrathful figures
of Tony the Wop and Blackie Judson, demoniac with
their film of grit.

"You keep way. You keep way." Tony backed toward
the boilers as the second advanced with a vicious hammer in his upraised hand.

Blackie Judson swung up his shovel. "Blast yer hide!
If you touch me I'll kill yuh, so help me God!"

"Will you git back t' work, you two?" cried the second
in a voice of venomous passion. "I'll have the chief put
you both in irons—see?" He brandished the hammer
threateningly.

Tod Moran, crouching in the darkness of the tunnel
entrance, saw Tony the Wop suddenly fling up his heavy
slice bar in a fury of rage. "Treat us like pigs! No food
—worms, maggots—then keek us at work. I care no more.
I keel you—I keel you!"

The Italian leaped forward. His uplifted slice bar cut
toward the second's head.

Tod shivered. A scream bored into his ears. The second went down in a heap, a great bloody gash in his cheek.

A whistle sounded from the engine room. Blackie Judson cringed, wild-eyed, in the opposite corner. "I didn't do it," he whined. "It was the Dago—not me." He cowered there near the third stoker, who watched the scene impassively.

Tony the Wop leaned limply against the bulkhead. He stared, apparently amazed, at his work. His deep chest rose and fell in panting breaths. The second rose to an elbow and struggled to his feet. "You'll pay for this," he snarled, clasping a hand to his bleeding face. "It's the brig for you both."

"It wasn't me, sir," quavered the big form of Blackie Judson. "I can stoke all right."

At that moment the chief engineer appeared in the passageway near the port boilers. His face grew grim. "Attacked you, did he? Get the irons."

Tony the Wop stood wringing his hands; his dark eyes swept round the stokehole, desperate with frantic fear. There was no place to go, no place to hide—unless overboard.

The chief motioned to Blackie Judson. "Get to work, you swine!"

"Yes, sir." Blackie swung open a furnace door. The leaping flames splashed on the plates like spilled blood.

Tod Moran backed up the incline of the tunnel. He saw Mr. Hawkes stride quickly from the engine room. He saw the metallic gleam of handcuffs as the chief engineer stepped forward. In a flash, he had locked them about the wrists of Tony the Wop. Moaning, staring about him with the desperate eyes of a trapped animal, Tony was led away.

Softly Tod stole back to his barrow. The men would rouse one of the other watch in the firemen's forecastle to take the Italian's place; while Tony, baffled by this life, would be imprisoned in the darkness of a locker below deck.

Bitter thoughts welled up in Tod. On the voyage out, he had taken it for granted that the scorn heaped by the officers and deckhands on the firemen was well founded. Swine, they had been called, and scum and offal. They had been treated as beneath contempt. Drunk in port, carried aboard ship before sailing time, illiterate, their brains working ponderously over their little world of brute force, dirty and laughed at and cursed for their dirt, now Tod began dimly to perceive that the stokers were what the ship had made them. They were spawned by a sharkish sea. When he himself climbed that iron ladder of the fiddley to the deck above, would he care whether he were washed or not, whether all the grime of his work were off his face and body? When he lifted his shovel and thrust the blade beneath the coal, when his tired shoulders carried the weight of the laden barrow and he stumbled down the alleyway, he had no thoughts of a cold bath in the washroom. Only one desire pervaded him—to stretch his weary body in his bunk and sleep.

He sent his barrow of coal sliding downward, then paused as a familiar voice came to him. Neil's. Neil had taken Tony's place; roused from his well-earned rest, he had turned out to come below once more.

With a sigh Tod resumed his work. His thoughts re-

verted to the stokers again. True, he had never been so
unimaginative that he had seen the men with the eyes of
the deck crew. He had always envisioned them as tiny
cogs in a great machine, dirty perhaps and greasy, yet
cogs which were a part of the immense throbbing heart
that drove the vessel onward. Now he himself was a cog;
and it came to him ironically that he felt no thrill of
ecstasy at the thought of his work so necessary to those
engines beyond the bulkhead. Instead, they became a crying burden, and the furnaces only yawning Molochs which
lifted insatiable mouths in never-ending greed.

He must be a lubber; he should never have gone to
sea. And yet, and yet. . . . Had he not always turned his
eyes westward to the sea? When he had reclined of a soft
summer evening in the hammock of his garden, his mind
submerged in a soothing ecstasy of dreams, had it not
been pictures of the sea that he envisioned? Oh, those
books—those sea books! How they lured one on to dis-
enchantment.

His shovel, missing the barrow, sent a cloud of black
smoke upward. He worked furiously now. A resolve took
possession of his mind. He would open that iron door in
the bulkhead and peer into number three hold.

Presently he slipped down to the stokehole. "Neil," he
shouted, "how long will that coal last?"

His brother turned a blackened face. "Ten minutes,"
he answered.

Ten minutes! Tod Moran raced back to the bunkers,
whirled to the left, and in a moment had reached the
after bulkhead. Lifting his shovel he drove it against the
handle of the watertight door. It gave by slow degrees;
its finger pointed upward. He glanced round with a quick,

furtive movement. The only sound was the steady pulse of the engines, muffled by their walls of coal.

He swung the door open.

Facing him and completely blocking the little doorway was a tier of cases, marked *Olio di Lucca*. He hesitated a second before those words. Olive oil destined for the innumerable Italian sections of California. Was he mistaken?

In feverish eagerness he set about tearing a case apart. With the shovel end he pried open a box. It broke with a shrill screech that made him glance over his shoulder in terror. The bunkers, however, loomed dark and silent about him. He turned to the case again. Two five gallon tins, he saw, lay within. How could he open one? A nail —but he had none. Desperate now, he lifted his shovel and drove the corner of the blade into the tin near the top.

A clear liquid shot out for a second, then dripped down the sides of the container. His heart leaped. It was too thin, too transparent for olive oil. He put up his hand. It came away wet. Water—clear water!

He leaned weakly against the bulkhead. The *Araby* carried a false cargo.

IV MIDNIGHT

"OOKIT the kid. Hell's bells, he's tryin' to shave!"

"Ain't 'e the toff? I arsks you now, wot's 'e shavin'—dirt?"

Tod Moran turned from the cracked mirror nailed to

the cupboard and grinned. "Pipe down, Toppy. You talk
too much."

"Yah—yah. Thad faller always got his trap open."
Swede Jorgenson nodded approval.

"Shut yer bloody marf, you squarehead," retorted
Toppy with venomous fervour. "Cawn't a bloke say nothin' in 'is own fo'c's'le? When the kid's got 'air on 'is
chest, then 'e can talk back—see? Blimey, you wants t'
shut me up like Tony the Wop."

The words struck the forecastle into silence. A day had
passed since the fireman had been imprisoned in a locker
amidships; his pitiful cries and curses were to be heard
when one went down the port alleyway. Now, in whispers,
the seamen in the dog watch below discussed the plight
of the fireman.

"The blarsted, bloomin' hofficers—they treat us like
swine."

"Yah, und the cap'n drunk und never showin' hisself
on the bridge."

"A nice blighter 'e is. Gimme a coffin nail, Swede.
Thanks. When we hit Frisco I'm through with this tub,
I am."

Tod Moran went on with his precarious task. It was a
thin, slightly pale face that surveyed him in the mirror.
The gray eyes were shadowy in their sockets, the mouth
and jaw, when he scraped away the lather, firm yet youthful. It was hardly the face, though, of the boy who had
so blithely set sail on the *Araby* two months before with
the wide world beckoning over the horizon. As he slid the
razor with a flourish down his smooth cheek, he wrinkled
his brows. He had only been a kid when he came aboard;
now he was a man.

He repeated the phrase to himself, then turned in trepidation for fear someone might have heard his moving lips.

"Seven bells," the boatswain murmured. "Whose trick at the wheel?"

"Mine," replied Swede Jorgenson from his bunk.

"And me the bloomin' lookout," Toppy volunteered. "Let's 'ave a game fust, bose."

Tod Moran crossed to his bunk as the men settled themselves about the table for a game of coon-can.

"Say, kid, yoost come here minute."

Tod placed his safety razor in a small hammock swung between his bunk pipes and turned to the opposite tier. "Yes?"

Swede Jorgenson gave him a mysterious smile. "I almos' forget. The cook, he give me letter for you."

In puzzled surprise, Tod took the folded paper which the big seaman proffered. He glanced round quickly; the men were intent on their game. He jumped into his bunk and pulled the light-curtains as though he were turning in for a half hour's rest before going on duty in the bunkers below. With trembling hands he opened the note. It was written in a plain large script.

DEAR JOE MACARONI:

Don't think I've been asleep. I'm standing by—waiting. I've missed you in the galley and hope the officer's steward falls overside and into a shark's mouth. I have news. Come to my cabin before you go on watch below at eight bells.

T. JARVIS

Tod folded the note and thrust it into his pocket. He had confided his discovery in number three hold to Neil only; indeed, he had been so fatigued when he had climbed up the fire-room fiddley that he had had only one thought

—rest. He pulled back his curtain and slid over the bunk board to the floor. Casually, he went up the companion steps to the deck, where he crossed to the firemen's forecastle and gazed within. Through the blue haze of tobacco smoke, he made out his brother's form, outstretched on his mattress, apparently asleep.

"Neil," he called. "Neil Moran."

"Yes?"

"You're wanted on deck."

As his brother emerged from the door, Tod drew him to the bulwarks. Night was closing down. The *Araby*, steaming west for Colon, was entering the Caribbean. The Leeward Islands lay astern; Saint Croix was somewhere off the port bow.

"Neil," Tod whispered, "Jarvis just sent word for me to come and see him. You wait near the alleyway; I want you to talk to him too."

"Oh, don't bother about me. I've talked to Jarvis."

"Yes; but I want you to be friends."

"All right. I'll come along."

Tod led the way toward the cook's cabin. At the alleyway entrance, they halted as they saw Mr. Hawkes step from Jarvis's door and proceed aft. They waited until his burly form had disappeared into the officers' cabin, and then Tod went forward and knocked upon the cook's door.

"Come in."

Tod stepped within and closed the door behind him. Tom Jarvis reclined on his bunk. He took his large pipe from his mouth and motioned Tod to the settee.

"Hullo, Joe Macaroni. How's the coal-passer?"

Tod dropped on the worn red seat and smiled. "Fair," he said; "it's not so bad."

"Did you think I was mad at you?" Jarvis rose to a sitting position; he rubbed the bowl of his pipe on his nose. His penetrating eyes were fixed on the youth.

"No——" Tod hesitated, then stumbled on. "You've never asked me what happened. You've never asked me where I found Neil. He was a prisoner, Tom. Swickard had him locked in a villa near Nice."

"I know it. But go ahead. Let me hear you."

A rush of words came to the youth's lips. He was back once more in Marseilles, following Mr. Hawkes and Jasper Swickard to the Gare St. Charles. Jarvis listened, his shoulders forward, his elbows on his knees. He puffed slowly, reflectively; his eyes never left his visitor's face.

"Well, Joe Macaroni, we've both been playing our own little game," he admitted when Tod had finished with their meeting in the Genoa flophouse. "And mine has been a desperate one." He drummed with his knuckles on his knee. His voice dropped to an undertone. "Hawkes doesn't intend this ship to get to Colon."

Tod raised an excited face. "The cargo's false. I unscrewed the door to number three hold."

Jarvis hung on to his words. His brow contracted; his chin shot forward. "I suspected as much; but I wasn't sure. Mr. Hawkes is ready, then, to spring his trick. The flood tide is on with him now; but when it turns it'll ebb fast. I'm standing by, waiting. We're sailing close to the wind, Joe Macaroni."

"You mean any time? Now?"

With a nod Jarvis rose. Standing erect, his huge body seemed to dwarf the narrow cabin. "I don't like these shoal waters we'll be hitting toward midnight," he said thoughtfully. "I was thinking of you below, Joe Maca-

roni. You're in a mighty dangerous place. Watch. Be prepared at any time."

"Even to-night?"

"Yes; Hawkes is taking his watch on the bridge this
evening. Why? It isn't his turn. And the cap'n is dead
drunk in the cabin aft." Jarvis swung about with a lithe
movement. "Now, go out and send that brother of yours
in. I want to talk to him—alone."

Tod rose and slipped out the door. He motioned to
Neil, who stood at the engine-room entrance, gazing below.
"He wants to see you," Tod whispered.

"Thanks, kid. I'll go in." Neil disappeared.

Tod went down the alleyway to the fore-deck. Under
the stars, the night was dark. He crossed to number two
hatch, seated himself, and glanced up at the bridge. Mr.
Burton, the third mate, stood outlined against the wheel-
house window. To starboard shone the steady glow of the
green light, to port the red eye with its threat of danger.
In the crow's nest high above, the lookout was peering
ahead into the darkness. Barely a breeze stirred the calm
waters; yet suspense hung heavy in the air.

The chart-room windows leaped into sudden visibility,
and Tod discerned Mr. Hawkes turn from the deck-head
lights and bend over the chart table. At the same instant,
the ship's bell began sounding from the bridge. *One, two
—three, four—five, six—seven, eight.* As the bronze bell
on the forecastle head took up the notes in a deeper tone,
Tod sprang for the alleyway.

"Neil," he whispered, opening the cabin door, "eight
bells."

"Coming." Tod glimpsed his brother clasp Jarvis's
hand.

Tod ran for the fire-room fiddley. He had already reached the first grating when his brother plunged into the entrance above him. They descended the iron rungs of the ladder while the warm air whirled up about them. In the stokehole the firemen were drawing their buckets of hot water. Blackie Judson was snarling at the condition of one of his fires. Tod gave him only a glance as he ducked his head and hurried up to the black yawning mouth of the bunkers. Shortly the Greek came toward him with laggard steps.

"They let Tony out yet?" His begrimed face was turned hopefully toward the youth.

"No—not yet."

The coal-passer swore beneath his breath and without another word propelled his exhausted body in laboured movements toward the stokehole.

Tod Moran picked up the coal barrow and swung to the left. He went at his work slowly but steadily; he knew the amount of coal necessary to keep the stokers satisfied below. The moments dragged their weary way toward midnight. It was strange how little thinking one did here when there was nothing to bother! But the aching muscles in one's back and arms seemed to drain every ounce of energy from one's body. A languorous torpor enveloped the mind. By golly, he was tired; and probably it was not more than ten o'clock.

Suddenly, without a moment's warning, the light winked out.

The suspense that all evening had hung in the thick black air seemed to close down with the oppressive darkness. Tod put down his barrow and listened. He heard the rhythmic tremor of the engines—they were all right, then.

The propeller was going too. He took the sweat rag from his belt and wiped his face. His thin shirt clung to his moist body; he felt the sweat trickle down his belly. He jerked the shirt over his head and flung it away. Then, with outstretched hands, he stumbled round toward the fire room.

His hands touched the low tunnel entrance. He stooped and came out into the stokehole. Red splashes of fire played on the plates of the flooring. He made out the forms of Neil and his two companions standing against the bulkhead. They seemed waiting, expectant, listening.

"What's happened, Neil?" Tod felt his mouth go dry.

"The dynamo, I guess. I just heard the second call for lamps."

"Yeah," grunted Black Judson, "you kin expect anythin' on this blamed tub. It'll be these rotten boilers that'll blow up next." He dropped to a sitting position on the plates. "Let 'em bring us a lamp," he muttered. "We can't work without lights."

Neil's voice, low, vibrant, came from the flickering darkness. "You stay here, Tod, near the fiddley. I'll go and get some lamps."

Tod heard him cross to the tunnel at the corner and go aft to the engine room. Ten minutes, probably, had elapsed before he returned with a brass oil lamp and a lantern in his hands. "The chief got them from the locker," he vouchsafed in a lowered voice. "There isn't much oil in them, and the mate says there's no more to be had. Forgot to get some in Genoa."

Passing the lantern first to Tod, he stuck the lamp in a brass holder in the bulkhead. In the dim light, Tod gave his brother a searching look, but Neil's face lay imper-

turbable. Only when the youth turned away did the older brother stride his way and whisper: "Sparks is working on the dynamo, too. The wireless has gone dead. Be ready —any time."

Tod Moran set to work once more in the bunkers. He carried the lantern now on a barrow handle. The light made only a feeble glow in the profound darkness of the 'tween-decks; the steel walls faded away above; the dust-laden air moved slowly as a mist. Each shrill scrape of the shovel startled the youth in terror. Suspense weighed him down like an iron hand. If he were only above in the fresh cool air! Any place but here, walled in by these oppressive plates of steel. What was happening on the bridge? Was the mate altering the course, steering in the night toward some surf-beaten shoal? Was Captain Ramsey so drunk that he did not notice the ominous approach of danger? And Jarvis—what was he doing? Standing by? Why didn't he act? Why did he allow this ship, so gallant in spite of her rusty hull, to be wrecked on some hidden reef?

In the port bunkers, Tod worked furiously, filling his barrow. In eager haste, he returned to the chute and slid the coal noisily downward. He listened to the iron clang of furnace doors, the hiss of steam from the clinker. At last he heard the sound of the ash buckets in the pits. The end of the watch was drawing near. Eight bells would soon be sounding midnight.

With quickened breath he remembered Jarvis's warning. He wiped his chest with his sweat rag. He was getting nervous as a silly girl. That wouldn't do; he mustn't imagine things. Once more he returned to the end of the port bunkers.

In the very act of sending his shovel into the coal he felt the plates of the 'tween-deck slowly lift. A force beneath his feet flung him upward. The empty bunker opposite tipped toward him. He pitched forward, flat on the coal pile.

To starboard, a long grinding noise ripped the hull. A shudder passed through the *Araby*. She rose; she quivered for an instant; she settled back in silence.

Tod Moran put out his hand to grasp the falling lantern. It swayed giddily out of reach, turned over, and, rolling down the plates, flickered out. The darkness closed about his heart.

V : ABANDON SHIP!

IN THE silence that followed, Tod Moran fumbled on his knees for the lantern. When it touched his outstretched hand, he grasped it eagerly, even though he had no matches. Rising quickly, he made his way with infinite caution through the velvet blackness toward the passageway.

"Careful, Joe Macaroni," he thought, "there's an opening here in the deck for the coal chute." He lifted his head at the sound of a muffled cry from the stokehole. Before him he saw the oblong entrance aflame with light as though every furnace door were open and belching forth a fiery tongue. With all the blood in his body throbbing in his ears, he stumbled down the incline, the dark lantern aswing in his hand.

Great flares of light leaped on the bulkhead. In the glare he saw the Finn and Blackie Judson climbing like long-armed apes up the fiddley ladder. A low moan to his right made him turn. Backed against the bulkhead, his face drawn with suffering, stood Neil Moran. Tod's gaze fastened upon his brother's right arm which showed a long burning scar.

Tod sprang toward him. "Neil, you're hurt."

His brother spoke between his teeth. "When she struck, the door swung open. It caught my arm."

The youth whirled. Near the engine-room door, he knew, lay a can of grease. He jumped for it, pushed his hands in the mass of yellow stuff, and was back at his brother's side. "Here, this'll help." He smeared the mixture along the scorching wound. Reaching for his sweat rag, he took it, dirty as it was, and wrapped it about Neil's elbow, fastening it tightly with a torn end. "That'll keep the air off."

"Better already. Listen—what's that?"

Above the steady draft of the furnaces a cry drifted down the ventilators: "Abandon ship!"

Tod's heart dropped. Something seemed to clutch his throat. The *Araby* was sinking.

"Get up the ladder to the boat deck," Neil urged.

Tod crossed the slanting plates. With his hands on the ladder he turned. "Can you make it alone?"

"I'm all right. You go above."

Reluctantly Tod swung up three iron rungs. There he paused as he glimpsed his brother disappear in the darkness of the engine-room tunnel. Why didn't Neil go above? Why was he slipping aft?

He listened a moment. No sound came from above. From the slant of the plates of the flooring he knew that the ship must have shoved her starboard bow high on a reef. Had she torn a hole in her side? Was she filling her holds with water, slowly going down stern first? No water had yet reached the fire room; she couldn't be sinking this suddenly. As he hesitated there on the ladder he heard the sudden jangle of the engine-room bell. Strange. If the command to abandon ship had been given, who, then, was on the bridge and signalling below? He slid from the ladder and ran for the engine room.

Peering from the low doorway, he saw Neil vanish between the engines and the condenser toward the shaft tunnel. His first thought was to cry out: "Come back, Neil—come back!" Then, as he perceived the second engineer ascending the ladder to the middle grating, he stifled the words on his lips. Staring wide-eyed around the corner of the ventilating fan, he saw, high above, the chief engineer swinging with surprising agility down the iron steps.

"Get back, Mr. Phillips," called the chief.

The second engineer hesitated as he reached the middle grating. "The mate's ordered abandon ship, sir," he answered loudly.

"Get back, Mr. Phillips," repeated the chief, his Scotch

face flushed with anger. "We're not leaving the ship yet. I'm in charge here."

"She's sinking," the second yelled in a high voice. "We'll be left behind!"

Tod gave a sudden start as the telegraph bell near him jangled shrilly above the pulsing tumult of the engines. The indicator on the dial curved to the words *Stand By*.

It caught the attention, too, of the men on the steps. "D'ye hear that bell?" thundered the chief. "Mon, would ye desert?"

The second stood irresolute, with one hand on the iron rail. Slowly he backed down the steps as the chief descended from above. Abruptly the younger man stopped. "Hawkes ordered boats got out!" he shrilled with renewed energy. "She hit a reef—ripped open the plates on the sta'b'rd side. She's going down."

The chief's pink face crimsoned with rage. "You fool, the cap'n's on the bridge now. He's drunk; but the ship isn't sinking yet. Hear that anvil chorus? Get back."

Tod Moran, looking at the slim back of the junior officer, suddenly understood. The second was Hawkes's man. His plan of action had been carefully prepared.

"You Scotch imbecile," the second was snarling, "Hawkes won't let her be saved!" He flung himself up the ladder.

The chief blocked his way. "I'm in charge here," he retorted in a voice of fury. "Ye dare disobey your superior?"

Tod stood as though powerless to move. He saw an automatic flash in the second's hand. He heard his voice raised: "Get out o' my way! I'm going on deck."

The chief's step did not falter; his eyes never wavered.

As he swung down the rail, the second raised his hand. Above the noise of the engines a shot cracked faintly.

The chief flung his head backward. His arms, pressed close to his sides, thrust clenched fists towards his throat. He swayed; one hand slid down the rail as he pitched forward. He crashed down the steps to the plates.

"Serves you right!" screamed the second as he grasped the rail for support. "You're not goin' to drown me here like a rat." He stared for an instant at the crumpled form on the floor, then turned and sprang up the steps, two at a time.

Tod Moran jerked into action. He ran to the chief, knelt at his side. The man's face was ashen, the eyes closed. On the chest just above the heart, a crimson stain slowly widened. Tod straightened his legs and moved his arms to his sides. In a stirring instant he saw the chief's eyes open. The man regarded him with a questioning glance.

Tod nodded. "Yes—he's gone."

"The swine!" The chief struggled to an elbow. A wrench of agony went through him. His teeth bit down on his lower lip.

"Shall I help you to deck?"

The bell jangled behind them. The chief's gaze swept across to the telegraph dial, and Tod Moran's eyes followed his glance. The indicator pointed to *Full Astern*.

"Help me to deck?" muttered the chief. "Hell! Get me over to those levers."

With the Scotchman's arm thrown over his shoulder, Tod dragged him to his feet. Swaying, lurching, they crossed to the innumerable levers opposite the dial. The chief gripped the handles. He pulled. The engines throbbed; the floor quivered. But the great propeller beat the waves in vain. The even slant to port told them that the *Araby* still lay on the reef.

"Moran—Moran!" A voice boomed out from the stokehole doorway.

Tod whirled. Jarvis stood gazing round the engine room. "Where's your brother?" he snapped.

"Went down the shaft tunnel," Tod answered loudly.

"Good." The big man apparently took in the situation at a glance. "Chief, you're with us? Yes? . . . Then Joe Macaroni, we got work for you too. Can you keep the fires going—and going strong?"

Tod moved toward the stokehole. "I'll keep them going. Yes, sir—I'll keep them going."

"Get busy." Jarvis sprang with a lithe movement for the ladder.

"The steam's down," called the chief thickly, as he pointed to the gauge. "Hurry."

Tod Moran ran up the plates and into the tunnel. Coming out into the gloom of the stokehole, he picked up a shovel and flung open the door of number three furnace. A white sheet of flame leaped toward him. He jerked to one side with a sharp quiver of apprehension. That almost got him!

He swung the door shut with the shovel, opened the draft, and then once more swung the door outward. Thank heavens he had plenty of coal on hand. He plunged the shovel blade beneath the pile and threw it with a long sweep into the fiery mouth. He worked furiously, with but one thought: to feed that ravenous mouth so he might cut off the white heat that scorched his face and naked shoulders. He kept at it steadily with long swinging movements. Furnace doors clanged. The draft roared. The heat and dust increased. With black rivulets of sweat streaming down his glistening body, he worked like mad, stoking first one furnace, then another. Their intermittent clang became a nightmare; against the steel bulkheads of that fiery hole, the echoes beat a sharp tattoo.

What was happening on deck? Were the boats being lowered? Was Sparks trying vainly to drum out calls for help? Or had Mr. Hawkes seen to it that no S O S went winging through the night? And the chief? Was he still standing by his engines, throwing his weight in answer to the telegraph?

With tightened lips Tod Moran kept at his work. His eyes seemed branded by the heat; his breath came in spasmodic jerks. The hot plates of the stokehole burned through his shoes. In the back of his head, a throbbing pain seared deep; his nostrils seemed suffocated. When he opened his mouth in desperate abandon to breathe in the soot-filled air, his throat choked on the dust. Before his swimming vision those fiery Molochs opened jaws with tongues of flame that scorched to a sickening degree. He lost the sense of time.

A sound behind him, barely perceptible, like a soft hiss, just caught his attention. He turned his burning eyes that way. An uncontrollable groundswell of fear pulled at his limbs. Gliding toward him across the hot plates was a small stream of water, hissing as it approached, lifting its head in a faint cloud of steam.

Fascinated, he stared. Until this moment, he had never really fancied that the *Araby* would sink, that Mr. Hawkes could win out when Jarvis and Neil and he all stood in the way. That the *Araby* could sink? No—no! It wasn't right; it wasn't fair. Yet here was this water winding toward him across the plates. It wasn't the fact that they had lost that most concerned him; it was the thought of the *Araby's* death—her end. There was a hole in her side, then! or—and how his heart leaped at the thought!—could it be merely the water from the bilges?

Well, he'd better get to work. Presently, he awoke with a start to the realization that all the coal had been used. For only a moment he hesitated at the black cavernous mouth of the bunkers. He glanced at the shining wet surface of the plates. Steadily the glistening expanse widened. Dared he go into that dark entrance where any sudden movement of the ship might well mean death to him? What! He, stopped? He, Joe Macaroni? No—no! If his moment had come he wasn't afraid. Well—he was afraid, but that made no difference. He had promised Jarvis he'd keep the furnaces going. He must have coal, even though he already knew his task as almost futile. He wouldn't waver. He knew what to do!

He plunged into the bunkers. He had no lantern now. He skirted the coal chute, turned to the left down those familiar passages, and stumbled against the barrow. A shovel lay close by. He thrust the blade into the coal. The first shovelful missed, but it gave him the direction, and after that he worked with furious haste.

Abruptly he stopped and listened. A voice was calling from the stokehole. "Joe Macaroni—where are you? Joe Macaroni!"

He picked up the barrow handles and slowly guided it along the plates of the 'tween-decks. Coming down the incline he saw the huge figure of Jarvis silhouetted against the flickering light.

"That's where you are!" He gave Tod a swift glance of affectionate delight. "I knew I didn't guess wrong."

"I needed coal."

The man's eyes gleamed. "Get up on deck. We're leaving."

Tod Moran placed the barrow on the stokehole plates and lifted a blackened face. "The boats?" he stammered. "The end? Then this doesn't matter?"

Jarvis spun about. "The end?" he boomed. "Joe Macaroni, we're just beginning to fight!—Get up to the deck. The port lifeboat. You look fagged. Go up through the engine room; it's easier. I'll see you above." Jarvis sprang for the fiddley ladder.

Tod Moran went, unsteadily, toward the engine room. In the tunnel, he awoke to the fact that the engines had stopped. The silence seemed to press upon the walls of steel. For a moment he thought the engine room deserted; then he observed a still form lying beside the levers.

"Chief?"

No answer. The Scotch engineer sat hunched against his engines. His mouth hung open with little trickles of blood at the edges. His eyes stared up at the telegraph dial where the indicator pointed to the word *Finished*.

Tod Moran grew rigid. Slowly he advanced. "Chief." He choked on the word. Even as he said it, he knew the chief was dead.

He stepped across the motionless form. He dragged his burning gaze to the ladder. In a daze, he climbed upward. On the middle grating he swung about and went up past the cylinder heads.

About him the silence seemed to pulse and throb. Or was it the beating of his own heart that he heard?

He came out into the alleyway, passed the galley with its warm smell of food, and reached the after ladder leading to the boat deck. Above, he encountered a phantom figure emerging from the darkened wireless shack.

"That you, Sparks?" he murmured. "Did you send an S O S?"

"Couldn't," came the low response. "The dynamo was off and the batteries run down. God! what an outfit."

In the starlight of the deck, Tod discerned figures pressing about the lifeboats. On the poop deck other figures like those in a dream were putting out the captain's gig.

The air was heavy with disaster. Across the clear night voices called. Lanterns flickered vaguely. As in a trance, he reached the port lifeboat, tumbled in, and dropped on a seat near Jarvis. He glimpsed Mr. Hawkes sitting in the sternsheets, giving his orders. Tod looked down at the rounding cleats. Once before he had to put to sea in this same boat. That had been upon a night of storm with death in the air. Now they were casting adrift once more, but this time in the stillness between midnight and dawn, with the cold stars winking overhead. They were leaving the *Araby* forever.

The *Araby*. They had run her upon a reef, wounded her, and now they were deserting. Alone she would sink into those greedy seas. These decks which he had trod, these decks which had become his home, almost a part of himself, would slide into the black depths of a tropic sea. There, below, they would lie submerged, with strange monsters swimming about them, strange seaweeds waving along their planks.

He felt the boat lowered; he heard the whine of ropes

through the falls. They dropped on a sullen swell, rolling
gently. Whispering voices murmured about him. Oars
strained in the rowlocks. He looked up at the black outline of the ship.

Her bows lay high on the reef; her stern sank toward
the sea. High aloft on the foremast a white light gleamed
among the stars; and lower down on the navigation bridge
the port light shone wanly like a bloodshot eye. As he
watched, the distance slowly widened. Silence enshrouded
them. The ship dissolved in the night, with only those
lights left gleaming amid the stars.

"Listen!"

A dull thudding noise like an explosion washed toward them.

"She's going!" screamed a voice.

"What's that?" cried Hawkes. "Blast me, if we didn't
forget the dago! He's locked in the brig."

Tod quivered. He seemed of a sudden to leap awake.
His hands clenched; the nails dug into his palms. A sound
drifted toward him across the water—the muted wail of
Tony the Wop lifting his voice to Heaven.

Tod Moran, in sudden terror, put out his hand and
clutched Jarvis' arm. "Where's Neil?" he whispered.
Neil! . . ."

Jarvis answered in a low tone. "Your brother is on
the *Araby*."

"On the *Araby*!" The words were almost an echo.

The man leaned toward him. "Quiet, Joe Macaroni!
Neil is doing a man's work. . . . This time we're not going
to let our ship go down."

VI : "I TAKE COMMAND, MR. HAWKES"

Ship your oars, boys," said Mr. Hawkes gruffly, from the stern sheets. "We'll stand by till she goes down."

The lifeboat, adrift under strange stars, lost headway. Silence enveloped them. Tod Moran, gazing aft, saw that the lights of the *Araby* still shone dimly perhaps two hundred yards distant. To the north a dark thin line of shore was vaguely visible, one of the innumerable islands, probably, which thrust their heads up through the Caribbean. To the south, two wavering lights approached across the gentle swells. They were, he knew, the other lifeboats. A moment later a call came faintly across the starlit water.

Hawkes rose and sent a stentorian voice toward them. "Turn and make back on our course for San Martin. We'll follow as soon as she goes down."

"Very good, sir," came the reply.

"How's the skipper?" shouted the first mate.

"Sleepin' in the bottom. Dead to the world."

Hawkes laughed deeply in his beard. Tod saw the two lights turn and progress slowly toward the east. Jarvis, sitting with his oar shipped in his hand, bent down and whispered, "Take this flash, Joe Macaroni. Turn it on Hawkes when I nudge you." Unperceived in the darkness, he slipped the youth an electric torch.

Pondering, Tod held it on his knee, with the round glass pointed to the stern of the boat. What plan of action was Jarvis contemplating? Was he waiting until the other boats were out of reach, when he might deal with the first mate alone? In the seat at the stern, on each side of Hawkes, sat Red Mitchell and the second engineer. Upon those two only did he believe Mr. Hawkes could absolutely rely. Tod looked round. Among the firemen and seamen behind him he made out Toppy and Jorgenson, both on their side probably. He knew that the twelve other men in the boat were anything but friendly toward the mate; and he also knew that, since the night when the stoker had been dragged from the sea, Tom Jarvis held no small place in their estimation.

Yet, did they dare mutiny? For to take the *Araby* into their own hands would be little less than that. And there was Mr. Burton, whose voice he heard behind him in the stem of the boat. Where did the young third mate stand? True, he had no love for the captain and mate; and yet, would he not do his duty and stand by his superior officers? As Tod glanced questioningly at the huge figure of the Tattooed Man at his side, he sensed in his attitude an air of confident poise. Doubtless, Jarvis had planned this moment for months; yet was not Hawkes a man to reckon with every eventuality?

A startled cry from the stern sheets focussed his attention upon the lights of the *Araby*. Low on the water, so low that he believed the light must be on a lowered accommodation ladder, a lantern was swinging back and forth.

"Tony's got loose. Ain't I right, now?" muttered Red Mitchell. "He wants us t' come back and save 'is little 'ide." He laughed shrilly, an apparent note of hysteria in his voice.

"Well, we ain't," snapped Hawkes. "It ain't safe. The blasted tub'll be goin' down any minute now."

Tod felt the man at his side quietly stir. "I hardly think she will, Mr. Hawkes," said Jarvis softly.

The words struck the lifeboat into puzzled silence. The men leaned forward, expectant.

"What d'yer mean, Mr. Jarvis?" blurted the mate.

"I mean," said the Tattooed Man in a low repressed tone, "that now I take command, Mr. Hawkes."

The three men in the stern sat motionless. Tod felt a sudden movement at his side. He pressed his finger on the electric torch. A cone of light leaped through the darkness. Between the startled faces of Red Mitchell and the second engineer the bearded countenance of Mr. Hawkes flushed crimson.

"Don't move, Hawkes!" cried Jarvis sharply. "Leave that gun alone. I have you covered."

"Blimey," rasped a voice behind the youth, "didn't I say that Tattooed Man wasn't any bloomin' cook!"

In the stern sheets Red Mitchell raised his voice in a curse. "Jerry, you fool, you've been double-crossed!"

Tod saw Mr. Hawkes's right hand itch at his knee. "Cut out this play stuff," he snarled, a rising note of defiance in his voice. "The men won't stand for ye goin' against yer officers."

Jarvis leaned intently forward. In his hand gleamed an automatic. "I think they'll go with me, Hawkes, when they hear what I have to say." He motioned over his shoulder. "Burton, get their weapons!"

In surprise Tod saw the third mate step over the thwarts. Mr. Hawkes thrust his beard forward with a menacing movement. "That young whelp with ye, too?"

Jarvis raised his automatic. With a muttered curse, Mr. Hawkes relapsed into silence. Coolly yet swiftly the third mate felt for the weapons. "I have them, sir," he announced, turning to Jarvis.

Someone behind Tod laughed shrilly.

Mr. Hawkes's beaked nose curved over his lips. "D'ye know what this means?" he snarled. "When we reaches port, ye'll both be tried for mutiny."

"I think not, Mr. Hawkes," returned Burton as he seated himself on the gunwale.

"Keep the three of them covered, Burton," went on Jarvis, unperturbed. "Now I've got something to say to these men." His eyes roved round the boat.

Hawkes leaned forward. The scar on his temple flamed red against his sombre brows. "Who are you?" he whispered gruffly. "You ain't no cook."

Jarvis answered in a low vibrant tone. "I'm the former master of the *Annie Jamison*. Do you remember the cargo carrier that the Jamison Line sent to the bottom in the Columbia River two years ago?"

As Jarvis went on, the dark eyes of Mr. Hawkes widened. "The Board of Inquiry put the entire blame on me. Oh, I had no one to help me prove it; but I knew that the ship had been scuttled by a few on board. I vowed that I'd show up Swickard and his dirty crowd. The insurance company in San Francisco felt that something was wrong; but they couldn't prove it, either. So they told me to ship on this freighter to find out if all was right on it. Well, I did. I found that all was wrong." He paused a moment and fingered the automatic. "Burton knows that I'm telling the truth. He's seen my papers from the insurance company. They give me a free hand in case of an accident to the *Araby*. I'm the only man here, save you, Mr. Hawkes, who has master's papers. And now I take command!"

"You fool," retorted Hawkes with a defiant toss of his head, "you lie! And what's more, you can't prove anything. The *Araby* won't last five minutes."

"I think she will, Mr. Hawkes," Jarvis went on evenly. "You see, there was no hole ripped in her starboard bow —as you know."

Tod saw the Mate's eyes glitter, saw the black brows draw together.

"And that nice little clock-work which you placed in number three hold to open up her plates never went off."

Mr. Hawkes threw back his head in a fury of rage. He snarled out a stream of oaths. Turning to Red Mitchell upon his right hand he screamed: "You played me false, you cur!"

"I didn't! I didn't!" whined Mitchell as he cringed toward the gunwale. "I earned every blooming penny——"

"That'll do!" Jarvis threw out his hand in a quick gesture. "Neil Moran is now on the *Araby*. He's fixed your little trick. I've got you right where I want you, Hawkes. We'll get the ship off the reef at high tide. We're going to take her, just as she is, into port. This time we've got the evidence within her holds!" He turned and spoke to the murmuring men behind him. "You've known, boys, that all wasn't right aboard our ship. When we get her to port, there'll be a nice little present for all of you. This means that the insurance company will not lose something like half a million. Are you boys with us?"

"Yah—yah!"

"Blimey, yes."

Jarvis's eyes swept the thwarts as the men nodded. Past treatment, past grievances, doubtless surged to the surface of their thoughts. Would they come with Jarvis? Just watch!

Tod saw the second engineer rise. "Let me go forward," he interposed. "I've got nothing to do with this."

"Oh, you ain't?" snarled Hawkes. "Think you'll leave the sinkin' ship, eh? Well, ye sit right where ye are!"

"I'm through with you," reiterated the second, looking about him in sudden fear.

Tod Moran moved toward Jarvis. "Tom, that man killed the chief in the engine room."

"You lie!" cut in the second sharply.

"I saw him. I was behind the ventilating fan. He shot the chief and then ran on deck."

A rattle of steel sounded as Jarvis brought forth from his pocket two pairs of handcuffs. "Here, Burton—lock these on Hawkes and Phillips."

The third mate caught one pair and swung it about the wrists of the engineer. Immediately the man let out a stream of oaths. Tod flung the torchlight full upon him. Metal gleamed on his wrists, on the steel chain clasping the bracelets together. In tha' instant, when all eyes were focussed upon the second, Tod glimpsed Mr. Hawkes make an abrupt movement. The man flung himself across the gunwale on the shore side. The boat rocked as his body disappeared below the surface.

" 'E's gone!" yelled Toppy. "The bloke'll git away t' shore."

Tod Moran turned the cone of light upon the water. Little whirls and eddies rose to the surface where the form of the mate had vanished. At Tod's side, Jarvis's tall form loomed up for a second. The youth beheld the man clasp one of the steel bracelets about his right wrist. The next instant he stepped to the thwart and dove in a great leap after the mate.

Breathless, the men crowded to the gunwale. Foam swirled to the surface. It leaped in little waves that washed away outside that circle of light. Tod felt his heart flutter against his ribs. Cries sounded about him. He gripped the gunwale. Immovable he stared. Below the surface a fight was being waged. Bubbles floated up; the churning distance widened. He flashed the light out across the water.

Of a sudden, the phosphorescent surface parted and two hands rose, locked together with flashing metal. Tod started. One arm was tattooed with a network of stars; the other, clutching wildly, was a hairy paw with flattened fingers. Below the water Jarvis had locked himself to Hawkes. Face to face, the two men rose into view: Jarvis's closely cropped hair dripping; Hawkes's dark bearded face contorted in rage. Struggling, treading water, they fought like two wild beasts locked in close embrace. On each side the blue radiance fell away in gleaming rivulets.

Jarvis swung his left fist forward. It caught his opponent upon the jaw. Tod saw the man's eyes close; his head flew back; he went down, dragging his companion with him.

"Yah, they drown," said a voice.

Tod Moran, his eyes riveted downward, felt his heart miss a beat. What was happening below those even swells? Could Jarvis haul the burly form of the mate to the surface? As he stared, two bubbles floated to the top and slowly dissolved. A churning eddy filtered upward. Outside the circle of light the stars danced.

"Yah—they drown," repeated Jorgenson.

"Drown nothin', you blarsted squarehead," retorted Toppy. "Tom Jarvis is a blarsted painted whale, that's wot 'e is. Just wait."

In the phosphorescent ripples close to the lifeboat a head emerged. Tod swung back the light which flashed upon Jarvis as he threw back his head and caught his breath sharply. He grasped the gunwale with his free hand while the other slowly dragged the still form of Mr. Hawkes to the surface.

"Jorgenson," snapped Burton, "give me a hand. Boys, get back to the other side." The two men leaned over and helped Jarvis into the boat. The man dropped on a thwart, with his shackled wrist hanging overside. Leaning forward again, the three dragged the sputtering Hawkes over the gunwale. Half drowned, softly cursing, he was willing to lie passively on the bottom while Jarvis extracted a key from his pocket and unlocked himself.

"Get us back to the ship, Burton," ordered the Tattooed Man. Mr. Hawkes rose to a sitting position and swore volubly. The men flung out their oars and in steady movements sent the boat toward the dark outline of the *Araby*. As they drew near, Tod discerned on the lower platform of the accommodation ladder the figure of Neil Moran, lantern in hand.

"All O.K. here, Tom," called Neil.

"Good work," replied Jarvis.

The boat grated on the woodwork. The men sprang out. The boatswain held the painter while Burton and Jorgenson led the dripping prisoner up the steps.

"Now, up you go too," said Jarvis, pointing his automatic at Red Mitchell and the second engineer.

"You ain't got no right," began Mitchell in his whining voice.

"Oh, haven't I? Well, I think that we'll let Tony the Wop lock you fellows safely below in the brig."

"*Dio!*" called a voice from above. "Just watch me."

Jarvis stepped to the platform. "High tide in four hours," he announced. "Get those fellows locked up, Burton. I'll place the men."

Tod Moran paused on the deck of the *Araby* as Tom Jarvis turned to the group of men. "Boys, I have orders to take this ship back to San Francisco. We'll have to work double shifts until we make Colon. We'll get a full crew there. Are you willing?"

"We are," they answered.

"Line up, men," commanded the new master of the *Araby*. In quick tones the men were placed; none were to turn in till the ship was off the reef. The third engineer took charge of the engine room; Burton and Tod were ordered above. "Yes, we're so short of hands," pursued Jarvis, "that you'll have to take the wheel, Tod Moran, while I'm on the bridge."

The wheel! Tod turned his eyes aloft in ecstasy. He stood in silence while the men scattered fore and aft, above and below. Neil brushed past. Tod caught his arm. "Neil, we've done it," he whispered; "done what we started out to do. We've saved your name—and Tom Jarvis's too."

Neil smiled queerly in the lantern light. "Kid," he said, "you've got a lot yet to learn about seafaring men. Do you think that was the only reason that Jarvis did this?"

Tod looked puzzled.

"Well, there's another." He lowered his voice. "When I first came aboard I thought that I recognized this ship. Her superstructure was changed somewhat; but one night I went forward to the forecastle head and rubbed the bell on the far side. I knew then. Her old name, very faintly, was still engraved there."

"Her old name?"

"Yes, the *Annie Jamison*. Now do you understand what this means to Jarvis? His first command! . . . His ship."

VII : MAKING PORT

F og ahead, sir," called the lookout.

At the cry, Tod Moran swung up the ladder to the bridge. It was midnight some sixteen days later, and his trick at the wheel. Mr. Burton, now second mate, was relieving the third officer, whom they had taken on at Balboa. Tod entered the wheel house, was given his bearings, and after glancing down into the lighted binnacle, stood with both hands gripping the spokes.

Pigeon Point had just come abeam. The great light was winking through the starlit night. Tod gave a spoke, steering north by west toward the dark promontory of Point San Pedro. Looking ahead, he saw the *Araby's* blunt bows ploughing through long swinging seas toward San Francisco, toward home. The foremast cleaved the star-strewn heavens like a knife thrust; high up in the crow's nest Toppy's head was vaguely visible. Eight bells sounded, and the lookout's cry came back on the still air: "Lights burning brightly, sir."

The ship entered a gray bank of fog hanging low over the water. Mr. Burton stepped to the lever that connected the bridge with the great bronze whistle on the funnel and leaned upon it. For six seconds, a blast sent out its mournful note of warning. The mist swept athwart the ship, blotting out the decks below and hazing past the foremast. But above, Tod could still see the quivering arch of the Milky Way.

"Well, Moran," said Mr. Burton, stopping at the window, "how'll it feel to set foot on ground again?"

Tod laughed softly. "When I touch the old wharf at the foot of Powell Street, I'm going to do a sailor's hornpipe."

"Be sure you do, then. Here's the skipper," he added as steps sounded on the ladder.

Captain Tom Jarvis emerged from the companion. As he stepped to the canvas wind dodger and stared ahead, Tod glimpsed his big frame, clothed in blue serge, outlined against the sky. "Our last night out," he remarked in a voice that carried out into the mist. "The fog's thickening, Mr. Burton. Place a lookout on the fo'c's'le head and signal below for half speed."

"Very good, sir." Mr. Burton swung the telegraph indicator upward.

The captain walked to the starboard wing, peered out across the sea of fog, and swung back to the wheel-house window. "Moran, are you signing on another ship?" he asked, pushing back the cap from his tawny head.

Tod took a spoke, then replied. "I hardly think I will, sir—at least, not soon."

He stood with braced feet as the captain crossed to the weather cloth. Now that Jarvis had become master of the *Araby* only rarely did a conversation pass between them. The rules of the bridge are rigid, and, with surprising ease, the former cook had slipped into the place of the vanished captain. Tod gazed through the glass of the binnacle at the swaying card within. The ship was on her course. He lifted his eyes through the filmy haze to the stars. His nightly trick at the wheel had counted here; he could name them now: cold Polaris straight ahead, blue Vega shining out of those inaccessible depths of space, the constellations of Orion and the Great Bear. A strange longing drifted into his consciousness, a longing to push back the mystery of those stars.

Night after night at the helm had brought him the realization of what they were, and the little place that his own world held with them. He had unloosed all those misconceptions which he had brought with him aboard ship. Here, before his very eyes, lay reality, a reality more magnificent, more glorious, than any childhood fairy tale. Standing here in the presence of the fleeting centuries, he was imbued with a new clarity of vision. Civilizations with their customs, their morals, and religions, were born, lived for their pitiful moment, and died even as those stars above him would flicker out some day. And what lay ahead? ... Surely in that direction lay work for a god: to harness those half-known powers that might perhaps hold back the day when his own little universe would cool in frozen space. Or would it meet some wanderer of the heavens and in a fiery cataclysm hurl itself into dissolution? Ah, that would be living! That would be reality shorn of all illusion.

A sluggish pitch of the ship brought him back to the helm. "Hold her five points east of north!" ordered the captain.

"Five points east of north." Tod swung the wheel on the new course.

The captain turned to converse in low tones with Burton, who stood with one hand on the whistle lever, the other on the engine-room telegraph. Again the stillness was pierced by a warning blast. The ship steamed on through the night. Tod had the sensation of riding atop the world, as though the *Araby*, alone upon a murmuring sea, beneath the star-flung vault of Heaven, was only a bit of time adrift between two eternities.

Once more the whistle sent out its wailing note of warning. Almost at once, somewhere off the starboard bow, came an answer, a quick frightened blast. Tod gripped the spokes, with feet braced.

"Hard astarboard!" snapped Captain Jarvis. "Full ahead!" He sprang for the whistle lever and jerked it twice, quickly.

A low shape crept toward them out of the mist. The *Araby's* bow swung to port. A cry came across the inter-

vening distance, as the stern of the other ship grazed the
Araby's forecastle head.

"A narrow escape—that," acknowledged the captain.
"Hard aport!"

Tod Moran spun the wheel and the *Araby* quivered as
she surged forward, passing the slim vessel on the starboard beam. From the other ship a red flare was flung
aloft. It disclosed a low schooner with masts fore and aft
and a funnel amidships.

"The pilot boat," affirmed Mr. Burton shortly. "Are
they asleep? Shall I give four blasts, sir?"

Jarvis crossed to the starboard wing. "No; these are
home waters to me. We won't take on a pilot. Half speed
ahead."

As the ship once more swung on her course and the
pilot ship fell away astern, Tod perceived that a rising
breeze was driving the fog in to land. A light blinked far
ahead; and presently they came abreast of the lightship.
Tod knew that they were now three miles outside the bar.
Captain Jarvis, raising his night glasses, scanned the black
waters of the entrance. Soon the lights of Fort Point and
Alcatraz Island came into range, and the *Araby* entered
the channel to San Francisco Bay. The dark outline of
Point Lobos loomed up. Ahead lay the Golden Gate.

Tod Moran, with mounting pulse, gripped the helm
and let his eyes peer across the forecastle head. Every
five seconds the great light on Alcatraz sent a long beam
flashing toward them across the water. Cliffs rose up on
the starboard beam; to port, Lime Point lifted and fell
astern.

Eight bells sounded the end of the watch. Tod gave up
the wheel to Swede Jorgenson and climbed with eager

steps down the ladder to the main deck. It was four o'clock in the morning and home soil encircled the bay. He'd never be able to sleep in the stuffy seamen's quarters now; instead, he climbed to the forecastle head and, passing round the winch and the cables, leaned over the starboard rail.

A rose dawn was coming out of the east. The ship cut slowly through the still surface of the bay, turned to the right, and swung toward the docks. Fishermen's Wharf lay in blue shadow at the foot of Russian Hill. As the sun rose over the Berkeley hills, the windows of the houses, rising tier on tier, flashed yellow, as if a welcoming lamp burned on each sill for homecoming mariners. Tod's heart leaped. Home! He was coming home.

The freighter turned northward toward Angel Island to await quarantine inspection in the anchorage. Tod went below then and turned in. When he later woke with a start, he saw through the porthole that they were headed for the city. He gathered up his dunnage and hurried up to deck. The *Araby* was slipping into her berth at Pier 43.

He sprang to the bulwarks. A wharf office, incredibly small and gray, stood silhouetted against the moving traffic of the Embarcadero. At the sight, Tod felt his mounting pulse abruptly stilled. It brought up from the depths of his memory a bitter scene with Jasper Swickard more than three months before. He wiped it from his vision as he saw a group of men waiting there now. They were reporters, he knew, desirous of meeting the man who had brought the *Araby* back to her home port. Doubtless the insurance agents would be there, too, with words of commendation.

As he watched, the door of the office opened and the

slender figure of a girl emerged. She stood on the little
step, her tan coat whipped by the wind, a fur caressing
her cheeks. Tod Moran swung up his cap. Sheila Murray's gaze, running eagerly over the ship, settled upon
him. Her lips parted; then, pushing back the bronzed hair
that blew across her eyes, her glance passed on to Neil
Moran, who stood on the bridge ladder, motionless.

"All fast for'ard, sir," came a call.

Captain Jarvis's deep voice sounded from the bridge.
"Signal 'Finished,' Mr. Burton."

Up from the engine-room skylight drifted a bell's harsh
jangle. Tod stirred. Beneath his feet the deck's faint pulsation trembled into silence.

Voices sounded. The gangway scraped on the wharf.
Tod saw his brother slip down and move toward the girl
at the office door. With laggard steps, Tod followed. He
halted at a bollard and stared at the city rising above him.

He was home once more, the voyage over. The crew
would get paid off and scatter. Toppy, Swede Jorgenson,
Tony the Wop, and their forecastle mates would each go
his own way. In port, they would drink and carouse; on

other ships, they would grumble, curse their lot, and carry on their sharkish tricks. But he was ready to forget all that. That was past. He was done with the sea.

And yet, and yet. . . . As he turned and looked across the straining hawsers at the *Araby*, lying there so quietly, so lifeless, yet withal so gallant, he felt his heart tug at its moorings. Here, this wouldn't do! At this rate, within a month, he'd want to be at sea again. He stood there in silence, while about him the life of the water front flowed on.

He saw the insurance men climb aboard. One raised his voice to the captain on the bridge: "Man, you've become a seven days' wonder!"

Tom Jarvis leaned over the rail and laughed deep within his throat. "Yes—and on the eighth day forgotten."

Tod Moran looked up. Forgotten? .. . Well, not by him. He was bringing home a cargo of knowledge safely imprisoned beneath the hatches of his memory. That would be with him always. He saw Jarvis swing down the ladder to the chart room and pause for a moment at the rail in contemplation. He was no longer the Tattooed Man; he had become master of the *Araby*. And gazing down across the hawsers, Jarvis flung aloft his hand in a gesture of farewell. Tod Moran could almost hear his voice softly vibrate: "We've made port, Joe Macaroni."

His huge figure disappeared into the chart room, and the *Araby's* upper decks lay deserted. Her funnel and foremast towered black against the blazing sky. Gulls swooped and wheeled about them, settled upon the bridge rails, upon the lifeboats, peering with curious eyes down at the galley. A departing cargo liner went by toward the headlands, and the gulls, with raucous cries, rose in circles and winged their way to sea.

SEE NEXT PAGE FOR LIST OF *Comet* BOOKS.

COMET books

If you liked this story, you'd surely like some of the other *Comet* Books—exciting mystery, sports, career, and adventure tales. Each book is printed in large, easy-to-read type, handsomely illustrated in two colors, and priced just right. Here they are—yours for fun and good reading.

1. **WAGONS WESTWARD,** written and illustrated by ARMSTRONG SPERRY. *A swashbuckling story of the opening of the Southwest, full of buffalo, Indians, frontier scouts, and the Mexican War.*

2. **BATTER UP** by JACKSON SCHOLZ, illustrated by ROBERT FRANKENBERG. *One of Jackson Scholz's fastest-moving sports stories. Marty Shane wins a place in big-league baseball, and learns to be a good sport, too.*

3. **STAR-SPANGLED SUMMER** by JANET LAMBERT, illustrated by BETH and JOE KRUSH. *A summer full of fun and gay romance with Penny and the happy-go-lucky Parrish family at Fort Arden.*

4. **TAWNY** by THOMAS C. HINKLE, illustrated by BOB MEYERS. *Tawny is a handsome outlaw dog, hunted mercilessly by the cattlemen, but befriended by Tom Harper, the range boy.*

5. **300 TRICKS YOU CAN DO** by HOWARD THURSTON, illustrated by RUTH MC CREA. *Coin tricks, card tricks, handkerchief tricks, all kinds of tricks, explained by one of America's outstanding men of magic. Be an amateur magician, and be the life of the party.*

6. **PEGGY COVERS THE NEWS** by EMMA BUGBEE, illustrated by EVALINE NESS. *Follow Peggy as she learns the ropes on a big city newspaper. A fascinating story, full of sound information about journalism as a career.*

7. **WINGED MYSTERY** by ALAN GREGG, illustrated by KATHERINE C. T. LIPPERT. *Fast-moving mystery, as the Conroys help crack a case of illegal immigration on the Mexican border.*

8. **YOUR OWN JOKE BOOK**, compiled by GERTRUDE CRAMPTON, illustrated by HOWARD SPARBER. *Here's a lot of wonderful fun — tongue-twisters, puns, smart comebacks, wisecracks, and funny stories.*

9. **SUE BARTON, STUDENT NURSE** by HELEN DORE BOYLSTON, illustrated by URSULA KOERING. *A lovable redhead adds her own brand of fireworks to the dramas and tensions of a big hospital. The first of the popular Sue Barton books about nursing.*

10. **THE TATTOOED MAN** by HOWARD PEASE, illustrated by RALPH RAY, JR. *The first of Howard Pease's long series of adventure stories with Tod Moran as the hero. In this one, Tod sails aboard the "Araby" in search of his brother Neil.*

11. **SKYCRUISER** by HOWARD M. BRIER, illustrated by JO KOTULA. *Take off with Barry Martin, young test pilot, as he flies a new Starwing ship, and help him trace the missing plans for the Skycruiser.*

12. **THE SPANISH CAVE** by GEOFFREY HOUSEHOLD, illustrated by GOULD HULSE, JR. *A story full of thrills and chills as a young boy, Dick Garland, helps solve the mystery of the monster in the dreaded Spanish cave.*

BUILD YOUR OWN *Comet* BOOK LIBRARY